# THE
# GIRL
## IN THE
# GRAVE

# BOOKS BY HELEN PHIFER

*Dark House*
*Dying Breath*
*Last Light*

# THE
# GIRL
## IN THE
# GRAVE

## HELEN PHIFER

*Bookouture*

Published by Bookouture in 2019

An imprint of StoryFire Ltd.

Carmelite House
50 Victoria Embankment
London EC4Y 0DZ

www.bookouture.com

ISBN: 978-1-78681-879-9
eBook ISBN: 978-1-78681-878-2

*For my lovely, amazing friends Phil and Diane Sullivan xx*

# PROLOGUE

The sudden vibration of the ground beneath her head followed by a thudding, scraping noise woke her. A shiver ran down the full length of her spine and she realised that she was freezing cold. Not just cold as if she'd kicked the duvet off in the night; no, a blood-chilling coldness was seeping through her entire body. Her bones ached. Reaching around her for the light switch, she immediately realised that she wasn't in her bed. Touching the hard surface beneath her, she realised that she wasn't in *anyone's* bed.

It was dark. No, it wasn't just dark, it was pitch-black. Turning her head from side to side she couldn't see a thing. The air felt as if it had been pulled from her lungs. She knew she was panicking. *It's okay. You're not at home, but it's okay. You're going to stand up and walk out of here as if there's nothing wrong. Deep breaths, stand up and walk out.*

As she tried to sit up a wave of dizziness hit her, but she kept on pushing: up onto her elbows until her head hit something hard. *What the hell?* Lifting her hands, she reached up and tried to push whatever it was that was blocking her from sitting up. It wouldn't move. Scrabbling around, suddenly in more of a panic, her hands and feet met cold concrete all around her.

She was boxed in.

As fear set in she opened her mouth and screamed: the sound was so high-pitched that for a moment she wondered if it had really come from inside her.

It was then she realised that the box she was in had a shape to it: a coffin shape.

# CHAPTER ONE

Barry had been a cemetery groundskeeper for the last six years. As a child he'd wanted to be a cowboy, only there was no need for them in the heart of the English Lake District. Instead, he'd settled on being a self-employed landscape gardener until the permanent position of groundskeeper had come up, offering a fixed wage, no more worrying about making enough to pay the bills. It had taken some getting used to, but he'd managed.

He took a bite of the cheese and pickle sandwich he'd got up early to make for his dinner and couldn't help but wonder what the world was coming to when bodies that should be left in peace were being exhumed. The papers were full of terrible stories and the TV news wasn't much better, which was why he didn't buy them or watch the news on TV. Life was hard, occasionally cruel, but on the whole it was good.

His wife worked nightshift at the local nursing home; he'd often be leaving for work as she walked through the front door. Which was probably why they were still married after twenty years: they didn't see enough of each other to ever have the time to dislike one another. She was off work this weekend and he was looking forward to spending some quality time with her. They were going to go to Manchester for some shopping and to drink some of those fancy cocktails she liked so much.

He finished the last of his sandwich and tipped the crumbs from the crisp packet into his mouth. Far better to have eaten his dinner now, before the exhumation. He might not have an appetite later when he would need all the energy he could muster. He drained the last dregs of tea from the cracked Costa mug someone had bought him in the Secret Santa last year. Rinsing it under the tap, he left it to drain and dried his hands on the rough tea towel that was as crusty as the bread he'd just consumed.

Leaving the small wooden hut that doubled as the office and staff room, he began the walk towards the hill. The heat from the sun felt good on his face. It was a shame it didn't warm the chill that had formed around his heart at the thought of what he was about to do next. He let out a sigh. He'd never known anyone have their grave exhumed. It was unheard of, especially around here. It was the kind of thing that happened on television, not a quiet cemetery in the middle of the Lake District. Still, it made for an interesting afternoon for him. It was going to be fascinating watching those crime scene investigators working around the burial site and taking photos of everything that was happening.

There was already a small welcoming committee standing around the grave waiting for him and he felt a twinge of guilt for thinking about his belly and holding things up. One of the guys wearing a black fleece jacket with 'CSI' emblazoned across the back of it was still faffing around with the camera around his neck, so this made him feel better.

Barry nodded at Jason, who tapped his watch and rolled his eyes at him. Normally he'd have told him to bugger off, but it didn't seem right today, not in front of these police people; it might sound disrespectful, and that wasn't him. He had the utmost respect for the people he buried and for their families, always polite and ready to answer any questions they may have for him. Lifting his hand, he waved at Jason, who climbed into the cab of the digger. Jason was better at operating the machine than he was; Barry preferred digging with a spade. Harder work, but so much more precise.

The guy in the black fleece photographed the mound of soil they were all gathered around. Florence Wright, the woman in the grave, had only been buried eight weeks ago so the soil hadn't been levelled. She didn't even have a headstone yet. Barry gave the signal and Jason brought the heavy arm of the digger down and began to scoop up buckets of soil, depositing them into another pile on the overgrown grave next door. Good job that family only visited once a year; he wouldn't like to see his gran's final resting place being made a mess of like this.

After a few minutes, Barry saw a glimpse of wood through the soil and waved his hands, shouting, 'Whoa, whoa lad.'

The arm of the digger stopped mid-air and a hushed silence fell around them as everyone gathered around to look down into the grave. Barry glanced down then stepped back. They were lucky this was a fresh one. The coffin was relatively new, so would be in good condition. He wasn't too sure about the body inside it. He didn't like to give much thought to what lay inside the holes he'd dug once the coffins were down there. It freaked him out. When he'd first started working here he'd had terrible nightmares which woke him in the night. Eventually, his wife had dragged him to the doctor's for some sleeping tablets, told him she couldn't take the tossing and turning on her nights off work. He'd done as he was told, got his pills and took them every night, supressing his dreams about being buried alive in one of the graves he'd dug, unable to claw his way out.

'What now?' The voice in his ear startled him. He stared at the woman with the camera, wondering if she was addressing him or asking a general question. He certainly didn't know what now. Jason had jumped out of the cab. It was him who answered.

'Well, someone is going to have to get down in that hole, clear the rest of the soil and put the straps around the coffin. Seeing as how I've used up all my skill in getting the soil out without breaking the coffin in half, it looks as if that's a job for you, Barry, lad.'

Barry stared at him in horror. He wasn't about to jump down into someone's grave. Sleeping tablets or not, that was going to give him nightmares for sure. Jason stood opposite him with his arms crossed, staring at him. Barry realised that the CSI team had stopped what they were doing and were also staring at him. Shaking his head, he muttered 'Christ's sake' and jumped down into the grave, holding out his hand for Jason to pass him the spade.

Once he had cleared the rest of the soil around the coffin, Jason passed him the straps to secure around it then helped him back out of the hole. He hadn't realised how much he'd been sweating; his forehead was damp with beads of perspiration and his hair wet. All he could smell was the earthy, coppery smell from the soil tinged with an underlying darker, sweeter odour that wasn't familiar and it made him feel sick. He was so glad he wasn't the one who had to open the coffin and examine the poor old woman's remains; he wouldn't be a pathologist for any amount of money in the world. The thought of having to cut into dead bodies made him shudder. He looked over to where the private ambulance was parked up on the small road as near to the gravesite as it could get. Two undertakers got out and pulled the trolley from the back. They would transport the coffin to the hospital mortuary, so the body of Florence Wright could be examined.

He watched as Jason used the heavy machine to lift the coffin from the grave. It had been raining heavily the past few days and a waterfall of rainwater cascaded down from inside of it. He'd always imagined that coffins would be watertight. *The price they cost they bloody well should be*, he smiled to himself as the undertakers, now in protective suits and gloves, guided the casket down towards their waiting trolley.

Barry glanced down into the empty grave and gasped, his eyes suddenly wide and alert; there was something else down there. Moving closer to the edge, he stood staring as a wave of hot bile filled the back of his throat. He wobbled as he tried to stop his legs from giving way underneath him. Finally finding his voice, he yelled so loud that everyone stopped what they were doing, and all turned to stare at him. He pointed down into the grave.

'She's… she's fallen out; she's not inside the coffin.'

Jason clambered out of the cab and strode towards him, closely followed by the CSIs, an environmental health officer, the priest from Florence's local church and the two undertakers, until all of them were standing in a circle staring down into the dark, sodden grave. There, poking through the soil, a pair of mottled green and blue legs were clearly visible, the remains of a torn pair of tights still clinging to parts of them. Higher up, a hand with green-painted fingernails and half a face were also partially exposed; one milky, glazed eye with long eyelashes stared up at the sky.

'How did that happen?' said one of the undertakers, his voice much higher pitched than normal as the flash of a camera illuminated the body.

Jason could only shake his head. 'Is that even possible? I mean, how did she get *under* the soil?'

A member of the CSI team ran over to the coffin, still dangling in the air, and knocked on the bottom of it. 'She didn't, it's solid. The bottom hasn't come away at all. Could it be… *another* body?'

Barry felt his stomach lurch. How the hell had a body got into this grave? He'd dug this one himself: prepared the hole and shored up the sides ready for the burial. There hadn't been a body in the grave when he'd finished. He'd even been the one to fill it back in because lazy bastard Jason had thrown a sickie. But he hadn't noticed anything amiss. Wouldn't he have noticed another body down there?

One of the CSIs was talking urgently into the radio clipped to his shirt as the other one walked towards him and Jason.

'Thanks, guys, we'll take it from here. I'm afraid I'm going to have to ask you to step away. This is a crime scene now.'

Barry felt himself being tugged backwards and turned to see Jason pulling him away towards the path. The undertakers and environmental health officer followed quickly behind them until they all stood huddled next to the silver van with blacked-out windows belonging to the undertakers. All of them turned to watch, their eyes drawn towards the grave and the coffin suspended in mid-air above it.

Dark clouds rolled over the sun, and Barry didn't think he'd ever felt so cold.

# CHAPTER TWO

Elizabeth Adams tucked the silver, chin-length hair that normally hid the scar on the side of her forehead behind her ears and wiped the sweat from her brow with her sleeve. Strong arms grabbed her as a foot slipped around the back of her leg and she felt herself falling through the air, landing on the gym mat with a loud 'Agh'. Her assailant towered above her with a grin on his face. He held out his hand, and she took it as he pulled her to her feet.

'That was sneaky, and you know it.'

'You left yourself wide open. It was an opportunity and I took it.'

She wanted to give him the finger but managed to restrain herself. He was right: she'd taken her eyes off him for a moment and he'd got the advantage. She knew the golden rule: never take your eyes off your opponent. It was a reminder to be alert at all times and one she shouldn't have needed. To say she was annoyed with herself was an understatement; it could have been anyone. Just because she was in the church hall where the self-defence classes were held didn't matter. She knew better; an attack could happen anywhere at any time, even in your own home. She stopped herself before the memories could come flooding back.

'Yes, I did. Well done.'

He saluted her and walked over to the crowd of newbies who were huddled in the corner staring open-mouthed at her. She could tell they were hoping that Phil, who was over six foot tall and had muscles Arnold Schwarzenegger would be proud of, wouldn't pick one of them for his next victim. A phone vibrated on the windowsill and she glanced sideways, knowing it would be hers; it always was, no matter how many times she was supposed to be off duty, she never really was. This was her weekend off and she'd had every intention of spending her Saturday doing nothing but drinking tea and reading, but then the guilt had kicked in: she'd missed her evening class, so had decided to get out of the house and come to the Saturday lunchtime one. Although not necessary for everyone, human interaction and an attempt at some kind of social life, for her, was something she knew she had to force herself to do. Striding towards the window, she picked up her phone.

'Doctor Adams.'

'This is the Force Incident Manager. We have a serious problem. Someone's found a body in a grave that shouldn't be there.'

She shook her head. When didn't the police have a problem?

'What's the address? I'll be there as soon as I can.'

As she listened, she grabbed a pen off the windowsill and was about to scribble the details down on the back of her hand when she stopped: there was no need. She knew this address well, although she hadn't been there for quite some time.

As she said goodbye and ended the call, a loud shout behind her made her jump. Turning around she saw that Phil was now towering over one of the newbies who was lying on the gym mat clutching at his stomach and groaning. She smiled to herself. She'd been there before many times. It hurt like hell when you winded yourself by landing heavily in an unexpected move. That guy wouldn't forget that in a hurry, or the laughter coming from the others around him. It would make or break him; he'd either get up and start again to prove he wasn't a pushover, or he'd hide at the back until the self-defence class was finished. She hoped he stuck it out; he looked as if he needed all the help he could get.

She grabbed her water bottle and car keys from the window ledge, turning to wave at Phil, who nodded in return. He was a nice guy and he worked her hard now, but he'd taken his time and never pushed her too far in the early days when she'd plucked up the courage to walk in and sign herself up to join the class. He never asked questions and she never told him why she was there, although he probably recognised her from the newspapers. Everyone did, eventually, even though she'd cut her long, blonde hair and asked the hairdresser to turn it ash grey to make herself look older and blend in. Now it seemed everyone wanted to be grey. The only time in her life she'd been a leader in the fashion world, she chuckled to herself.

As she left the church hall she scanned the car park, making sure there was no one around. It made her angry that she was now so aware and conscious about her safety. Only a few years ago it would never have entered her head: she'd always been so sure of herself. She clicked the fob and the lights on her black BMW X1 blinked in response: not too flashy but it had made her feel safe when she'd taken it for a test drive. It was solid, yet fast if she needed it to be. Climbing in, habit made her turn her head and check the back seat was empty; the constant fear that someone might be hiding in it sometimes made living her life impossible. Breathing out a sigh of relief at the sight of her gym bag and empty coffee cup, she started the car. The cemetery was less than ten minutes away.

# CHAPTER THREE

Detective Sergeant Josh Walker got out of the unmarked Ford Focus and stared at the sight in front of him with his mouth open. He turned to his colleague, Detective Constable Sam Thomas, pointed to the dirt-covered coffin dangling mid-air and whispered, 'Well there's something you don't see every day.' She shook her head, speechless. Josh lifted his hand, waving at Claire and Carl, the two CSIs who'd had the privilege of documenting what should have been a straightforward grave exhumation. Claire waved back, while Carl nodded and pointed at his protective suit. Josh realised he was telling him to get suited and booted, so he walked around to the boot of the car where he kept a supply of the essentials needed to enter a serious crime scene. Sam followed and the pair of them began to open the plastic packets and dress in the protective clothing.

Josh tugged on some protective shoe covers along with a pair of rubber gloves and headed towards the scene that had been cordoned off with blue and white crime scene tape. He ducked under it, turning to see if Sam was behind him, but she was still by the car, talking to someone on her phone. He smiled to himself: she was a little too squeamish sometimes for this job, but as they had been the only two left in the office, he'd had no choice but to bring her along.

'So tell me how a body can end up in a grave *underneath* a coffin. Are you sure it didn't fall out of it?' Josh said, catching up with Carl and walking alongside him towards the grave.

Carl rolled his eyes at him. 'Yes, I'm bloody sure. What do you take me for, Josh? I'm not an idiot; the coffin is new. It's rock solid. There's no way she's come out of there.'

Josh walked along the metal plates that had been put down along the grass verge to lead a path to the open grave without contaminating the scene. 'Maybe the rain washed the body from another grave into this one? That storm was terrible; it poured for days.'

'And maybe you watch too many horror films, Josh. There's no way that's happened, it's impossible.'

'How do you know that?'

'Because the grave has four solid walls. It didn't give way when it was dug out and the coffin removed. It's a perfect, oblong hole in the ground. The only way it got there was because someone put it there.'

Josh had reached the gravesite. Stepping forward he peered down into the grave.

'Bollocks, I hate it when you're right, Carl.'

Carl laughed. 'I know you do, but it doesn't take a hotshot DS to figure this one out. Sorry to take away some of your glory. You do, however, have a chance to redeem yourself. I'll leave it to you to figure out who the body belongs to and how it got there.'

Josh felt the beginning of a headache set in. Jodie was going to go mad; friends of hers were celebrating their wedding anniversary, and they were supposed to be going to the meal tonight. This was going to be a long one. There was no way he was going to be clocking off work on time. Unzipping his suit, he reached inside his trouser pocket to find his phone. He'd better ring her now and get it over with: there was no point making her wait until last minute. He stared down at the partially buried body; his eyes widened as he felt his stomach churn. The victim was a girl, judging by the torn tights and the lurid green nail varnish he could see on the two fingers that were sticking through the soil. From what he could make out of her somewhat crushed face, she didn't look much older than nineteen or twenty. Around the same age as his younger sister. He shuddered; too young to be dead. Questions he couldn't answer were flowing through his mind, the most pressing, *who are you*, and *how the hell did you get down there?*

'What's wrong?' Jodie's voice shouted down the mobile clamped to his ear and he pulled the phone away a little, so she didn't deafen him.

'Nothing's wrong.'

'You only ever ring me during the day if you're going to be late home or if you want something. So, what's wrong?'

He paused for a moment wondering if she was right. Did he only ever ring when it was bad news? He stepped away from the grave. It didn't seem right to have his angry wife shouting at him in front of the dead. It felt somehow disrespectful.

'Something's come up. I'm not going to be home on time.'

'I bloody knew it, always the same with you, Josh.'

'I'm sorry, but this is important.'

'Everything is important, except for me that is.'

He cringed, hoping no one else could hear her. 'I'm sorry, Jodie, go to dinner without me. If I can get away I will, but don't wait for me.' The line went dead, and his heart sank. Things had been getting worse lately. She'd never truly understand, but with recent cuts in the department he was on call more than he was off duty; she only stopped complaining for a moment when his wages went into the bank. One day he'd pluck up the courage to confront her: he was running out of reasons why they were still together. They had nothing in common any more; he knew he needed to sort it out because there was no way he was spending the rest of his life living like this. If there was one thing dealing with murders and sudden deaths had taught him, it was that you only get one shot at living and you should really make the most of it.

Sam, who had finally plucked up the courage to take a look at the scene, walked towards him. 'Everything okay, boss?'

'Yes, thanks. Let's get this sorted. We need a pathologist. We'll probably need an anthropologist as well, but we'll wait and see what Doctor Adams suggests. Do you know if she's been called out?'

Sam nodded. 'Control messaged whilst you were on the phone to say she was on her way.'

'Good, that's good.' Josh felt his stomach unclench a little knowing it was Beth who would be attending. She was the best forensic pathologist he'd ever worked with and a good friend. She was also a professional of the highest standards which made his life a little bit easier. There was nothing else he could do apart from speak to the witnesses whilst he waited for her. The scene was hers; she would dictate what needed to be done and by whom.

A large raindrop landed on his face as he walked towards the two men standing next to the private ambulance, both wearing high-vis safety vests. The older of the two had no colour in his face and looked as if he could do with a shot of brandy for the shock. Josh felt bad for him; it must have been terrible enough having to exhume a grave without the added extra surprise of finding another body in there. Looking up at the rapidly darkening sky he felt more drops of rain fall on his head. It was about to lash it down. He heard Carl and Claire shouting as they ran towards the CSI van, and he hoped they had a tent in there to cover the grave or they were liable to lose any trace evidence.

Different scenarios were playing through Josh's mind, but the only one that made sense was the one that told him this wasn't an accident. Whoever this girl was, she had been put there intentionally, seemingly by someone who'd thought she wouldn't be found. He had to hand it to them, it was clever; hiding a body in a grave which had already been dug for someone else was sick and twisted, but brilliant in its own terrible way.

# CHAPTER FOUR

Beth stared at the huge, rusted cast iron gates that sealed off the east side of Fell View Cemetery as she pulled up and a police officer checked her ID.

'Afternoon, ma'am, they're up on the hill near the church. A bright yellow digger truck with a coffin dangling from it: you can't miss it.'

She tried her best not to let the small smile which played across her lips turn into a smirk: dark humour was prevalent throughout the police and her own medical profession.

'Thank you. Can you tell me if the duty DS is here yet?'

She nodded. 'Yep, he turned up thirty minutes ago.'

Beth smiled again, driving through the imposing Victorian gateway into the cemetery. It was one of the most breathtaking places to visit in the Lake District and was often filled with tourists. Not today though: they'd all have been ushered out. The windscreen wipers swished the heavy rain off the glass, giving her a clear view for a second before it was covered again. She looked around; nature was fighting a battle against the council to take control of the grounds and from this perspective it seemed that nature was winning. The Gothic monuments and crumbling gravestones from this side looked like something out of a horror film; they were in desperate need of renovation and repair. Long, overgrown grass and weeds hid the faded names on the majority of the graves making them hard to read. Before she'd become such a recluse she'd spent many hours wandering around the area. There was something so calming about a walk through this part of the cemetery. It was like stepping back in time and history, looking at names and wondering what the people were like, what sort of lives they had led before their deaths. Centre stage was a sunken circular row of mausoleums owned by the area's wealthiest families. Last time she'd walked around, it had been sealed off because of the state of disrepair they were in. This part of the cemetery was closed off for public burials and pretty much everything else until the council and the volunteers who had decided they wanted to take control of it came to an amicable agreement about maintaining it.

She carried on driving up the hill to the newer part of the graveyard, which was where the good citizens of Windermere and the surrounding villages were laid to rest. The boarded-up chapel, which had never been consecrated, served only as a funerary chapel. It had never been used as a place of worship and sat at the peak of the hill, surrounded by much smaller, modern graves than the ones she'd just passed. As she rounded the bend she muttered: 'Holy shit'. The dangling coffin against the backdrop of the grey, ominous clouds was certainly a sight to behold. Near to the digger was the private ambulance belonging to the undertakers, a police van with 'CSI' emblazoned across the side and a group of people standing around, huddled under umbrellas. On the opposite side of the church, along the main thoroughfare, were a couple of unmarked police cars, a police van and a huge carrier van which no doubt held the search team. She parked behind the carrier, got out and went around to the boot of her car so she could get dressed into her crime scene uniform.

'Hi, Beth.'

Looking up, she smiled. 'Josh, how are you?'

'Could be better, I'm glad you're on call.'

'I was about to say the same thing; I don't think I could cope with your colleague and his continual grumbling about everything.'

'You mean you don't like working with Sherlock? But he's *such* a good bloke.'

'No, I don't like working with DS Holmes. He's about as funny as a corpse.'

Josh began to laugh. 'Nah, neither do I. He's such a miserable git. Listen, this scene is a complete mystery; I've never seen anything like it. In fact, I've never *heard* of anything like it, but I'll let you take a look for yourself and see what you think.'

As she zipped up the pale blue paper suit, tugging on a pair of shoe covers and a pair of matching blue gloves, she grabbed her heavy case from the boot.

'Lead the way, I'm ready.'

*But are you really ready?* The question burned in her mind as she followed Josh across the narrow metal footpath to the crime scene. Taking the scene guard booklet from the officer standing in front of the police tape, she signed herself in. This was it, there was no going back now. Whoever was in that grave was going to demand her full attention and they were going to get it; she'd give every single piece of herself to this case. Stepping inside the tent, all noise except the steady patter of rain as it drummed against the sheeting ceased to exist. The air inside was stuffy and the muted light cast a shadow over the open grave. Beth pulled a torch from her case then stood still taking in the scene. She would live, eat, sleep and breathe it until she had solved the puzzle of the mysterious body in the grave.

# CHAPTER FIVE

Beth switched on the torch and stared down into the grave, her eyes wide and lips slightly parted. She'd seen some terrible things since she'd completed her training, the stuff that nightmares were made of, but this, this was more than terrible. It was wrong, so wrong. Why would someone put a body in a grave that had been dug for another person? From where she was standing the body looked intact, although the marbling on the exposed flesh of the legs and the putrid smell of decomposition that lingered in the air told her that it might not be the case. Through the thin layer of soil she could make out what looked like a rather tatty faded yellow dress. Turning to look at Josh as he entered the tent she mouthed: 'Why?'

He shrugged his shoulders; he couldn't answer that yet. She knew that in time to come he would be able to, as she put as much faith in his ability as a detective sergeant as he did her post-mortems. They made a pretty good team and between them had solved every murder that had come their way. For this area they had been few and far between, not like over the border in Lancashire where she also covered, that was far busier. She liked that about Cumbria: the police force was much smaller than the rest of the north-west, so it was easier to get to know the detectives you were working alongside. It was one of the reasons she lived in this county instead of anywhere else: she'd be called to local jobs with a team she trusted. She'd known Josh for years: they'd been friends at university but they'd grown closer after he'd helped her that terrible night – she stopped herself from going back in time; now wasn't the time or the place to go back there. She squatted down at the side of the grave to take a closer look at the body.

'We need a forensic archaeologist to excavate the site. Aside from being flattened with the weight of the coffin and the decomposition, our victim looks relatively fresh. How long ago was this grave dug?'

'According to the guy over there, Barry, who dug it, around eight weeks ago.'

'Well I can't tell you much until the body has been recovered to the mortuary, but I can tell you I don't think she put herself down there. She was definitely dead, or near to death when she was placed inside that grave. There is no way she could have covered herself in enough soil not to be noticed by the mourners at Florence Wright's funeral.'

Beth looked across at the men who were leaning against the side of the private ambulance, then back at Josh.

'Is Barry a viable suspect? He had access to the grave before and after: wouldn't he have noticed a body in there before the coffin was interred?'

'At this point, *everyone* is a viable suspect. I've asked for some of my team to come and take Barry, and Jason, the other guy who was operating the digger, down to the station to give a statement.'

'Good, I know it's not for me to say, but surely it has to be someone who knows all about the cemetery and how it works. You can't just rock up with a dead body and throw it in a grave hoping for the best.'

'Yeah, that's what I'm afraid of. Apparently, there's a team of two who maintain and dig the graves, plus the office staff. Then there's also the undertakers who come and go, not to mention members of the public.'

'Good point: so it could be anyone in the funeral trade?'

'Or it could have been some opportunistic killer who saw the readymade grave and decided to fill it himself.'

'So, basically, it could be anyone.'

Josh laughed. 'Basically, yes. But starting with those two at the top of my list, I guess I'll have to work my way backwards.'

Beth stood up, her back creaking; as she put her hands on her hips and stretched. 'I have a feeling this is going to be a rather difficult case, Josh. We'll have our work cut out for us.'

The look on Josh's face said he'd figured that out long before she'd arrived.

# CHAPTER SIX

There was nothing more that Beth could do at the scene for the moment. It needed to be dug out by a forensic archaeologist and the nearest one, Doctor Chris Corkill, was based at UCLA in Lancaster. He'd been called and would attend the scene first thing tomorrow morning. As much as it pained her to have to leave the nameless girl alone like this, she had no choice. At least the tent that now covered the grave allowed her some privacy. Two police officers were going to be stationed outside the tent, guarding it until Chris could get here and start the painstaking job of sifting through the soil looking for any trace evidence. The cemetery was now closed to members of the public with PCSOs guarding each entrance.

As she said her goodbyes, she spotted Josh chatting to a rather pasty-faced woman who she'd never seen before. The woman had a clipboard under one arm and the black hair that framed her face only served to make her skin look paler than pale. Beth lifted a hand at Josh, who excused himself to come and speak to her.

'Is that you done?'

'Until tomorrow, yes. It's pretty obvious she's dead. You didn't need me to confirm that for you. She's been there at least eight weeks, and as much as I'd like to get her moved out of that cold, damp hole, another night isn't going to make any difference. Who was that woman you were talking to? Is she from the cemetery? She looks like she's seen a ghost.'

'No, environmental health. I didn't realise, but they have an officer present at exhumations to ensure everything is done correctly and respectfully, meeting all the health and safety regulations. The reason she looks so tense is that they've all messed up; apparently the coffin should have been exhumed in the early hours of the morning with the gravesite screened off from public view. She was sent last minute when the original officer phoned in sick, causing a bit of a delay. She freely admits she didn't know the correct protocol and is currently having a heart attack whilst waiting for her manager to get here.'

'Lord, the poor woman. Well let's hope she doesn't drop down dead here because we already have two bodies to deal with. I don't fancy adding another onto my scheduled list of post-mortems for tomorrow.'

Josh stifled a laugh with the palm of his hand. 'You're terrible! I'll see you tomorrow.'

'I know, and yes, you will. I'd say have a nice evening but, knowing you, I don't think you'll be going home anytime soon.'

She walked back to her car, where she stripped off the protective clothing and put it into a paper bag in case it was required for forensics. She hadn't been in contact with the body or been inside the grave, so it wasn't likely. Getting into her car, she turned back to look at the scene, turning on the windscreen wipers to clear the glass. The rain was coming down heavy now. The CSIs were in the process of setting up portable lights around the area. Shivering, she began to turn the car around. She didn't envy Josh and his team; it was going to be all hands on deck for them until they could get an ID for the body, and whoever was responsible for putting it there into custody.

It was almost dark by the time Beth arrived home, the sky full of stormy, grey clouds. As she waited for the automatic gates to open, she jumped out of the car to check the post box mounted by the gate. Opening it, she took one look at the single cream envelope inside and felt her stomach turn inside out. 'Damn you, Robert,' she cursed as she pulled it out and threw it into the passenger side of the car, where it slid from the leather seat and landed in the footwell.

Looking behind her to check there were no cars following her in, she drove through the gates and waited for them to close before parking as near to her house as she could and getting out. The house was built on the shore of Lake Windermere and the views were stunning. Just staring at the water set against the backdrop of the fells and mountains usually calmed her; but tonight the security light which normally lit up the entire front of the house and gardens didn't turn on as she got close to the front door. The entire frontage of the property remained cloaked in shadows, and Beth felt her heart begin to beat fast. She waved her arms in the air to set the motion detector off – nothing. Finding her mouth dry, she felt the familiar palpitations that signalled the beginnings of a panic attack. She took deep breaths as she tried to get the key into the front door with shaking hands. *It's okay, Beth, the bulb has blown, nothing else. Deep breaths. Everything is good, you can do this.* Finally the key slid home and she turned it, her ears attuned to every noise, straining to pick up on anything that didn't belong. Pushing the door open, she threw herself inside, slammed it shut, locked it and turned the deadbolt. No matter how many times she whispered 'Stop it, Beth' to herself, she knew the tears were going to come. And they did, fast and furious: a hot, salty mess rolling down her cheeks as she leant, panting, with her back against the front door. The long, clear note of the intruder alarm told her that she was safe, that there was no one home, but it didn't do much to calm her racing heart. If she didn't key in the code in the next few seconds all hell would break loose, so she turned and deftly typed the sequence of numbers into the keypad. The beeping stopped and silence took over the house. She finally let out the breath she'd been holding on to. Her life was a mess. *She* was a mess.

Kicking off her shoes into the hall closet, she hung up her jacket and managed to walk down to the kitchen. She had an expensive camera system that covered both inside and out of the property and she wanted to check them for signs that anyone had been trespassing. Before doing that, though, she opened the fridge and took a bottle of chilled wine from the rack. No need to look far for a glass as there was one still on the draining board from last night. Pouring herself a generous measure, she lifted it to her lips and swallowed a huge mouthful. It felt good. The only thing she knew she could rely on, lately, was the soothing effect a glass of wine had on her supercharged nerves. Sighing, she went into the utility room which doubled as a downstairs office to check the cameras. She'd had this room specially designed with a heavy, metal, fire-resistant door, secured from the inside with several locks. If anyone ever got past the gates and the alarm system outside, she had the luxury of her own little panic room inside, to lock herself into whilst waiting for the police to arrive. It was just an empty space, nothing fancy or high tech, but having her own safe room gave her an added sense of security should she ever need to hide from an intruder. 'Or a killer,' she whispered to herself.

# CHAPTER SEVEN

The phone ringing woke Beth. She looked across to the window and was surprised to see the sun streaming through the cracks in the blinds. Reaching under her pillow she answered it, expecting it to be Josh.

'Good morning, this is Steve from Safe & Secure. I got the message you left on the answerphone last night; I can be with you in an hour, if that's okay?'

She sat up. 'Really, but it's Sunday morning?'

'Yes, of course. But I'm sorry, we do charge a little extra for a weekend call out. If you prefer I can leave it until tomorrow?'

'No, not at all. Today is fine. I'm sorry if my message last night seemed a bit panicked.'

'Don't worry, I figured it must be important, so I'll be there soon. Can I check the address though? I think last time I came the satnav told me I'd arrived, but I couldn't find the property?'

She laughed. 'Yes, it does that. The house is pretty remote. Once you get on my road, drive just as far as you can, and the gate is on the right. It's quite well hidden: there's a small gap between the hedging that leads to the gates.'

'I remember now. Thank you, I'll see you soon.'

He hung up, and she clambered out of bed. Too much wine last night had made her head a little fuzzy this morning. When she'd checked the cameras the previous night, she'd discovered the outside and inside front ones weren't working and she'd almost had a meltdown, terrified that someone had been onto her property and sabotaged them. But then she'd talked herself down, reasoning that to have done something to the camera inside they'd have had to have gained entry to the house, which was totally secure. The alarm hadn't been triggered, so it was probably just a power cut, or maybe the rain had got to the wiring. There was probably some perfectly good reason for it, she knew, but she was unsure and had rung the alarm company in a panic. She'd then taken her wine and a family sized bag of salt and vinegar crisps up to bed with her, resisting the urge to phone Josh, to take comfort in his calm friendly voice and ask him to come and check the cameras for her.

The intercom for the gate buzzed. She'd showered, dressed and made a pot of tea. She checked the camera on the gate to see a large white van with 'Safe & Secure' emblazoned across the side. The large, confident black lettering made her feel instantly better. She opened the gates and watched Steve drive through them. She opened the door as far as it would go with the heavy-duty safety chain on.

'Morning, Ms Adams.'

'Morning, sorry to ask, but please could I see your ID?'

There was some rustling as he pulled the lanyard over the baseball cap on his head, passing the card with a full colour photograph of the man standing outside the door on it to her. Despite remembering him from the last time he'd attended, she still took it from him, scrutinised the picture of the man then nodded. Sliding the chain off, she opened the door wide. He grinned at her and she couldn't help but smile back. She hadn't remembered him to be quite so good-looking.

'Thank you, the operating system is through here,' she said, leading him through to the utility room.

He whistled at the huge display monitor and top-of-the range computer system. Turning to her, he nodded. 'Still got a really good set-up. So, what seems to be the problem?'

Like on his last visit, he was discreet. If he'd noticed the metal door he didn't mention it. He also didn't mention the rows of medical books on the shelves above the desk either even though he'd glanced at them several times.

'Both the main camera on the front door and the downstairs internal camera which covers the entrance and part of the ground floor are faulty. The rest of them seem to be working fine. Have a seat and I'll leave you to it.'

He nodded, sitting down on the chair and pressing buttons to check the system. Walking off, Beth paused to ask, 'Would you like a drink?'

He turned to her, smiling. 'I'd murder a coffee. One sugar, please. I didn't have time this morning.'

She made him his coffee and poured herself a mug of freshly brewed tea while he went out to his van to get his ladder and toolbox. Taking his drink down to him, he took it from her, and he began to chat. Despite her best intention to leave him to it she found herself chatting back: he was friendly and easy to talk to. It had been a long time since she'd had a stranger in her house, and she found herself enjoying the company.

After he'd showed her what the problem was with the cameras, pointing out the loose connections, he began to dismantle the small domes that housed them. This time, she did leave him to it, aware that she didn't want to distract him too much. As much as he was a nice guy, her priority was getting her security system back up and running as soon as possible.

Settling at the breakfast bar in her kitchen, where she could see the lake, before she knew it, she'd lost herself staring out at the mass of grey-blue water. It was calm today, a lot calmer than it had been last night during the heavy rain.

'I'm finished for now.'

Beth jumped so high she almost slid off the stool. She hadn't realised Steve was standing behind her.

'Sorry, did I scare you?'

She laughed. 'A little; I tend to get lost in the lake sometimes.'

He nodded. 'I can imagine, I think I would too. That view is magnificent.'

She felt the heat rise up in her face. 'Thank you.'

'Anyway, I've managed to fix your outside camera. There were a couple of loose connections. The internal one, I'm not so sure about. I'll have to order some new parts and see if they fix it. Unfortunately, that could take a couple of days. As soon as they arrive I'll come back and get it sorted for you.'

'Thank you so much. It's funny, I've never had any problems with them before and then two of them go down at once. Did you manage to get the light fixed?'

'Yes, that was easy. It just needed a new bulb. It's always the way with these things. At least everything else is working okay. And thank you for the coffee; it was the best I've tasted.'

'Blimey, if that was the best you've had I feel sorry for you. I'm more of a tea drinker so I have no idea if my coffee is even palatable.'

'Well it was perfect.' He winked at her, and she felt the warm blush begin to rise further up her cheeks.

'Take care, Ms Adams.'

'Bye, Steve.'

She walked him to the front door, closing and locking it behind him. Then went to watch the cameras. Nice as he'd seemed, she had to make sure he drove out of the gates and didn't do anything to arouse her suspicion. Men, in particular, had to earn that trust from her. No one could blame her for that after what had happened.

She looked at her watch, time to get going. Doctor Corkill should be arriving at the cemetery in the next hour. Josh had texted to say he'd meet her there. A few more hours for their Jane Doe wasn't going to make much difference. At least they'd found her. It might take a while, but once the site was properly processed and the girl's body removed, they'd be able to work on identifying her so that her own family could give her the burial she deserved. Life was cruel. The girl was far too young to be lying in a grave, crushed under the weight of someone else's coffin.

She opened the drive gates and watched the van leave. She didn't bother to shut them again: she needed to get going if she was going to make it back to the cemetery on time.

Shrugging on her favourite black linen jacket, she put on a pair of walking boots and tucked her jeans into them. The heavy rain which had set in yesterday afternoon had eased off, but today it was still drizzling, which would make the grave site slippery and forensically a bit of a challenge. That was the thing with the Lakes; it had its own distinct weather pattern. One minute the sun would be burning hot, the next clouds and rain. Still, she wouldn't swap it for the world. She realised how lucky she was that she could afford to live in such a beautiful, secluded area. At first she'd thought about buying a house in the middle of a busy town where she'd be surrounded by people and never truly alone, but then she'd realised that she'd always be on edge, wondering who her neighbours were. What the noise was. Who was outside. At least here, even though she was miles from another living soul, nobody knew where she was. With her cameras, alarms and self-defence skills she'd be ready. She knew the statistics. Christ, she'd spent a lifetime researching violent crimes. How many post-mortems had she completed on innocent people killed by someone else, for no apparent reason? Too many to count. But she'd nearly died once, and she wasn't going to let it happen again.

She set the alarms and did her usual checks before locking up and getting into her car, waiting to see the electric gates shut in her rear-view mirror. The cemetery was fifteen minutes from her house on a good day when the roads weren't full of coaches carrying tourists.

Heading to the crime scene, she let her mind wander to Josh for a moment as she drove. There were rumours that his marriage wasn't working out, and she wanted to tell him she was there for him should he need a place to crash or someone to talk to. It was the least she could do for him, but she knew deep down that she wouldn't mention it. She laughed at herself; these days the deepest conversations she had were with the dead who came into her mortuary. Glancing at her reflection in the rear-view mirror, she checked herself. *You need to claim back your life, Beth. It doesn't matter that you survived; he's still won if you keep living in fear like this.*

# CHAPTER EIGHT

The story had broken on the local paper's Facebook page this morning, and it would no doubt be front page news in the papers tomorrow morning. Pictures of the freshly dug up coffin dangling from the jaws of the digger filled her phone screen, but the reporter didn't know the full extent of the story, and the police were doing their best to keep it that way. The family of Florence Wright, the poor woman inside the coffin that had been dug up, were going to be horrified. It was bad enough that a question mark over her cause of death had resulted in the exhumation in the first place.

Inching her car through the crowds of onlookers – she supposed the local cafés and gift shops had never seen so much custom – she drove back through the east gate and flashed her ID for the police community support officer to wave her through. The coffin, thankfully, had been taken away to the mortuary late last night after the scene above ground had been processed. Florence Wright's postmortem had been pulled forward to first thing tomorrow morning, to make room for an examination of the surprise second body. It was cold and clinical, but this was how Beth's world operated. Grieving was a luxury for the family and friends; her job was to determine how, and why. Beth would grieve in her own way, but only when the case was closed.

She parked behind Josh's Mini Cooper, smiling to herself as she wondered, not for the first time, why someone so tall would choose to drive a car so small. She got out and made her way towards the white tent which had been erected over the open grave yesterday, to provide privacy and preserve any evidence. And in a case like this which, thanks to the Facebook scoop, was going to be headlines in all the national newspapers, they needed to keep a lid on it for as long as they possibly could.

Someone exited the tent just as she was approaching and, despite being dressed from head to toe in protective clothing, she knew it was Josh from the way he stooped on the way out. He lifted his hand in greeting.

'Is Dr Corkill there?'

Josh nodded. 'He is, with one of his archaeology students. I think we should be good to move the second body in the next hour.'

Beth felt relieved that Corkill was on the case. He was good: one of the best. She would poke her head inside and see how he was getting on. If he needed her assistance, then she'd suit up and dive right in. If not, she'd go to the mortuary to wait for the body to arrive. She had two assistants who were more than capable of booking the body in, but she felt as if she needed to be there for this one. This girl deserved more than the end she'd been given, and it would make Beth feel a little better knowing she'd been the one to take care of her every need from now on.

The tent opening pushed aside once more, and Beth smiled as she locked eyes with the doctor.

'Chris, it's good to see you.'

He pulled back the hood of the white paper suit he was wearing, grinning at her with the smile of a guy half his age.

'Beth, you too. It's just a shame we only ever meet under such tragic circumstances. You'll be pleased to know the body is intact. Apart from the usual decomposition, she's pretty well preserved. I won't have an awful lot of input once we've removed her and sieved the soil for trace evidence. She'll be all yours unless you need help with identification. There are signs of some dental work and a couple of older scars – one on her forearm, another on her right shoulder – that suggests it will be straightforward.'

'Ever the optimist, Chris.' Beth smiled.

'Someone has to be, Beth, there are enough pessimists in this world.'

She couldn't disagree with him. She'd been full of optimism at one point in her life, before fear and regret took over.

'Do you want to oversee her removal? Or are you happy for us to crack on?'

She nodded. It wasn't that she didn't trust anyone else to do it: she felt as if she had to.

'No, you take the lead. I'll be here, but I won't get in the way.'

He nodded, then turned and ducked back inside the tent. Josh gently took hold of her elbow, leading her away so they couldn't be overheard.

'Is everything okay?'

She glared at him. 'What's that supposed to mean?'

'Just that, you seem a little edgy this morning.'

'Yes, everything's fine. Well, apart from the fact that some sicko hid a girl's body in someone else's grave, I'm good.'

He arched one eyebrow at her. 'Really?'

She blew out her cheeks. 'I'm just a little stressed. Two of my cameras went down last night.'

'I knew something was wrong. Do you think someone tampered with them?'

'I don't know, I don't think so. It's just unnerved me a little.'

She was aware she'd lowered her voice. She didn't mind Josh knowing what a mess she was, but there was no way she'd let anyone else hear about it.

'Want me to come over when we've finished here? We can have a beer and you can cook me some of those burritos you're so very good at?'

Beth laughed. 'If you want to, but I don't want to get in the way of any plans you and Jodie might have.'

'Jodie's gone to visit her sister – again.'

'Ouch, that bad?'

'You can't even imagine.'

Beth smiled; the things she could imagine would give anyone nightmares for the rest of their lives.

# CHAPTER NINE

Beth, Josh, Chris and his student, Amber, bowed their heads respectfully as the undertakers wheeled the trolley past them. Until they identified her and found her family, the girl was their responsibility and Beth took some light relief in knowing that she had such a talented team fighting her corner. It was a shame no one had been around to fight for her when she was alive. Beth gulped, hoping to God that the girl was dead before she was buried. The thought made her squirm as all sorts of scenarios played out in her head; in each the face she saw on the body was her own.

The van doors slammed shut behind her and she jumped so high Josh grabbed her.

Beth knew she was acting strangely; he could tell she didn't want him to think she was losing it and not fit to work this case, because he knew she was more than capable.

'Right, I'll go to the mortuary and get her booked in. Josh, I'll see you later,' Beth said, as calmly and matter-of-factly as she could.

Josh's phone began to ring, and he fumbled in his pocket for it, sticking his thumb up at Beth as he headed back towards his car, his voice hushed and urgent. She watched him for a moment as he stripped off his protective clothing and ducked inside his car, his phone still glued to his ear. He looked tired and stressed.

The undertakers were waiting for her to leave first, to open the mortuary doors at the other end, so she hurried over to her car and got in. Despite the warmth of the sun, she was chilled beyond belief. She turned on the heater and waited for the blast of warm air to hit her face and warm her bones. Something about this case was really unsettling her, but she didn't know what.

The drive to the hospital was a long one; the mortuary at Westmorland General in Kendal was being refurbished, so the body was taken to Furness General Hospital in the small industrial town of Barrow-in-Furness. The road from Bowness was a nightmare: all twists and turns, traffic lights every couple of miles while the water mains were being replaced and the slowest moving cars she'd ever known. When she finally turned onto Abbey Road she breathed a sigh of relief. She'd phoned ahead so the mortuary staff knew they were on their way. Turning right onto Dalton Lane as she crested the brow of the hill, she saw the hospital and her heart did a little jump, just like it always did whenever she had cause to work from here. It was the hospital they'd rushed her to that night, where the busy accident and emergency department staff had worked so hard on her. She'd forever be in their debt.

Blowing out her cheeks, she turned into the huge grounds and drove around to the staff car park at the rear of the hospital, where the mortuary entrance was situated, and where a familiar face was waiting for her. Abandoning her car on a gravelled area with a huge wooden sign that said 'No Parking', she got out and jogged over to Abe. They smacked hands in a high five.

'Ouch, Doc. I swear you hit harder every time.'

She smiled. 'I've been practising.'

They then hit knuckles together and both laughed. 'You know out of all the doctors, nurses, coppers and undertakers who come through here you're the only one who knows how to greet me with a bit of respect.'

'That's because they don't have the same street cred as me.' She looked around to see the undertakers' silver van turning the corner to drive towards them.

'This is a bad one, Abe.'

'Most of them are.'

'No, this is—' She hesitated, not quite sure how she could describe the situation to the young man standing in front of her, his dreadlocks tied in a neat ponytail and his tattoos covered by his hospital scrubs. He probably wasn't much older than the girl inside the body bag and she often wondered why he'd ended up working as an anatomical pathology technician. One of these days she would get around to asking about his career choice, but, then again, it was probably the same reason she ended up becoming a forensic pathologist: she trusted the dead more than the living. He seemed like a confident young man though, not an edgy recluse like her. 'This one is dark,' she finished, lamely.

He nodded. 'I heard you found her in someone else's grave. That's bad. The old lady they exhumed got brought in last night. The coffin is all set up, ready to go for the morning.'

'Thank you, I'm going to book the Jane Doe in. I'll be here first thing to do the PM on the exhumation. I want it done and everything cleared for the afternoon.'

'You'll figure it out, Doc, you always do.'

'I hope so, Abe, I really do.'

He smiled at her, opening the doors wide for the trolley carrying the body to be carried through.

# CHAPTER TEN

He knew that the mortuary nearest to the crime scene was off the cards, of course he did. When he'd read in the local newspaper about it closing temporarily, he knew it was now or never: the perfect time to make his move. He'd been watching her and biding his time for more than seven years, and he could wait no longer. The physical pain inside his chest every time he saw her had become unbearable.

Everything changed the day he'd gone into the attic to fix a leak in the roof and found the box he'd stashed away under the eaves in a blind panic all those years ago. Sitting on the floor, he'd carefully slit the tape with the penknife he always kept in his pocket and pulled out the book he'd wrapped lovingly in brown paper and tied with string, a disguise so as not to arouse suspicion should the police ever have a reason to search his property. Slowly unwrapping it and revealing the well-worn cover, he felt the familiar stirrings in his loins as keenly as he had the first time he'd ever read it. *The Collector* by John Fowles had a cult following, it appealed to a select few, the elite as he liked to think of them. He wondered if the author had ever expected what he wrote to inspire killers around the globe. Somehow he didn't think so, but the book had unleashed in him an insatiable need to be in control of others, and now it was time to act.

As he drove along the deserted road he wondered how safe Beth really felt living out here on her own. Did the seclusion give her a false sense of security, or did it heighten it? Did she sleep at night, maybe she self-medicated? He could imagine her more likely to pour herself a couple of glasses of wine to wind down and relax than taking prescription medication.

He wanted to keep her busy, busier than she'd been in a long time. He wanted her to lie in bed at night awake wondering how the girl had got into that grave, why she'd been put there and who had put her down there. Who had killed her. It was going to be fun watching her pull her hair out trying to figure it out all by herself. She wouldn't give in because that wasn't her style. She would take it personally; of this he had no doubt.

At first he'd thought of her as Doctor Adams, then Elizabeth. Now, well, he felt as if he knew her well enough to call her Beth, just like her very few close friends did. He drove past the nondescript gates that guarded the entrance to her property: she'd chosen them so that they didn't stand out or draw attention to the house behind them. The house he'd studied carefully from afar; he knew the layout like his own. He'd got access to the plans through the local council planning portal and spent many hours imagining what she did in each room when she was home alone. He knew she hadn't scrimped on the security: there were cameras and a fancy alarm system. He also knew there were blind spots to the cameras because he'd been and inspected the exact same alarm system at the showroom and the salesman had admitted there wasn't a hundred per cent full coverage. She didn't have cameras on the whole grounds to the house, just the front and back doors. The drone he flew overhead whilst she was out at work had filmed everything for him. He'd then downloaded it all so he could study it for hours on end. Occasionally, when she was home he'd fly it overhead to get images of her. He didn't dare fly it too low when she was there; a couple of times he'd filmed her pottering around in the garden in a pair of cut-off shorts. She had good legs: nice, long and toned with a light, golden suntan. He wouldn't like to get caught between those legs; he knew she was pretty good at self-defence because he also watched her going into the community hall to attend the weekly classes.

He parked his car on the grass verge further down from her house than he'd have liked and put his hazard lights on. He could see a group of hillwalkers in the distance, adding to the risk, adding to the thrill. If anyone stopped or wondered what the car was doing on this normally deserted stretch of road he could pretend it had broken down. It had been risky pulling the cables out of her camera yesterday, but worth it. He'd found a blind spot, or what he hoped was one, when he'd squeezed through the tight gap in the hedging. She'd just left for the cemetery and he knew she'd be tied up for a couple of hours giving him free rein of the gardens.

Grabbing the carrier bag from the boot of the car he crossed the road, walking around to the narrow gap he'd found. If she knew about it then he had no doubt she'd have had a six-foot-six brick wall built around the entire perimeter. As he slipped through he muttered under his breath as a sharp hawthorn branch scratched at his arm and snagged his T-shirt. He looked down to see a thin line of blood appear. He swore; the last thing he needed was to leave traces of his blood around. It stopped before it got going: it was only a surface wound. Standing against the hedge, he stared at the house. It was nice. Very impressive. He could have lived in a house like this. He almost did for a short spell of time, but it hadn't worked out and he'd had to leave.

Walking over to the front door, he reached inside the bag and pulled out the gift he had brought for her, left it at her door and pushed his way back out. The road was still deserted; no nosy tourist or Good Samaritan had stopped to see if he needed a hand with his car. He laid the bunch of red roses a short distance away from the entrance gates to her house: a non-threatening gift from an admirer that wouldn't be ignored. Briskly crossing the road, he strode back towards it, tugging off the thick leather gloves he'd been wearing. He opened the boot and threw them inside. His hands slick with sweat, he wiped them on his trouser leg.

# CHAPTER ELEVEN

Josh arrived back at the station a hot, sweaty mess. He could have gone home to shower and change, but that would have meant having to face Jodie. He was in no mood to face her, or another argument. He felt a little bad for lying to Beth, though, as he'd much rather spend time with her. They would've been able to discuss the case. He kept a spare set of clothes and a shower bag in his locker. Grabbing everything, he went to the men's toilets where there were two shower cubicles.

Hanging up his clean trousers and shirt, he took the shower gel and a towel with him, locking the door. If anyone needed the toilet they could go and use the gents further down the hall. What he needed was ten minutes alone to scrub his skin clean and process everything he'd just witnessed. Stripping off, he stepped out his clothes and kicked them to one side. The water wasn't as hot as he liked, but it would do. He stepped under the spray, squeezing a huge dollop of lime shower gel into his hands and lathering his entire body and hair. He had to squeeze his eyes tight to stop the scented gel from making them sting. People thought being a copper made you hard as nails. It did, to a certain degree: there were things you dealt with on autopilot, you didn't think about it. He'd been to car crashes where there had been multiple fatalities, attended suicides, murders and domestic abuse cases that had stayed with him long after the offenders had been jailed. Most of the time he was okay with it, sad for the family and friends left behind, no doubt, but this case had got under his skin more than he cared to admit. The horror of seeing the girl's pale flesh peeking through the soil had given him a fitful night's sleep. He'd kept waking up a few times gasping for air, convinced he'd been buried alive. He could still feel the imaginary weight of a coffin pressing on his chest.

He turned the shower off and stepped out into the now-steamy bathroom. The mirrors were fogged up. Drying himself as briskly as he could he then dressed and unlocked the door, propping it open to let some air in. The extractor fan wasn't working, so he rubbed his arm against one of the windows to see his reflection, comb his hair and check he looked presentable.

The clock was ticking, but thankfully, Florence Wright, the woman in the process of being exhumed yesterday, wasn't anything to do with him until Beth had conducted the post-mortem. If the PM indicated that foul play had led to her death then he'd become involved: a murder investigation would be opened. But if not, he'd begin on the second investigation: first, he'd identify the girl in the grave, and then he'd find her killer. He sent up a silent prayer that he'd only have the girl in the grave to look after, because he didn't know if he had the energy to run two murder investigations at the same time with such a small team.

He strolled through the warren of dark corridors until he reached the rear staircase which would take him straight up to the too-small office which housed CID. Kendal police station had seen better days; it was old-fashioned, with lots of small offices, unlike the fancy new glass one that had been built down in Barrow. On the odd occasion when he'd had to travel down there to work, he'd decided that they could keep their new station with its open-plan offices and hot desks; he much preferred the privacy here. If he needed space to think he could disappear into one of the many smaller offices and shut the door. Even the higher-ranking officers down in Barrow didn't have anywhere to hide.

He turned the corner into his office to see his team fighting over the box of biscuits he'd brought in to bribe them to stay late. He grinned; they were easily bought. It was a small price to pay for such dedication.

# CHAPTER TWELVE

Beth finished the paperwork for her Jane Doe: she had full responsibility for her now. The body bag containing the crushed, rotting corpse wouldn't be opened until she began the full PM tomorrow. What had happened to her? Beth doubted she was out of her teen years yet, so why the hell wasn't anyone looking for her? Josh would have said if there was a chance she might be a match for any high-risk missing persons. She didn't understand it; surely someone had to have wondered where the girl was. It struck her suddenly that maybe she had more in common with this girl than she thought. Beth was a loner, like her; what if she disappeared off the face of the earth one day? She knew that Josh would be the first one to question where she was, then there was her team of staff if she didn't turn up to work. *But who else, Beth? Maybe she's just like you, with a tiny circle of friends and no family to care for her?* The thought made her heart ache; imagine something this terrible happening to you and no one even caring?

Tomorrow was going to be a very long day. She glanced up at the clock in her office, surprised to see it was almost eight. She saved the files onto the computer then stood up and stretched; poor Abe would be ready to go home. Going back through to the mortuary she saw him hosing down the tables and floor, which were already spotless. He was so good, always paying attention to the details, to the things that really counted. She wished she could hire him to be her full-time assistant.

'Hey, I didn't realise it was so late. You can go home you know.'

'So can you. There's nothing to do here tonight, so you might as well go home and get some sleep.'

He was right: tomorrow was going to be busy. 'I will if you do.'

He laughed and his brown eyes crinkled, his perfect white teeth showing. Watching him as he checked each fridge door to make sure the bodies inside were secure, she wondered what his girlfriend made of him working day in, day out with dead people. He walked across to her, tugging off the plastic apron he'd been wearing. He screwed it up and threw it into the special yellow waste bin then followed her out and locked the door behind them.

Waving at Abe as he strolled towards his bike, Beth carried on towards the patch of gravel where she'd abandoned her car. Her stomach growled and she realised she needed to eat. A few years ago she'd have happily spent her evening curled up in front of the television with a family size bag of crisps or large bar of chocolate, sometimes both depending upon how stressful her day had been. But since that night seven years ago, she'd swapped junk food for wine, sometimes neat vodka. Her nights of vegging out in front of the television had been replaced with exercise classes, running and self-defence training. After the night she'd almost died, she'd promised herself that she would never put herself in that position again. She'd learnt how to fight, got fit enough to run fast if she had to. The extra weight she'd carried had dropped off along with her zest for life. She walked up to the car and stared through the window into the back seat, making sure it was empty. Her heart sank. This was her life now; always living on the edge. Once upon a time she wouldn't have even double-checked if she'd locked her car and now look at her. Even though the windows were all intact, the alarm wasn't sounding, and everything was secure, she still felt her heart race.

As she climbed into the car she watched Abe unlock the huge chain from around his bike. He waved at her before racing off into the distance. She waved back even though he couldn't see. Good manners cost nothing, that was another reason she had a soft spot for him. Her stomach growled and thoughts of dinner took over. There was an amazing takeaway not too far from the hospital. Checking her phone, she read a message from Josh: he didn't think he'd make it; he was working late and wouldn't be free for supper after all. She sighed: she should have realised that he would be up to his neck in it back at the station, but the thought of spending time with him had kept her going all afternoon. It had taken away the churning in her stomach thinking of being home alone all night with a broken security system. Dialling the number, she placed her order for a Szechuan beef chow mein, salt and pepper chips and the obligatory bag of prawn crackers. *In for a penny in for a pound*, she smiled to herself.

By the time she got to the takeaway and nipped in the Co-op opposite for a bottle of wine, it would be ready. She would be home in forty-five minutes if the traffic wasn't too bad. Then she would try and spend the night relaxing, not worrying about anything other than her workload tomorrow.

# CHAPTER THIRTEEN

Jason slammed the rusted metal locker door shut. Checking there was no one around, he shoved the small ziplock bag into his trouser pocket. He had been on edge since they'd found that body yesterday; even though he'd only caught the slightest glimpse of her his stomach tied in knots every time he thought about it. She'd been a mess covered in soil, her face all squashed and the flesh slipping off it like some wax mask that was melting. He shuddered as his stomach lurched again. The door to the men's changing room slammed, making him jump. He looked up to see Barry heading towards him.

'What's up with you? You look like shit.'

'I feel like shit. Not good at all. I think I'm coming down with something.'

'Yeah, well keep away from me then. I've got a big night out planned. If you pass your germs onto me and ruin it, I'll kill you.'

Jason smiled; Barry was okay for an older bloke. A bit of a pain in the arse about not cutting corners, but he'd worked with a lot worse though, some real idiots.

'I won't. I'm going home to bed and might not be in tomorrow.'

'Make sure you ring in then, but not before I've left for Manchester and they can't ring me to come back and work.'

'Yes, *Dad*. I will.'

'Cheeky git, I'm not your dad. Even your mother doesn't know who he is.' Barry laughed at his own joke, grabbed his rucksack from his locker and walked out.

Jason stood up, his legs like jelly. He didn't know what to do. If the coppers brought in sniffer dogs, they'd find out what he'd been keeping in here, then there'd be an investigation and he could end up being arrested. He needed to get the stuff out of here, but he didn't want to take it home with him. He felt the weight of the bag in his pocket. Christ, if the coppers got wind of it, they'd still drag him in and try to pin something on him. Well they could do one – he wouldn't let that happen.

# CHAPTER FOURTEEN

Josh cleared the whiteboard of the pictures of old suspects that had been stuck on there that long ago the edges were curling. He then folded them neatly and pushed them through the slot of the box where all the official documents were put ready to be shredded. Next, he took a damp cloth and began to rub away the faded red writing from the board. He knew they were all watching him. It had been at least a year since they'd last investigated a murder in this part of Cumbria. Barrow, the largest town in south Cumbria, seemed to have more murderers than here in the heart of the county at the Lakes: CID down there were kept a lot busier, and Josh was grateful for it. Around here it was mostly rural crime: thefts, burglaries; the odd travelling gang from one of the cities would come in, ram raid a few shops and cash machines then move on. He was only thirty-four but had ten years' experience under his belt which counted for a lot in this job. Seven of them had been in CID, working his way up from detective constable to sergeant. He'd begun typing up the application for his inspector's board a couple of times only to have stopped midway and deleted it. He didn't know if he could handle being stuck in an office most of his shift and not being able to go out and conduct a lot of his own enquiries. A higher rank brought more power, which he definitely didn't care about; it also brought more responsibility. For now he was happy being in charge of his small team and mucking in with them to get the results they all wanted.

He'd emailed Claire from the Barrow Scenes of Crime Department for a blown-up picture of the victim. Tomorrow, he'd have a cleaner, clearer image once Beth had completed the PM, but this would do for now. He wanted the rest of the team to realise just how horrific and serious this was: somehow just describing what they'd found didn't do the crime justice. Pulling the photo from the printer, he rolled up a couple of blobs of Blu-Tack and stuck it on the board. A whistle and some groans made him nod his head in appreciation. He turned to look at them.

'It's bad; no actually it's beyond bad. It's terrible. I want you to look at this young girl and feel the same anger that I do. Why did someone believe she deserved to end up dead, hidden in someone else's grave?'

There were a few headshakes, shoulder shrugs, the usual collective 'we have no idea' expression on their faces. DC Alison Bell held up her hand. 'Whoever it is, they're sick.'

Josh nodded. 'They are, and we need to find out who that individual is before something like this happens again.'

'Boss, how do we know this is the first time it's happened? I mean, maybe they got unlucky this time. They wouldn't have known the grave was going to get exhumed, would they? They're probably panicking big time. How do we know that there aren't more bodies hidden beneath coffins all over the graveyard, or in other graveyards?'

Josh paused for a moment to let the idea sink in with the rest of the team. DC John Paton was right, the possibility was very real. There was no way to know, not unless they started exhuming the whole bloody cemetery, and that wasn't going to happen. He cleared his throat. 'What I want is for you to focus on missing person reports. Start local and then widen the net. Is anyone aware of any recent reports of missing young people?'

DC Tina Sykes rolled her eyes. 'What? Apart from the usual ones who are never really missing, just acting up to worry their parents?'

'Yes, them. Everyone. Have any of them been missing a couple of months? We know that Florence Wright was buried eight weeks ago, so anyone who went missing just before then. We need to identify our girl in the grave, until then we're working blind. She's young from the looks of her; surely someone out there is missing her.'

'What if she's in care? Or it's possible she could be a runaway?'

'Good shout; can you and Sykes start ringing around the local foster homes, young people's hostels, and speak to the staff, ask them if they have anyone who has disappeared without any warning that they haven't reported yet. I'm hoping we might be able to get some prints from her tomorrow and run them through the system. You never know, we might get lucky.'

He said a silent prayer that they would and left them to it while he went into the office to go through the statements from the two gravediggers, to see if anything stood out. The two undertakers who'd been present at the discovery had been busy with funerals all day, so were scheduled for interviews first thing tomorrow morning. The environmental health officer had nothing of value to add to the investigation. She had been drafted in at the last minute and was already in hot water with her boss: a simple pocket notebook entry taken from her at the scene had been sufficient. He saw no justification in adding to her misery at the moment by bringing her into the station. Unless they came up with a reason to question her further, she was off the hook. He sat down on the knackered swivel chair that he wouldn't let them replace because he liked it and had spent years moulding it to fit his shape. They could keep their newfangled, flimsy ergo chairs. Like him, this chair had been built to last.

# CHAPTER FIFTEEN

Beth had managed to eat most of the chips and prawn crackers before she'd arrived at the gates to her house. As she turned onto the road which led to her house she hit the brakes as a huge stag with antlers almost as big as her jumped over the drystone wall and in front of her car. Screeching to a halt into the middle of the road, she missed it by millimetres. Another jump and it was across the wall on the opposite side of the road and out of sight. Her heart racing, she looked at the grease-covered steering wheel and berated herself: she could have lost control of the wheel and careered into a drystone wall, killing herself because she'd been too greedy to wait until she'd got home. She knew the perils of driving through the countryside, yet still she'd taken the risk. She'd been lucky, not as lucky as the stag though. Pressing the button on the keyring remote she glanced around, noticing a discarded bunch of flowers on the grass verge near her gates and wondered if someone had been killed along this stretch of the road. No one had since she'd moved here, but perhaps it was an anniversary from years ago. She waited for the gates to open, then drove through, waiting again on the other side whilst they shut. Not that it was very likely anyone would follow her through: there had been no cars on the road behind her. She drove along to her usual spot outside the front door, got out of the car, grabbed her tea and slammed the door shut. The security light turned on at her movement, illuminating the house and immediate gardens. She turned to look at the lake behind her. Whenever she needed to think or clear her head, staring at the expanse of water surrounded by lush green countryside always did the trick.

Turning back towards the front door, she froze, her head tilted to one side: what were those reddish-brown streaks all over her usually pristine white door? Moving closer, she was trying to think how on earth they'd got there when she stepped on something and she heard the crack of bones beneath her foot. Jumping back she looked down and screamed in horror at the crushed dead bird on her doorstep. How the hell had that got there? The poor thing must have flown into the door and broken its neck. She shuddered as she tried to convince herself it was a common thing for birds to do. She'd had a few fly into the huge glass windows along the front of the house, but they'd only ever stunned themselves before flying off. This one must have been old, or ill.

With trembling hands she opened the front door. 'Light's on,' she commanded, and the hallway was flooded with light. Suddenly no longer hungry, she walked down to the kitchen, abandoning the bag of food on the worktop and grabbing a pair of rubber gloves, bleach spray and some cleaning rags from under the sink. She couldn't leave the poor bird there like that, its guts smeared all over her door until the morning. It wasn't right.

Back outside, she bent down and picked the little creature up by its wing and carried it over to her bin. She would have buried it, but it was going to be dark soon and she wasn't risking standing outside at the far side of her garden at night digging a grave for a bird. After the last two days she'd had enough of graves. Placing it gently inside the bin, she let the lid slam shut; *sorry, bird.* Then she went to the door and began spraying copious amounts of bleach onto the dark trails. After some serious scrubbing the door began to look clean once more. Satisfied there were no entrails left, she scooped up the rags and deposited them inside the bin on top of the dead bird. Peeling off the rubber gloves, she dropped those on top and went back inside the house, shutting and locking the door behind her.

The food no longer interested her, but the wine did. Pouring herself a large glass, she took it with her to the bathroom. Turning on the shower, she stripped off her clothes and stepped under the hot stream of water, though Beth knew the best way to cleanse herself of the last two days wasn't going to be a hot shower; it was more likely a dip in the icy cold waters of Lake Windermere would do the trick. If she wasn't so scared of being out of the comfort of her own little fortress in the dark then she'd have run outside and dived right in. Her fingers curled into tight fists; she hated the person she'd become so much that it made her want to punch the wall. She wanted to punch *him*, hit *him* until he was dead and couldn't hurt her or anyone else ever again. That upset her more than anything because she'd never been a violent person before, now rage bubbled up inside her without warning.

The incident had come out of the blue. Her life as a busy accident and emergency doctor before the event in 2012 had been so good: hectic, tiring, busy, but most of all fun. Back then life had been normal and pretty much carefree, but it all changed that night. Work had been busy, just like any other shift, but Beth remembered every stitch she had sewn to repair the ripped skin on the teenage boy's leg; it had been a deep gash. He'd come into the accident and emergency department on a trolley, pushed by two paramedics. A woman she'd assumed was his mother following behind, berating him for his stupidity. Her high-pitched voice echoing around the A & E department.

'Do you know how lucky you are, Ben? You could have died; you've never been on a moped in your life. What possessed you to decide that you were some kind of stuntman? Did no part of your common sense kick in and tell you that you might have an accident?'

Ben was shaking his head as Beth peered out from behind the curtain of the elderly male she was treating for shingles. The poor lad had looked as if he was in enough pain without the added embarrassment of his mum shouting at him for all the hospital to hear. The paramedics had taken him through to resus; she heard one of them ask him if he wanted his mum to come in and he'd whispered no. She'd offered to treat him, sewing up his leg and commiserating with him about embarrassing parents.

'You know, she's only shouting because you scared her.'

He'd grunted at her.

'Can I suggest you stay off mopeds until you have had a bit more practice?'

He'd laughed and so had she. Once he'd been patched up it had been time to clock off. She'd been looking forward to that night: a surprise party for Ellen, one of her close friends, and she'd decided she was going to get steaming drunk. It had been a long week and she needed to let her hair down.

She blinked back tears, unable to even blame it on the shampoo because she hadn't washed her hair yet. She was crying for the messed-up shell of the person she'd become. Drying herself, she smothered her face in moisturiser, and her body in expensive body lotion to cover the smell of bins and death that lingered on her skin. She'd finished the glass of wine without even realising.

Wrapping her hair in a makeshift turban, she picked up the empty glass and headed back downstairs to refill it. Spying the carton of takeaway on the kitchen counter, she decided she was ready to eat. Wine didn't agree with her on an almost-empty stomach. The food could soak up some of the alcohol, so her head wasn't too fuzzy tomorrow morning. She wondered how Josh was and if he was still at work. Looking at the clock on the microwave, it was almost ten and she realised there was a very good chance he would be. He was a good man and an even better detective. There was no way he would be able to go home while his team were hard at work looking for an ID on their victim. She was tempted to phone him, but the ping of the microwave broke her train of thought.

Tipping the contents of her tea onto a plate, she took a fork from the drawer and refilled her wine glass. Why on earth would she ring him? She wasn't that bloody needy. The voice in her head whispered back, *are you sure about that?*

# CHAPTER SIXTEEN

Estelle Carter drank champagne as if it was going out of fashion. She was on the third bottle and knew she could manage at least another four glasses before passing out. Daddy had taught her well; he'd always thrown lavish parties with never-ending supplies of alcohol. He'd always encouraged her to drink, told her he didn't think it would hurt her to get used to it. She had never complained. The only thing now was it took an astounding volume of the stuff to actually get her drunk. She looked around at her friends; they were definitely drunk and being very loud. If it wasn't for the fact that her dad owned the hotel and the adjoining nightclub they were now sitting in, the bouncers would have thrown them out hours ago. They didn't dare: she would have them sacked before they'd made it home. When her dad had suggested she learn how to run the hotel she had told him absolutely not, and that had been the only time they'd ever had a serious argument; so serious that he'd threatened to cut her out of his will and stop supplying her with endless cash to spend on anything she wanted. In the words of her friend Annie, Estelle had to suck it up and do as she was told.

Estelle loved Annie; she was so down to earth and very funny. She didn't care that Estelle had more money than she knew what to do with, even though she had very little herself. Annie worked as a general assistant in the hotel and lived in one of the poky staff bedrooms down in the basement. The first time they met, Estelle was mid-rant with the housekeeping staff about a complaint that there was dust under the beds, and Annie had interrupted Estelle's tirade with a clever quip about needing to feed the staff spinach every morning if she wanted them to have the strength to move four-poster beds. Estelle, not used to being talked back to, had relished the confrontation. They'd been inseparable ever since, much to her daddy's dislike.

Estelle looked over at Annie now to see her face had turned a strange shade of grey. 'Are you okay?'

Annie shook her head; trying to stand up, she managed to lurch forward and knock the ice bucket, champagne and glasses flying. The bouncers came rushing over to help Estelle hold her up.

'We need to get her to her room,' she shouted across at the man who'd left his drink on the bar and rushed over to assist.

He smiled, nodding his head.

'Of course, is it far?'

'No, just downstairs. Can you help me? She's too drunk to walk herself.'

'Lead the way.'

Between them they managed to get Annie out of the busy nightclub. As they stepped outside into the fresh air, Annie began to heave. Estelle looked horrified.

'Shit, don't you dare be sick on us. We'll get you down to your room and you can puke in the toilet. OK?'

Annie's eyes rolled back. She opened her mouth to speak but was unable to form any intelligible words. All that came out was a mumbled mess of sound.

'I'm really sorry about this.' Estelle looked at the guy, who was doing a great job of holding her friend up. He was a lot older than the pair of them but good-looking in a Colin Firth kind of way. She wouldn't say no, she thought, as she led them around the back of the hotel to the small set of steps down to the basement. It was a work of art getting Annie down there without letting go of her, and by the time they reached the bottom step both of them were out of breath.

'I'm so sorry, this is my fault. I let her drink too much champagne. She's going to kill me tomorrow.'

He smiled. 'I kind of think this is all her fault, not yours. I'm guessing you didn't force her to drink?'

She shook her head. 'Of course not, she drank it herself. I just paid for it.'

'Ah, the if-it's-free-I'm-going-to-drink-it friend. We all have one of those. They just don't know when to say stop, especially if they're not paying for it. Do you often buy your friend's champagne?'

Her cheeks began to burn. 'Not really; she's worked really hard this week and I wanted to say thank you.'

'Well it doesn't look as if she'll be working really hard tomorrow!'

Estelle smiled as she opened the door, and they dragged Annie along the narrow corridor to her room. She rifled through her friend's pockets until she found the key and unlocked the door. Between them they managed to get her onto the bed. Rolling Annie onto her side and propping pillows behind her back, Estelle disappeared then came back with a bucket which she placed by the side of the bed. Then they left her to it.

Once they were back outside she thanked her helper again for coming to their rescue without a second thought.

'It was no problem. Are you going to bed as well now?'

Laughing, she shook her head. 'No, I'm not tired.'

'Oh, that's good. Would you like to come and drink some champagne with me then?'

Hesitating, she thought about it. She didn't really want to go back inside the club: she was going to be in for a bollocking when the bouncers told her dad what had happened. She looked at him again; she'd always had a bit of a thing for heroes. Pushing her arm through his, she whispered, 'I know a nice place we can go for a glass of champagne that's a bit more private.'

He bent down, his lips brushing the side of her cheek. 'Lead the way, beautiful…'

# CHAPTER SEVENTEEN

Beth slept surprisingly well once she'd managed to actually switch her mind off and let it all go. When she opened her eyes it was hard to believe it was morning already. After a quick breakfast of toast and jam she set off on the drive to Barrow with a clear head.

Abe was already in the mortuary by the time she had washed and scrubbed-up. The coffin was on the table and Beth had to admit it was a strange sight to see. An exhumation wasn't something she dealt with very often; in fact, this was only her second in the seven years since she'd begun her training to be a forensic pathologist. Abe had a cordless drill ready to unscrew the coffin lid, but the moment the drill made contact with the wood, the door burst open and in rushed Carl from CSI.

'Sorry to interrupt, but Josh asked me to come and take photos. Just in case.'

'Just in case, what?'

'Well, I suppose in case there's any connection to the body found underneath the coffin.'

It hadn't even crossed Beth's mind that the two might be connected. She looked at Abe as a wave of terrible foreboding washed over her. What if he unscrewed the lid of the coffin to find no body in there? What if there were *two* bodies inside? Butterflies raced around in her stomach. It didn't matter what was inside the coffin, it needed to be opened. If there were three, or even four bodies in there she would deal with them, one by one, methodically and with precision, because that was what she did.

Abe patted her arm. 'Beth, is everything okay? You look kind of…'

She smiled at him. 'I'm fine, thank you, Abe. I was just wondering what was going to happen if there was something in there that we weren't anticipating.'

He smiled at her. 'I hope not.'

'Right, then. Shall we begin?' She looked at Carl, who was fiddling with his camera. Waiting for his reply.

He looked up at her, flustered.

'Sorry, Doc. What a morning. I hate having surprises sprung on me. I'm good to go when you are.'

For a moment she wondered how he coped with his job if he didn't like surprises; more often than not crimes occurred on the spur of the moment. She nodded at Abe, who began to remove the screws, while she did her best not to hold her breath. When the last screw came free she helped him to lift the lid.

A sweet, sickly smell filled the room as she looked down at the body of Florence Wright; her face and hands were covered in mould, a natural occurrence in some bodies that had been buried. Carl gasped beside her, his camera poised.

'What is that?'

Beth said, 'It's because of the dampness in the soil. The amount of rain we've had the last few weeks makes it the perfect environment. If we lived in a much hotter, drier climate then there would be more slippage of the skin or even mummification. Eventually.'

She wheeled the hoist over and between her and Abe they managed to roll Florence from side to side enough to wrap a sheet around her and slide the sling under her. They then hoisted her out of the coffin onto a waiting steel gurney. Thankfully, the body was fresh so it stayed in one piece: a few more weeks and it would have been a different story. God knows what they'd have done if her arm or leg had dropped off and gone sliding across the floor; poor Carl would have had a full-blown meltdown. Once the body was safely on the gurney, Beth wheeled her across to the X-ray machine. She wanted a full post-mortem examination: every single thing checked.

# CHAPTER EIGHTEEN

Estelle rushed into the hotel flushed and more than a little late; thankfully, she wasn't duty manager today. At least not until twelve; she had a meeting at ten. Checking her watch, she realised she had nine minutes to grab a coffee and go up to the conference room to take some deep breaths. Up to now she'd managed to avoid answering the influx of angry text messages and calls from her dad. Last night, she'd taken the Mr Darcy lookalike back to her apartment which overlooked the marina, and what a night it had been. She was beyond exhausted and hungover this morning. At some point the champagne and tiredness had kicked in and she'd woken up thirty minutes ago, alone. Though relieved he'd left her without having to be shown the door, she wondered if she'd ever see him again. It didn't matter to her one way or the other because she wasn't looking for a serious relationship: what she was looking for was fun.

Taking her coffee, she made it to the conference room just as the other attendees arrived and breathed a sigh of relief – she'd made it. Now all she had to do was sit through two hours of listening to the finance committee drone on and she was free. What it had to do with her was beyond her, but her dad had asked her to go and she needed to get on his good side after last night's fiasco. As soon as this was over, she'd go and see how Annie was, make sure she was okay. That was what friends did, wasn't it? It had been quite some time since she'd had one so close.

Ninety minutes later, Estelle had lost the will to live. She finished her second cup of strong coffee then slid her phone under the table to text Annie for the fifth time:

*Hey, at least let me know you're alive and didn't choke on your vomit in your sleep.*

She put a row of laughing faces on the end of it, but deep down she was worried; normally Annie would text back within minutes, this wasn't like her. Estelle was trying not to panic with all the different scenarios playing through her mind. What if she had choked and was lying there dead?

Unable to take any more, she pushed her chair back and stood up. She had no idea what these suits were all talking about anyway.

'I'm sorry. Please excuse me, I have to leave. I don't feel very well.'

She walked out of the room and didn't look back. In all honesty she didn't give a stuff what they were talking about. It meant nothing to her. All she cared about was making sure Annie was okay. Jogging towards the lift, Estelle jabbed the call button continuously until finally the lift doors slid open to reveal at least twenty Japanese tourists all chattering so loud she wanted to plug her ears with her fingers and shout at them to shut up. Squeezing in next to an elderly couple, the lift took an eternity to reach the ground floor. The doors opened and she stepped out first and spotted her dad hovering around by the reception desk. Ignoring his shouts, she headed out of the front door so she could run around to the rear of the hotel, where the main staff entrance was, knowing he wouldn't follow her.

Running down the concrete steps, she let herself in. Her heart was hammering so hard against her ribcage it occurred to her there was a chance she would either have a heart attack or throw up. As she reached the door to Annie's room at the end of the corridor, she saw that it was ever so slightly ajar. Hammering on the wood, she pushed it open.

'Sorry, but if you're in no fit state to reply to a text message then I don't care if you're lying there stark naked.'

She stepped into the darkened room and searched for the light switch, her fingers brushing against it as she pressed it down.

Breathing out a sigh of relief at the empty bed in front of her, she noticed Annie's phone was lying on it. No wonder she wasn't answering her messages. The room had an ensuite, so she strode across to the door, knocked once then threw that open. But it was empty as well. The feeling of relief which engulfed her entire body was so overwhelming she felt her legs give way underneath her and she ended up collapsing to the floor. She had been so convinced something terrible had happened to her friend. Estelle hated being wrong, but on this occasion, she was happy to take it lying down. Annie must have made it into work.

After a few minutes, when her legs felt as if they belonged to her again, she pulled herself up from the floor and left Annie's room, pulling the door shut behind her. Now she was ready to face her dad and the rest of her shift.

# CHAPTER NINETEEN

Josh knew he had to be at the hospital mortuary by midday. Beth had texted him to say she thought the post-mortem on Florence Wright would be over and done by then. He looked at his watch; he was running late. It didn't matter, she wouldn't start their Jane Doe's PM without him. They were no nearer to finding a name for her even though Bell and Sykes had been working tirelessly overnight to find it.

He'd been up all night himself, concerned that he was missing something from Jason Thompson's statement; there was just something about it that made Josh feel as if he was hiding something. According to the officer who'd taken it, Jason had been cagey, on edge and not very cooperative throughout the interview. An intelligence check on his background had brought up that he had previous for dealing class B drugs and he'd been questioned twice in relation to sexual relations with a person under the age of sixteen. There had been no concrete evidence and both times he'd been released without charge, which didn't sit well with Josh. It looked as if Thompson could be a person of interest and he wanted to speak to him. This time, it would be him who did the questioning, and at the morning briefing he'd asked DC Paton to track him down and bring him in for a formal interview.

Looking around his team, he wondered who to choose to attend the PM with him. He didn't really need anyone else, but it was always better to have two pairs of eyes and ears. His first choice would have been Paton, a seasoned detective with lots of experience and not one likely to complain if he felt sick at the sight of the Jane Doe's face being peeled back from her skull. But he'd already tasked him with finding Jason Thompson. He looked over at Sam and smiled, wondering what colour her hair was today. Yesterday it had been bright red, today it looked much darker. Tomorrow? Who knew! Sam was as reliable as Paton, less experienced, but keen and an excellent detective, even if she was a little green.

'Sam, are you busy this afternoon?'

She looked up from her phone. 'Not particularly, what did you need?'

'Your company for a couple of hours.' He smiled at her and enjoyed the expression on her face as she realised why he wanted her for a couple of hours. To give her credit, she didn't flinch.

'As long as you buy the coffee on the way to the hospital, I'm in.'

He laughed. 'Deal.'

The others turned around and Sykes piped up. 'Erm. That's favouritism, you know.'

'No, it's bribery. And seeing as how you're going to be spending all day visiting local authority care homes, you'll no doubt have time to fit in your own coffee run.'

She opened her mouth then shut it again: she knew better than to piss him off. Sam grabbed her coat off the back of her chair and her bag from underneath the desk. She followed Josh out. He already had a set of car keys in his hand, his collar number written next to the car registration on the huge whiteboard on the wall in the corridor.

'Where's the PM, Josh?'

'Barrow, so we'll go to Costa in town. I'll park up and you can nip in.'

She smiled at him. 'Deal, do you think we'll have an ID for her after it? It would be good if she was on the system.'

'It would be a bloody miracle and yes, it would be amazing. I sent Carl to evidence the PM on Florence Wright, the body that was exhumed, just in case something wasn't right. Claire is going to be joining him for the next one because we'll need a wet and a dry exhibits officer. Please will you take notes so I can concentrate on what the doc is doing and saying?' He knew she wouldn't object, and at least that way she didn't have to watch the entire procedure and could focus on writing.

# CHAPTER TWENTY

Estelle let herself out of the staff entrance: it was too stuffy down there. It was a shame there were no windows to throw open and let some fresh air in. She wrinkled her nose; there was a distinct odour of sweaty feet lingering in the air. She made a mental note to get some of those plug-in air fresheners – it wasn't the nicest smell to inhale every time you set foot into the corridor. She took out her phone and texted Annie, hoping her friend had been back to her room to collect it.

*On a scale of one to ten, how dead do you feel this morning? Where are you, I'll bring coffee? x*

She realised she'd better go and see her father, to sweeten him up and apologise for being silly last night, for drinking too much and letting her friends get too drunk. He liked apologies, always said it showed the true inner strength of a person if they could admit when they were wrong. What a load of crap. She was only doing it so he wouldn't spend the next three days in a mood with her and send her to every shitty meeting and event that was booked in. She really hated working here and wondered if Annie fancied going backpacking with her. She had quite a bit of money stashed in her rainy-day fund that Daddy didn't know about. More than enough that they wouldn't have to slum it whilst travelling the world. In fact, this was the best idea she'd ever had; if she could convince Annie to go with her it would be amazing. They could face the music when they got home: Daddy would only be angry with her for a short time. He'd forgive her and give her a job, then she could give Annie her job back. It was perfect, they couldn't lose: it would be like a Willy Wonka golden ticket if they could escape for six months and see the world. As soon as she'd grovelled enough she was going to hunt Annie down and surprise her.

The hotel reception was heaving with an entire coach load of tourists who were all trying to check in. She headed straight for them, smiling and pointing to them to get in a line instead of all trying to talk to Gary the receptionist at once. He looked at Estelle and smiled, mouthing the words 'thank you'. She'd miss Gary and the rest of the team: he was so funny and made them all laugh. But hopefully he'd still be working here when they got back, or maybe he'd want to come with them. She stopped herself; if she upped and left with all the best members of staff her dad would come after her and drag her back. Bad idea, she'd get away with just her and Annie.

This thought kept her going for the next few hours as they got all the tourists booked in and taken to their rooms. Then she walked into Bowness to go to the bank and get some cash to top up the till. Stopping off to buy coffee and cakes for her and Annie, she headed back down to the staff quarters to go and tell her friend her fabulous idea. The smell of sweat still lingered in the air and it was even hotter down there because it was now warm outside. She reached Annie's room and knocked on the door: no reply. Putting the paper bag of cakes and two coffees on the floor, she hammered on the door, shouting: 'Annie, open the door!' She was greeted by silence. Taking out her phone, she rang her number and could hear the phone vibrating from inside the room. This wasn't good. Since the day Annie had started working at the hotel she'd never seen her without her phone. She would have realised and come back for it by now.

The door next to Annie's opened and Paula stuck her head out of the gap. 'What's wrong? You gonna wake the dead shouting like that. Some of us were on night shift last night; we need our sleep.'

'Sorry, have you seen Annie?'

She shook her head, then shut her door. She began knocking on the other doors, but no one answered. She realised they were all probably working. What did she do now? Wishing she hadn't shut the door behind her earlier, she decided to go upstairs and get the master key. Leaving the drinks there she ran upstairs, asking Gary if he'd seen Annie today as she passed. He shook his head as she grabbed the set of master keys off the hook behind the reception desk. Then she ran around to where the housekeeping team kept their supplies in the huge walk-in linen closet on the ground floor. Two of the assistants were refilling their carts with towels and toiletries.

'Did Annie turn up to work today?'

They both shook their heads. 'Nope, haven't seen her. She left us short staffed, so we've had to cover her check-outs as well.'

Estelle felt the panic begin to fill her chest, making it hard to breathe. This wasn't like her friend, where the hell was she?

# CHAPTER TWENTY-ONE

Beth had examined Florence Wright from head to toe, scrutinising every internal organ by eye before dissecting them to look for any abnormalities. She had found no evidence of blood clots or tumours and had taken the smallest samples she could to retain for further microscopic examination. Samples of body fluids had been taken to be sent off for further analysis, but as far as she could tell Florence's death matched the conclusion on hospital records: that she had died in hospital with complications from pneumonia. There was no evidence of foul play. Unless the toxicology reports came back with something, she couldn't say that Florence's cause of death was suspicious. This left someone with some explaining to do: why had she been exhumed in the first place? Stepping back from the table, she looked at Abe, who had all Florence's internal organs in a biodegradable bag ready to be stuffed back into her abdominal cavity before he sewed her back up.

'Have I missed anything?'

He shook his head. 'Definitely not, you were as thorough as always, Doc. I couldn't see that there was anything suspicious about her death.'

'That's what I think. I don't understand why she was exhumed. The death certificate listed pneumonia and the fluid in the lungs confirms this. She was ninety-three years old; nothing about her death aroused suspicion with the hospital staff.'

Abe shrugged. 'At least now you've confirmed that she died from natural causes, nothing suspicious.'

'That's true. DS Walker should be here soon for the Jane Doe's PM; I'll let him know we support the original findings. Please can you get her put back into the refrigerator whilst I go and make some phone calls.'

She turned to the body lying in front of her. 'Florence, I'm so sorry you've had to endure this final indignity for no good reason that I can think of. Please forgive me.'

Stripping off her apron and gloves, she screwed them up, lifting the lid on the special waste bin to drop them inside. Leaving Abe to finish up, Beth walked down the corridor to the office she sometimes used when she worked down here. Her mind was buzzing with questions: why had permission been given to exhume Florence? Which family member had wanted their elderly relative dug up from their final resting place? And what did it all have to do with the young girl whose body was next in line, waiting patiently for her to begin her post-mortem? Did whoever request the exhumation know about the other body in the grave? It was hard to say; she wanted to think it was unlikely but – and this was a big but – it was a huge coincidence that they'd found a body in *that* particular grave. Beth didn't like coincidences. They needed to be found and their exact motive questioned. Sitting down at the desk and opening the file she began to read through the scant notes again. There was nothing at all in here to suggest anything other than death by natural causes.

A knock on the door made her look up and she smiled to see Josh standing there with another detective she'd met on a couple of occasions but had forgotten her name.

'Afternoon, Doc; have you met DC Sam Thomas? How did the exhumation go?'

'I have, hi, Sam. Come in and take a seat, and I'll tell you what little I've discovered.'

He frowned at her once she'd outlined her findings. 'You didn't find anything evidential at all?'

'I'm afraid not, Josh. Florence Wright died as a complication of the pneumonia she had been admitted into hospital with. There was no evidence of anything other than an elderly lady dying of natural causes.'

His mouth fell open. 'According to the application, we gave permission to exhume the body because her relative came into the station and spoke to a senior officer. The relative wanted to report that he thought there might be suspicious circumstances surrounding her death, and he wanted it investigated. It was all a bit cloak and dagger, to be honest. I assumed the reason for the exhumation was because once we'd had the complaint the force had to rule out the possibility of foul play. The relevant paperwork was submitted but it was all kept very hush-hush. I don't understand how this could have happened, though. How did we end up with two bodies? It's all a bit too much of a coincidence.'

She shrugged. 'That, my friend, is exactly what I'd like to know.'

# CHAPTER TWENTY-TWO

Annie opened her eyes. She was so thirsty, the inside of her mouth felt like her tongue had swollen to three times its normal size and was stuck to the roof of it. It was still dark, thank God, because there no way she was going to make it to work yet. In fact, she didn't know if she'd make it to work tomorrow either, she felt *so* ill. It was all Estelle's fault. Christ, she was never going drinking with her again. Drinking champagne as if it was pints of orange and water was not the best of ideas, and she knew that now. Moving her head slightly, the room lurched violently, and she felt her insides contract. She couldn't be sick; she'd have to move to be sick and right now she couldn't move because she felt as if she was dying. Annie thought back to the previous times she'd got drunk: had she ever felt *this* bad? There had been plenty of hangovers, but this was something else. Thanks to her friend, and the copious amount of free champagne, she'd taken it to the next level. This was it: she was absolutely never, ever drinking again.

She relived the moments before she'd lost control and ended up knocking over the entire table of drinks in the club. Her cheeks began to burn at the shame of it. In all her life she'd never got so drunk that she'd had to be escorted out of somewhere. If Estelle asked her to go out with her again it would be a big fat no. Absolutely not, unless she stuck to non-alcoholic drinks. Bile rose up her throat: just thinking about alcohol made her want to throw her guts up. She couldn't move, not that she wanted to or had any intention of moving. It would be nice if someone could bring her an icy cold glass of water though. She'd be ever so grateful. As soon as she could pluck up the courage she'd try and find her phone, ring someone to come to her rescue and put her out of her misery. Was this what it felt like to be lost in the desert?

It struck her how peaceful it was. The hotel was normally a twenty-four-hour bustling hive of activity. It was unusually quiet down here for a change – not that she was complaining. But the continual noise as doors slammed and the heavy footsteps of different members of staff thudding up and down the basement stairs were part of the background. It was very rare there wasn't some noise from out in the corridor; the amount of people that lived down here, it wasn't really surprising.

She lay there, eyes squeezed shut and head thumping. Where was everyone? Unable to move, even though she desperately needed a drink, she did the only thing she could: she closed her eyes and let the darkness take her to a place where she wasn't going to spend the next few hours regretting the life choices she'd made last night.

# CHAPTER TWENTY-THREE

Jason didn't have that many options; he could drive somewhere and book into a cheap hotel for a couple of days. Just until he got his shit together and they'd figured out who the girl was and who had put her in the grave. He'd packed his gym bag full of everything he might need, taken the money he kept stashed in the empty tea tin. There was a couple of hundred, not enough to sustain a life on the run for an indefinite period of time that was for sure. He didn't have any friends he could stop with. Once the police realised he was a person of interest, and a shitty one at that, they'd plaster his picture all over the television and newspapers. His hands were shaking; he'd never felt so sick in his entire life. OK, so he had sex occasionally with some of the teenage girls who hung around the cemetery if they had no money, but it wasn't like they were completely innocent. He ran his fingers through his hair. He could have talked to Barry about it. He was all right; he'd have known what to do. But Barry would be in Manchester now. He couldn't ring him and spoil his night away, because then he'd be pissed off with him as well. What was he going to do?

He decided to get the train, leave his car at home. At least if the coppers came for him and took it away to have it searched, there wouldn't be any trace of anything inside it. Thank Christ he'd taken it down to the Polish car wash last weekend and had it valeted.

He would get a train to Blackpool. It was always busy there this time of year. He could walk around in a baseball cap and dark sunglasses, and he wouldn't look out of place. If he found some cheap B&B he could lay low for a few days, keep off the Internet in case they traced his phone. He'd seen it on the television: they could do all sorts of stuff like that now. He knew he wasn't the cleverest of people, but it seemed like a decent enough plan. One that might buy him some time before the coppers came looking for him. He was pretty sure they'd take the easy option and he was it.

As he left his house he slung his bag over his shoulder, pulled his cap down low and kept his head down. He lived a ten-minute walk to the train station; all he had to do was cut down all the backstreets. Keep off the main roads and he'd be out of this shithole in the next half an hour.

His phone began to vibrate in his pocket. Pulling it out, he looked at the display.

*Private number*

He had no idea who that could be. He sent it to voicemail; it rang again. Too nosy for his own good, he lifted it to his ear.

'Yeah.'

'Mr Thompson, this is DC John Paton. I wonder if I could have a word?'

Jason swore under his breath; he was such an idiot. Why did he answer? He thought about throwing his phone into the bushes that ran alongside the front of the hotel he was walking past and running. Was there any point?

'Of course, what about?'

He squeezed his eyes shut momentarily, knowing he sounded like a fucking idiot. It was pretty obvious what it was about.

'We'd like you to come to the station, just to go over a couple of things. It won't take long. Are you busy now? Because I could come and pick you up. Save you the hassle of trying to get parked; it's a bloody nightmare getting parked around here.'

Jason knew what he was doing: he was trying to befriend him. He did sound like a nice bloke though, maybe he should just go with him. Tell him the truth about the girl and get it over with.

'It's okay, I'm out walking. I'm not far from the station; I can be there in twenty minutes if that's okay and it can wait that long.'

There was a slight pause on the other end of the phone, and he knew the copper was weighing up the odds on him actually turning up and whether or not he should call the shots.

'That's absolutely fine, thank you. I'll see you soon.'

The copper hung up first, and Jason breathed out a sigh of relief. He had some serious thinking to do and only a couple of minutes to do it. He needed to decide whether to run or face the music.

He carried on heading towards the train station. He would bypass the police station on the way there unless he changed his mind at the last minute. Christ, this was the hardest decision of his life. He knew if he ran, he was messing things up even more than they already were, but the thought of being accused of murder and locked up terrified him more than anything he'd ever experienced.

# CHAPTER TWENTY-FOUR

Estelle stooped across the reception desk. All the guests had been checked in and there was a lull in people passing through. She had spoken to everyone she could think of, but there was no sign of Annie anywhere. She had disappeared without a trace. Her stomach felt as if there was a heavy lead ball lodged in between that and her diaphragm. There was a thudding inside her head so loud it was hard to think; a mixture of the alcohol and stress, she supposed. She was going to have to call the police: what choice did she have? Daddy would be furious; he didn't like the police being called to the hotel, said it was bad for business, but she'd searched everywhere. She, Gary and Paula had searched all the empty guest rooms, bathrooms, linen cupboards, storerooms, every single nook and cranny. Gary had even been outside and checked the garage, outhouse, summerhouse in the grounds and every other place someone drunk might think was a good idea to go to sleep. He'd even checked inside the huge industrial bins that Estelle had wrinkled her nose at when he'd told her. He was right to check, though; God knows what seemed like a good idea when you were pissed was definitely not when you were sober. She looked at Gary, who nodded and passed her the phone.

'You need to do it for Annie's sake, call them. We've checked everywhere and spoken to everyone: no one has seen her since last night.'

'Did you manage to get hold of David about checking the CCTV?'

'Nope, I've left him a couple of voicemails and text messages. They were busy last night on reception. He'll be fast asleep. I'm pretty sure as soon as he wakes up he'll come into work and run the system.'

Estelle was angry about the fact that only one person knew how to work the bloody security system. It was ridiculous. A hotel this size should have at least one person on every shift that had been trained. As soon as she'd found Annie, she was going to arrange for the security company to come in and train the staff. Daddy could do one if he didn't want to spend the money. The whole point of having it was for situations like this.

She dialled 101 and heard a recorded voice telling her she was being connected to Cumbria Police. Her heart was racing because deep down she knew something bad had happened. She just didn't know what, and how did she explain that to some arsy copper who would probably try to fob her off and tell her she was wasting their time?

The real voice that answered startled her; she hadn't expected anyone to pick up the phone so soon.

'Good afternoon, Cumbria Police, how can I help you?'

'Hello, I'd like to report my friend missing. We can't find her, and we've searched and searched everywhere possible. I've spoken to everyone who knows her. She's gone. I don't know what to do.'

The kind voice on the other end soothed Estelle's frazzled nerves; the woman was nice. Not at all what she'd been expecting.

'Then let me get some details from you and we'll do our best to find her. I'm sure she won't be far.'

Estelle nodded at Gary, and then began to answer the long list of questions. She had a bitter taste in her mouth; while she'd been having the best sex of her life with Mr Darcy, she now knew something terrible had happened to her friend and she didn't know if she could ever forgive herself. When she'd finally answered the never-ending questions, the woman had told her that an officer would be there in the next hour to take details. Jesus, how much detail did they need? She wanted to scream *Just tell them to get here with a dog and find her.* She didn't, though, it wasn't her fault, she was doing her job. Instead Estelle thanked her profusely and ended the call, handing the phone back to Gary.

'Now what?'

'Now we wait for the police to come and take over. In the meantime we pray that Annie rolls up with a stinking hangover, but safe and well.'

'Do you think something's happened to her? Remember that lass a couple of years ago who got drunk and separated from her mates. She ended up in the lake, drowned. They didn't find her body for days.'

She glared at Gary. 'Thanks for that, I really appreciate your comforting words. Let's bloody well hope she didn't decide to go for a midnight swim.'

'Sorry, I didn't mean to upset you.'

'No, you're right. Shit happens and usually to the nicest of people. I'm so worried about her.'

Unable to take any more of Gary's stupid chatter, she went into the office, slamming the door shut, and collapsed onto the soft leather sofa. She'd never felt so ill and worried in her life. Her eyes were aching, and she just wanted to close them, drift off for a little while and wake up to discover that Annie was back in her room and life was how it should be.

# CHAPTER TWENTY-FIVE

Josh was out in the corridor having an animated conversation with someone, while Sam, the detective he'd arrived with, and Beth sat quietly trying not to listen in.

'I don't care. Find out who this relative is; when they came in to the station; who they spoke to; if we still have it on CCTV. I want everything. I want to know why someone would come in to the station complaining of suspicious circumstances regarding their elderly relative's death, when there is no evidence *at all* to say there was?… I want two officers despatched to their address and then I want them brought to the hospital mortuary to speak to Doctor Adams and myself. I want to know why permission was granted. Who applied for the licence, and what was the reason given on the application form?' There was a long pause as whoever was on the other end replied. 'I can't believe we agreed to exhume a body on so little information. Who signed it off?… When you have all the answers, I need you to get your arse up to the mortuary and come see me. The doctor needs to start the victim's PM now. As soon as you know, I want to know.'

Beth grimaced at Sam. She'd never heard Josh lose his cool like that before, he was always so laid-back. Judging by Sam's expression, neither had she. The door opened and he strode in, throwing himself down into the chair so hard that Beth wondered if it was going to snap.

'Everything okay, boss?'

'I don't think so. Something is way off. My bullshit radar is going crazy. Why was Florence Wright's relative so convinced she needed exhuming? I don't like that we found another body in that grave.'

Suddenly, a thought struck Beth and she began searching through her notebook, flipping the pages frantically.

'I spoke to him! I remember someone phoned here asking if they could speak to me for advice about a recent death. It was quite a while ago, but I'm sure I took down his details…'

'What did he say?'

'I'm not sure it's him, but I don't often get phone calls from people asking about exhumations. It was a couple of months ago; I was just leaving the office when the phone rang. He told me his name and said he had concerns that there was something amiss with the circumstances of his great-aunt's death. He said something about the GP visiting a lot more than he'd expect given she was such a relatively healthy woman for her age. He also mentioned something about her will being altered recently, maybe the GP being added? I told him he'd need to apply for a special licence and that it would be worth speaking to someone in the police.'

Josh looked at her in horror. 'Jesus Christ, don't tell me we have a small-scale Harold Shipman on the loose as well?'

Beth shook her head. 'No, we don't because there is nothing at all to support his claims. Obviously, I need the results from the full tox screen, but I've seen a lot of bodies with pneumonia over the years and fluid in the lungs was definitely the cause of death in there. I didn't see any signs of overdosing of medication when I examined her.'

'What are you saying then?'

'I think maybe he used that as his cover story; mention a crooked GP and people are going to panic. They wouldn't want a repeat of what happened back in Hyde with Shipman.'

Josh stared at Beth. 'So he wanted Florence Wright's body exhumed and re-examined for no reason? It doesn't make sense.'

Sam looked at him. 'He'd have a reason to exhume her if he *wanted* us to find the dead girl hidden beneath her coffin.'

Beth nodded. 'Because he put her there?'

Josh shut his eyes and slowly shook his head. 'We'd never have known about her if he hadn't made up this story.'

Sam spoke then. 'They're not going to find him. He'll have given a false address and probably had a cheap pay-as-you-go phone that he's thrown away.'

All three of them looked at each other. Beth stood up. 'I need to do the post-mortem on the girl. I can't put it off any longer. Abe will have prepared the mortuary, and you need all the evidence you can get to find this mystery man. You do know we might be completely wrong, and it could all be a genuine mistake.'

'Somehow, I don't think we are. At least we have something to work on; it gives us a sense of direction for the time being.'

Josh and Sam both stood up. Sam followed Beth into the ladies' changing room to get gowned up, while Josh went into the men's to do the same.

# CHAPTER TWENTY-SIX

When he'd realised his plan wasn't going to work, he'd panicked. It had seemed like the perfect murder, killing the girl and burying her in a grave dug for someone else, but once she was in there, hidden away, he hadn't experienced the thrill from it he'd imagined. It was all very well him knowing where she was, but what now? It was the excitement of the chase, recognition for his hard work and admiration of his audacity he wanted, he realised. Killing was easy.

As he sipped his latte from the cardboard cup, staring over the top of his newspaper, he felt a tingle of excitement in the pit of his stomach as a police van pulled up opposite the hotel and an officer got out. He had thought about booking himself into the hotel for a couple of days, to be near her and nearer the action. It might be a little bit too risky though. She was drunk last night, there was no doubt about it, but not that drunk that she wouldn't remember him. It was vain, but he liked to think he'd made an impression. Instead, he'd spent the day drinking endless cups of coffee and watching the hotel from afar.

He'd already witnessed last night's conquest come into the coffee shop around an hour ago; he'd slid down into the armchair, put his baseball cap back on and held the newspaper up so she couldn't see his face. It hadn't mattered, though, because he could tell she was preoccupied. She hadn't even glanced around the busy café; her focus had been on the barista and no one else. Which had suited him just fine.

He smiled to himself as he stared across at the cemetery opposite. He'd always had a morbid fascination with cemeteries. He loved the peace and quiet; they'd been his safe haven as a teenager. In fact, it was whilst sitting, propped against a huge gravestone reading a library book about famous American serial killers that he'd first realised he was not at all repulsed by what he was reading. He knew that he should have felt shocked and sickened, but the words made his pulse race and his loins stir like nothing he'd ever experienced before. From that moment on he had read about the lives of every twisted killer he could find until books were no longer enough…

His first kill had been such a bittersweet experience. He'd admired the girl from afar, for months, in that awkward schoolboy way. He'd watched her until he knew everything about her. He'd followed her home from school every day but she never took any of notice of him, always too busy laughing with her friends or flirting with the college boys much older than him. His moment came one night he saw her stumble out of a pub arguing with a lad she was with. He'd watched from across the road as she'd slapped his face. The lad had gone to hit her back, then stopped himself, shoving her to the ground and walking off. He'd rushed to help her up, taking her arm and offering to walk her home. She didn't even flinch. Walking past the cemetery he'd noticed the gates had been left open and took it as a sign, steering her into the darkness.

What happened next happened quickly, too quickly. Next thing he knew he was straddling her dead body, panting and panicking as the realisation of what he had just done set in. He stared at her for a few moments, talking in the beauty of her lifeless face before running all the way home.

The next few days were torture as he waited for the police to come knocking. But they never came. They arrested the boy she'd been seen arguing with outside the pub but eventually let him go for lack of evidence. He would have liked to have had someone to share the experience with back then, but he'd never had any friends and seemed to attract every bully in a three-mile radius. He'd used the cemetery, back where he lived in Barrow, as a shortcut from his home to school and back. When he wasn't dodging beatings by hiding behind the tombstones he knew like the back of his hand, he was spending time wandering around them with his notebook. He loved reading the inscriptions on the graves, especially the really old ones.

'Of Your Charity, Pray For The Soul Of…' was a popular one. Whoever had died and needed so many prayers always piqued his interest: did the people who buried them know all their deep, dark secrets? What would be on his gravestone, he wondered: 'Forever Burning in the Depths of Eternal Hell'?

He looked across at the small churchyard of Saint Martin's, with its pretty little graveyard that looked like something off a picture postcard. Some of the graves were adorned with posies of fresh flowers. There were no faded plastic flowers to be seen; no one buried here had to endure that. He inhaled deeply as the memory of the sweet smell of death mingled with the heady, coppery scent of the soil as he'd pushed the girl's body into the freshly dug grave filled his senses. The flash of her pretty yellow dress, torn and streaked with mud forged into his mind forever. He really was having the most pleasurable of days. Drinking coffee, as near to the police investigation into the missing girl as he could be, with a view of the graves opposite. There wasn't much more he could ask for, was there? Except maybe for one thing…

# CHAPTER TWENTY-SEVEN

Beth noted who was now present in the room: Abe, Josh and Sam had been joined by the two CSIs, Carl and Claire, plus her made six of them. She watched Abe cut the tag from the body bag. As he slowly unzipped it, the sweet, cloying smell of decomposition filled the air. She glanced around the room to see if everyone was coping, because this was the moment of truth; if someone was going to pass out it was generally because of the stench of decay, but everyone looked okay. Between her and Abe they checked inside the bag for any trace evidence, then lifted the legs as they slid the bag down. The body had been wrapped in a sterile white sheet to keep it together. Unwrapping the sheet, they revealed their victim. The soil-encrusted wet rag of a once-sunshine-yellow dress covered most of her body. Beth checked the toe tag which had been placed on the body at the scene.

One of the Jane Doe's eyes was half closed, as if she'd desperately tried not to fall asleep, and failed. Her once pretty face had been flattened with the weight of the heavy oak coffin that had lain on her for the last few weeks. Her skin was covered in dried mud, like a soldier in the trenches. Her clothes were covered in the brown, sticky soil which was common to the area. The heavy rainfall over the past few weeks had washed away the exposed soil from the slopes behind the cemetery, turning the grounds into a rain-soaked mud bath. She might have fared better had she been buried on higher ground, Beth thought. Abe measured her height and they weighed the body, as Claire began to photograph her from all possible angles.

Beth took her time walking around the table, examining every part of her. Removing the paper bags off first her left and then right hands to reveal her fingers were broken, bloodied and bruised; three of the nails on her right hand had been ripped right off.

'Looks like she tried to claw her way out of… somewhere.'

Beth noticed Sam shudder at the thought. This poor girl must have been terrified, but Beth knew she couldn't think about that now; all eyes were on her. She gently let go of the victim's hand she'd been holding and looked up at Abe. He smiled at her; she knew he was trying to let her know it was okay. She nodded at him as he passed her some nail clippers and a paper bag to put the trimmings in. She proceeded to clip the nails that weren't bloodied stumps, dropping them into the bag to be sent off for forensic examination. Then he passed her an ultraviolet black light. Turning off the overhead lights, Beth used it to scan the girl's clothes and body for signs of semen which would fluoresce under it if present. Nothing of any interest showed up. She passed the torch back to Abe, switched the lights back on and began the painstaking task of collecting trace evidence, one hair at a time. These were put into small envelopes, and the date and time marked onto them to be sent off for analysis. There were no pockets in the dress to search.

'We'll remove her clothes now,' Beth instructed, and Abe moved closer to help her remove the girl's outer garments. Once they were off, they delicately rolled down her torn and shredded tights. They worked together carefully in respectful silence removing every last item of underwear, Claire photographing each piece as Abe carefully laid them out on another table for Beth to examine. There were no obvious injuries to her body that Beth found, and the torn tights were intact on the crotch which had surprised her. The underwear, too, was intact; no rips or tears in her fuchsia lace panties. If there was any evidence of sexual activity, it looked as if it would have been consensual. Unless, of course, the killer removed her underwear, raped her then put it back on. Which she didn't think was likely.

Beth began to speak into the digital recorder, loud and clear so Sam, who was scribing, could take notes as well.

'This is the body of a female in her late teens, early twenties. This will be confirmed on closer examination and positive identification. She is Caucasian and has bleached blonde hair with quite a large regrowth of at least two inches of dark brown hair from the roots. She is thin but doesn't look malnourished. There is a large, well-healed scar on the inside forearm of her left hand which runs vertical from her wrist to her elbow. She has a tattoo of a bee on her left ankle and a heart on the top of her right foot.'

She pointed to them and looked at Josh, who took out his phone. He snapped a couple of pictures, then sent them to Sykes and Bell, who were on their way to speak to the local authority homes in the area. Hopefully someone might recognise the tattoos.

Beth opened the mouth and looked inside, giving a detailed description of her teeth. As she moved the head, a single, dark brown shell fell out of the left nostril.

'Ah, this is interesting.'

Josh frowned. 'Why?'

Picking it up with a pair of tweezers, Abe passed her a jar to put it into.

'This is a single fly pupa.'

She shone a light into the nostril cavity. 'There is very little damage from maggots considering the length of time she's been buried. I'm not an entomologist, but I know enough. Judging by the lack of maggots within the body, I'd say she was kept somewhere they couldn't get to her. We all know how persistent the common housefly is when it comes to finding a body. This looks like maybe an odd fly found her or managed to get to where her body was stored before it was buried. The pupa is the third stage of the maggot's life cycle and they normally disperse anywhere up to ten metres from the body to pupate.'

Josh was staring at her, and she smiled at him; she knew he didn't have a clue what she was talking about.

'Basically, what I'm saying is that after she was killed she was kept somewhere for at least twenty-four hours before she was put into the grave. She had to have been for the fly to have found her, then laid its eggs within twenty-four hours of death. Another twenty-four hours later these eggs hatch into first stage larvae which crawl into the recesses, usually focusing on the head orifices. The eyes, nose, mouth, sometimes the genitals. They then feed and twenty-four hours later you have second stage maggots, another twenty-four hours and it's third stage which then go on to feed on the body for three to four days. When they've finished feeding, they leave the body to pupate. Somehow this one didn't, which is good because it gives us a better chance of figuring out how long she was dead before she was put into the grave. If you can get a definite last sighting of her we'll be able to estimate a rough time of death. When I say rough, I mean that because it's hard with all the different circumstances. It's better than nothing though. You'll know, very roughly, how long she was alive before she was killed. Does that make sense?'

Josh nodded. 'I think so. We just need an ID then a confirmed last sighting before she disappeared. Thanks, Beth, I'll take anything.'

Closing the mouth, Beth then checked for any abnormalities or deformities in her bones. She couldn't find any fractures apart from the obvious damage to the fingers.

'Abe, you can wash her down now, thank you.' She turned to look at Josh, who was standing there looking pale. 'I don't think those tattoos are homemade; they're not the best I've seen but they're not the worst. Do you know of any studios that have a reputation for tattooing underage girls? They're not new; I'd say at least a year or two old. I don't think she's older than eighteen or nineteen. It might be a start, someplace to start looking.'

He nodded. 'You might be right, but I don't think they'd confess to tattooing minors to a copper. It's not going to help them with their licence, is it?' Josh took out his work phone and snapped a couple of photos of the girl's face now that she'd been cleaned up.

'It also looks as if she's had a serious attempt at committing suicide. That is a major scar on her arm; it would have required hospital treatment to stem the bleeding.'

She turned back to the body to see the last of the mud being washed away, though it took some time before the water began to run clean. Satisfied, she held her hand up for Abe to stop. 'Thanks, Abe, that should be enough.'

Now the body was clean, she began the painstaking task of recording every injury, though there weren't many, noting the size, shape, pattern and location of each external wound. Satisfied she'd documented them all, she stepped to one side to let Claire photograph them and the rest of her body. Under the glare of the florescent strip lights, with all the mud washed away, she looked much younger than Beth had initially anticipated. Her skin was so pale under the harsh lighting.

*Who did this to you, and why you? How did they choose you, was it someone you knew or did some stranger come along in the middle of the night and steal you away?*

She looked at Josh, her eyes pleading. 'Where are her parents? A girl this age, surely someone would be missing her. She's been gone at least eight, maybe nine weeks. If no one has reported her missing then maybe she had no one that cared?'

Josh turned to Sam in response. 'It's possible she was in care, let's hope Sykes and Bell have found where her placement was. I've emailed them some pictures.'

'It doesn't look as if there's been a sexual assault, but I'd rather take the samples and rule it out.' She began to comb through the girl's pubic hair to secure any foreign or loose hairs before plucking several from the root to be examined more closely. Abe handed her swabs and she deftly began to take oral, nasal, vaginal and anal samples for further examination. When she'd finished those she began to examine the exterior of the scalp for any injuries hidden by the hair. Feeling her way around it and looking closely she couldn't see anything. Lifting the girl's eyelids wide open she studied them. 'I can't find any telltale signs of petechiae in the conjunctivae.'

Sam looked confused. Beth realised and smiled at her. 'What I mean is there are no signs of manual asphyxia, it's a pathological condition. Tiny haemorrhages in the form of specks are seen lining the inner surface of the eyelids and on the mucous membrane.'

Beth continued checking the girl's ear canals for any evidence of haemorrhaging, then looked again, now the dirt was washed away, at the interior of her mouth, lips and cheeks to see if there were any signs of trauma.

After a while, she stood up and stretched, signalling to Abe silently that it was time to cut. He passed her a scalpel and she made her first incision, right across the head. There was a sudden loud clatter as Carl fell to the floor beside her, and his camera bounced off the metal leg of the steel trolley as he fell against the table holding all the items of clothing. Josh looked at him in horror.

'Oh shit, he's passed out.'

Abe pulled off his gloves and plastic apron as he ran over to him, ready to drag him out of the mortuary. Beth paused, completely unfazed, the scalpel dangling mid-air.

'Someone get him out of here.'

Josh grabbed one arm and Abe the other, and between them they managed to drag him out and into the corridor.

Sam shrugged. 'Men.'

Beth smiled at her. 'He's not the first one.'

'You can continue, Doc, I'm okay with it.'

Beth nodded. 'Claire, are you okay to do both wet and dry exhibits?'

'I am. Sam can always lend a hand.'

'Thank you.'

She carried on, completing the incision and pulling back the scalp to expose the cranium. She stole a glance at Sam, who was staring at the body, calm and collected, so she continued.

# CHAPTER TWENTY-EIGHT

Annie opened her eyes. Her teeth were chattering it was so cold. Why was it still so dark? Surely she'd been asleep for a while. Her mouth was even rougher than before. She had to get up for a drink whether her head could handle it or not. On the count of three she pushed herself up and hit her head on a hard, rough ceiling. 'Argh.' Lifting her hand to her head, she rubbed it hard, to ease the throbbing inside. She had no idea where she was or what was going on. Lifting her hands, she felt the rough surface above her and whispered, 'What the hell?' Then she tried to move onto her side and realised she was in a confined space. Her stomach lurched as terror took over; she had no idea where she was or how long she'd been in here. Just then she heard someone moving around somewhere in the dark, and she began to scream and cry for help until her voice had gone hoarse and it was hard to breathe.

Help didn't arrive. Whoever it was sneaking around knew she was in there and didn't care. Some bastard had put her here in the first place. She'd been so cold when she'd woken up, but now she was too hot; it was stuffy and getting harder to breathe. How was that possible? Her mind was spinning. She was inside a box, it seemed. But *who* would want to put her in here, *why* would they? It didn't make any sense.

'It's just a joke. Any moment, Estelle or Gary will appear and let me out. They have to,' she whispered to herself.

Trying once more to push open the lid of the box she was in, she found it was too heavy and wouldn't move. She lay back trying not to breathe too deeply, knowing she needed to conserve the oxygen. A voice in her head whispered, *you're going to die here, no one is coming to help you.* A ball of air lodged itself into her lungs: she needed to open her mouth and scream to expel it and she couldn't. She was slowly suffocating and there wasn't anything she could do. The panic exploded from her chest as she let out a high-pitched scream and began clawing, then scratching at the heavy panel above her head. She felt her acrylic nails begin to snap and tear off, but she didn't care despite the pain which was hot and intense. It hurt like crazy, but it meant that she was alive, so she carried on beating, hitting, punching, scratching and pushing it with every last bit of strength. Annie knew she'd rather die fighting than lie there and do nothing.

# CHAPTER TWENTY-NINE

Estelle watched the officer's face as he wrote down everything she said in his notebook, looking for signs he didn't believe her. He was nodding away and interrupting her with questions, serious questions about the CCTV system and how easy it was to gain access to the staff quarters. She answered him as honestly as she could. Eventually, he shut his book.

'Can you show me Annie's room?'

'Of course.'

She led him through the hotel to the staff stairs near to the kitchen, and he followed her down there, looking around. The smell of stale, sweaty feet still lingered in the air, and she frowned.

'Sorry, it's a bit rank down here. Too many men, not enough air fresheners.'

He laughed. 'Smells like the locker room at work. So, what do you think has happened to Annie?'

She reached her door and turned to look at him. 'I don't know, but she just wouldn't up and leave like this. She was too drunk for a start, and since she started working here she's never missed a shift.'

'Not even when she's hungover?'

Estelle shook her head. 'Definitely not; we've struggled through them together. Look, I know she's an adult and not vulnerable or anything like that, but something's wrong. I just wish I knew what it was. She's either gone out drunk and had an accident, or...'

'Or?'

'Is kidnapping an actual thing here in the Lake District?'

'You're being serious; you think she's been kidnapped?'

'Maybe not kidnapped, what's the other thing?'

'Abducted?'

She nodded her head fervently. 'Yes, abducted.'

'By who?'

'I don't know; you're the policeman, aren't you supposed to be able to figure that one out?'

She pushed open Annie's door and flicked on the light switch.

He stood on the threshold and looked around: the bed was unmade and there was the bucket tipped over on the floor next to it. A brand-new iPhone was lying on the bed; the curtains were drawn. He pulled a pair of bright blue latex gloves from the pocket of his body armour and tugged them on.

'You stay here, whilst I look around.'

She felt slightly better now that he was taking her seriously. If he wasn't, he wouldn't have put on the gloves. Her stomach was still a mass of churning knots, but it made her feel hopeful that she was doing the right thing.

He walked around the room then stopped and bent down to look at something on the floor underneath the far side of the bed. She watched as his face registered alarm and felt her heart begin to race. What had he found? What was he looking at that she hadn't seen? He stood up and walked towards her, pulling the door shut.

'I need this door locking now and no one is to come back inside here. Do you understand?'

She nodded. 'Why?'

He ignored her and began to talk into the radio clipped onto his body armour. She didn't understand a lot of what he was saying, but she caught the words 'CID', 'get the DS to call me now' and 'I need a CSI as soon as possible…'

The worry she'd felt before was nothing compared to how fast her heart was racing now. Her anxiety had just reached a whole new level.

# CHAPTER THIRTY

Carl opened his eyes, blinked several times then realised where he was. 'Oh shit, I didn't?... Josh, I'm sorry, I've been feeling a bit rough since I got up. I just looked at that scalpel slicing into her skin and can't remember anything else.'

Josh handed him a bottle of cola he'd got from the vending machine down the hall.

'It's fine. Do you want to go to A&E to get checked out?'

'No, God no. I'm okay, I'll be fine.'

Abe had gone back in to help Beth, so only Josh remained to offer Carl his hand and pull him to his feet.

'Well you don't look fine; you look like shit. Claire can finish off the photography and Sam can be exhibits officer. Sykes is on her way to pick you up and take you home. No arguments.'

Carl nodded, and Josh felt sorry for him. 'I've told her to pick you up from the rear entrance to the mortuary, so you don't have to walk all the way through the hospital. Is that okay?'

'Thanks, Josh, I really am sorry.'

Josh left him sitting on a chair sipping at the bottle of sugary cola, needing to get back inside and see if he'd missed anything. He walked in and heard a sucking noise: talk about bad timing. He looked to see Beth tugging the girl's brain gently out of her skull and wondered if he should have waited a little bit longer. He didn't like this part, or the sound when the ribs were cracked open with a pair of pruning shears to remove the breast plate. He shuddered; how Beth did this every day then went home and slept at night amazed him. Then again, how did he do what he did and sleep at night? According to

Jodie he slept too well and snored most of the night. Just thinking about her made his nerves jangle; she'd started screaming at him this morning before he'd even had the chance to warm his bowl of Shredded Wheat up in the microwave. He didn't know what to do to save their marriage; he'd tried everything; he'd been willing to try anything, but now he didn't know if Jodie even wanted him to try.

'How's Carl? Hello? Earth to Josh – don't you go fainting on me now!'

He turned to face Beth and realised both she and Sam were staring at him.

'He's okay, Sykes is coming to pick him up and take him home. Sorry, I was thinking.'

Sam laughed. 'Don't, it's a dangerous game, boss.'

He smiled at her, then turned his attention to the table and watched as Beth methodically finished the rest of the post-mortem. She'd taken a variety of samples from the various organs and tissues of the body, and Abe was in the process of stuffing a bag containing the girl's organs back inside her abdominal cavity, ready to be sewn back up. It was brutal and sad, there was no doubt about it.

'There are no obvious signs of injury apart from the self-inflicted damage to her fingers which look as if she tried to claw her way out of an enclosed space. I'm not the expert, but there are minute traces of something green under her nails. I checked the bottom of the coffin she was buried under and there are no splinters of wood, signs of damage from scratching or any sign of plant life or moss. She has to have tried to claw her way out of somewhere for her to rip her fingernails off like she has, but I don't think it was from underneath the coffin. I think she died from asphyxiation due to a lack of oxygen in a confined space. We'll know for sure once the blood results are back; there's a simple test they can do which will confirm the measure of carbon monoxide in the blood. If it comes back at more than three per cent, it's a definite.'

'So, she was put in a confined space and suffocated to death?'

'Yes. I don't think the burial site was the primary scene, Josh.'

Josh turned to Sam. 'Do we think she was put into a wooden box, a crate, maybe a coffin and left to die? But where, and why remove her from that to put her into the grave?'

'I don't know, maybe it was easier to hide her body that way. It's pretty hard to disguise a box or a coffin.'

'Who has access to wooden boxes, crates or coffins and the facilities to store and transport dead bodies?'

They all spoke at the same time.

'Undertakers.'

'Beth, does it say on the paperwork which funeral home dealt with Florence's funeral?'

She stripped off her gloves and apron. 'Let me go and check, I'm pretty sure it was Dean & Sons.'

Josh could feel a whole multitude of questions bursting through his mind. His phone began to ring; he saw Sykes's name on the screen, and he put his phone on to loudspeaker.

'Boss, you're in luck. We were just about to leave Dalton View when I got that email you sent. I showed it to the staff, and we have a positive ID on the tattoos. The girl is Chantel Price. Staff from Dalton View, a place that provides support to help young people about to transition to live independently once they reach eighteen, have identified her. Her caseworker has agreed to come down and do the official ID.'

'When was the last time they saw her, and why did they not report her missing?'

'They last saw her around six p.m. on the second of May. She walked out with her suitcase and a backpack. They said she'd refused to stay there any longer and got picked up by a male in a car. She would have been eighteen on the third of May, so she was leaving the home the next day and had refused any further help. They didn't think there was much point in reporting her as missing when she was legally entitled to leave the next day anyway.'

'You're kidding me; do they know who the male was or what car he was driving?'

'Staff said they've seen him a couple of times, Chantel referred to him as "J", driver of a white Astra, registration number JAZ 1991.'

Josh knew what she was going to say next; hopefully she'd already run the reg through the police national computer.

'It PNCs to Jason Thompson of 13 Seabreeze Walk.'

He nodded. A gravedigger was almost as good as an undertaker.

# CHAPTER THIRTY-ONE

Josh sprinted to his car. He needed to get back to Kendal as soon as possible. Paton wasn't picking up his phone. Was he was tied up? He hoped he wasn't avoiding him because he hadn't managed to catch up with Jason Thompson like he'd told him to earlier. He had a sinking feeling it might be the latter; he knew that Paton wouldn't want to let the team down and would be blaming himself. Sam offered to drive so he could keep phoning, and he tossed the keys in her direction. As they left the hospital grounds his phone rang, and he answered it, praying it was Paton.

'Walker, where are you?' He recognised Smithy's voice: one of the patrol sergeants and a close friend. 'Just leaving FGH; why are you phoning off a work phone?'

'I've just had an interesting conversation with Mickey: control sent him to a call-out to a missing hotel worker that came in over an hour ago in Bowness. Her boss took him down to her bedroom in the staff quarters located in the basement. Says he found something under the bed that you're going to want to see ASAP.'

'Like what?'

'Like a photograph of a dead girl with three bloodied fingernails placed on top of it…'

Josh felt a wave of bile rise from his stomach all the way up his throat, burning every inch of the way. 'I need a photo of the scene sent to me now.'

'Already done it, mate. I don't know exactly what's going on, but I suggest you get there as soon as you can. Mickey has the scene on lockdown, and I've sent a couple of PCSOs to guard the entrance and exits into the hotel. I'm on my way down there now, because apparently the owner has turned up and not very happy the police are crawling all over the place on a busy Monday afternoon.'

'Thanks, Smithy, I'll be there as soon as I can. Is there a dog handler on?'

'Already been requested and on his way from Carlisle.'

The phone went dead, and Josh looked at Sam. 'Did you get the gist of that?'

She nodded.

'It's another victim, it has to be. He's liking the attention and wants more. Would Jason Thompson be that bold though? I got the impression he was a bit of a wide boy, maybe dabbling in drugs, selling a bit of class B here and there. He doesn't strike me as the type to abduct two women and play games with the police.'

Opening up the glove compartment he pulled his airwave radio out and switched it on, needing to get hold of Paton and see where the hell he was. The radio on the other end rang out: no answer.

'He's taking the piss now.'

'Maybe he's not in a position to speak to you; he might have Jason Thompson pinned.'

Josh grunted and began to type one of the many passwords into his hand-held tablet, to get access to his emails and look at the picture Smithy had sent. He needed to know if the dead girl in the photograph was Chantel Price, or someone else. The bloody thing took forever to load; he hated technology with a passion. He could feel his blood pressure rising with every second that went by. This was turning into a nightmare. He needed to put a stop to it, and now, before any more girls went missing, or were murdered; he'd kill whoever it was with his bare hands when he found them. He hadn't felt this way since the night he'd arrived at Beth's house all those years ago, the night of her attack. The hate he felt towards Richard Hartshorn had given him nightmares for months afterwards. He wouldn't stand by and let another sick bastard terrorise innocent women; it wasn't happening. Not on his watch. But a voice inside his head whispered, *but it already has, and it already is, Josh. You can't protect them. You never could.*

# CHAPTER THIRTY-TWO

Beth finished up the paperwork releasing Florence Wright's body back for burial. There was no way she should have been exhumed in the first place. It was really bothering her; it had to have been a set-up, arranged so the body buried underneath her would be discovered. But why? Why go to all this elaborate effort to cover up what you'd done, only to undo it all again? It was risky. She knew it was possible the killer, or someone close to him, had spoken to her as well as the police. Granted, she couldn't remember an awful lot about the voice on the end of the phone all those weeks ago, but he'd seemed genuinely distressed about what he'd discovered about his great-aunt Florence, and she remembered how she hadn't wanted to upset him further by scrutinising his every sentence. She had a record of his phone number, and she'd spoken to him personally, so she had assumed it was all legitimate. Stupid, is what she'd been. She could see that now. After everything she'd been through, she should have known not to take anyone at face value. Her head was pounding, making her unconsciously rub the puckered scar on the side of her face to ease the tension; the late afternoon sun was still shining through the office window and it was unbearably hot. After the coolness of the mortuary she hadn't expected the day to be such a scorcher. She wanted to go home, shower, eat, have a large glass of ice-cold wine on the patio and watch the sun set over the lake. She wanted to breathe fresh air and push all of this out of her mind for a couple of hours. Chantel Price wouldn't be so lucky.

There was a soft tap on the door, and she knew it was Abe.

'Come in.'

He opened the door, looking as hot and tired as she felt. That last post-mortem had been long and arduous.

'Thank you for today. I think it's time for you to go home and get some rest. Maybe a cold beer or two?'

He smiled. 'What about you, Doc? You know I won't go until you do.'

'I'm walking out of that door right behind you. I have the headache from hell and need all the alcohol I can find.'

She stood up; her linen trousers were a lot more wrinkled than when she'd first put them on this morning. Grabbing her jacket off the coat hook near the door, she threw it over her arm and picking up her bag she followed Abe outside.

The drive home had been glorious, the air con blasting her full in the face, and the roads relatively quiet for a Monday night in the Lake District. She was excited to get home, had even stopped off at the supermarket for a piece of salmon and some fresh salad for her supper; there was no way she could eat red meat after today.

Despite the exhaustion, she took time to take a cursory check of the area before driving through the gates to her house. She wondered if the camera guy had managed to get the spare part for her. As she turned to get out, she noticed the letter she'd thrown into the footwell of the passenger seat, and sighed. Snatching it up, she decided to put it with the rest of them inside the house; there was no way she was giving *him* the pleasure of reading them.

Grabbing her bag of shopping, she climbed out of the car and let herself into her house. No dead birds today, thankfully. Setting the alarm again behind her, she headed to the kitchen where she opened a drawer and threw in the envelope, slamming it shut with her hip without even looking inside. Next, she unwrapped the piece of fish, placing it onto a baking tray with some freshly ground salt, pepper and a sliver of garlic butter. Sealing it in foil, she placed it in the oven, poured herself a large glass of chilled White Zinfandel and went upstairs to shower.

Back downstairs in a pair of cotton pyjamas, she took the salmon out of the oven, added a large heap of salad which she then smothered in full-fat mayonnaise. Tucking a knife and fork under her arm, she grabbed her wine and plate and let herself out of the sliding glass kitchen doors and took a seat at the wicker table on the patio which faced the lake. She could hear voices in the distance and focused on the water, searching them out. A loud splash followed by a high-pitched screech made her pick out the boat nearest to the shore. There was a group of teenagers messing around on it, drinking bottles of beer and jumping into the icy cold waters of Windermere. It didn't matter how brightly the sun had shone on the water all day, it would still be freezing cold. The boat was quite some distance away, but the noise carried because it was so peaceful and there wasn't any breeze. She smiled at them, just kids having fun.

She wondered if Chantel Price had ever known what it was to be carefree. Can't have been much fun living in care with no family. A lump formed in her throat and she had difficulty swallowing the mouthful of food she'd forked in. Washing it down with a large gulp of wine, she made a silent promise that she wouldn't forget the girl that no one had even noticed had gone missing. Would anyone even care that she'd been murdered? Beth was determined to find out. Although it was going against her best interests, she decided she would be paying Dalton View a visit tomorrow. She wanted to speak to the staff, find out as much about Chantel as she could. Beth owed her that, at least; someone had to fight her corner and she was more than happy to do it.

# CHAPTER THIRTY-THREE

Sam drove them down the narrow street to reach the hotel, where several police vans and the dog handler were already parked up. A large group of tourists who had just disembarked from a coach hovered round with their cameras taking photos.

'What the hell is going on?'

Josh jumped out of the car and jogged towards the flustered PCSO standing at the entrance to the Windermere Lake Hotel trying to move them on. He saw a look of fear cross her face when she recognised him and smiled back reassuringly; he didn't want her to think he was angry with her: he knew how difficult big crowds could be. He heard a woman's voice shout so loud behind him everyone stopped what they were doing and turned to look back.

'Move on now, please.' Sam had her hands outspread, preventing the group from getting any closer to the hotel. Josh joined in and between the pair of them they managed to push them back some distance.

'You can't come closer, I'm afraid. No photographs, please.'

Sam pointed to their cameras and shook her head.

The PCSO whispered, 'The bad news is they're all guests at the hotel. The good news is that another coach should be picking them up any minute to take them on a sightseeing tour.'

'Thank Christ for that. If there was any evidence out here, we can kiss *that* goodbye.'

'Sorry, Sarge. There was nothing I could do.'

'It's not your fault. Are they sending more officers to help out?'

'I asked thirty minutes ago but there's been an accident in Kendal that a couple of them got diverted to.'

'Walker.'

Josh turned around to see that the dog handler, Jack, had joined them, leaving his dog in the car for now.

'Jack. Good to see you.'

'This is a bit of a cock-up. I doubt the dog's going to be able to pick up much after they've been through.' He nodded his head in the direction of the group of tourists.

Ashley, the PCSO, smiled. 'Actually, they think the main scene is around the back of the hotel, at the staff entrance, and no one has been around there since Helen sealed the area off. Staff have checked the main entrance CCTV and there is no sign of the girl leaving that way. The manager said she had to have gone out of the staff exit, but there are no cameras around there.'

'That's something. Shame it's in a blind spot.'

Josh, Sam and Jack all headed inside the hotel entrance, where they were met by a very attractive woman. Josh and Jack both stared a little longer than necessary. Sam coughed and smiled apologetically at the woman, who was pale and seemed visibly upset.

Josh held out his hand. 'DS Joshua Walker, this is DC Sam Thomas and PC Jack Booth, one of the force's dog handlers. Could you show us where the staff exit is and where it can be accessed both inside and outside of the hotel?'

She took his hand, shaking it firmly. 'Of course. Estelle Carter, hotel manager. I'm so worried, the officer wouldn't tell me what he'd found in Annie's room. Will someone be able to talk to me properly about it?'

'I'm sorry, of course. He's just following procedure, which can be a little cold at times. As soon as I've taken a look at what he's found for myself I'll come and have a chat with you about it. Is that okay with you?'

This wasn't strictly true. Even if she owned the hotel, it was a police investigation and he would only tell her what he needed to. The less people knew about the details of the case, the better. He couldn't afford for it to be leaked out to the press. And he wanted to keep it between him and the killer; that way they could weed out the crackpots from the real thing and narrow down the suspect pool.

He followed as she led them through the hotel to a corridor and a wooden door with two frosted glass panels which had a big sign saying 'Staff Only' screwed to the front of it. She pushed open the door and they followed her through.

'Does the hotel CCTV system cover back here?'

'No, unfortunately not. It covers all the public areas or most of them. Daddy didn't think it was worth the money having it installed back here. He said he didn't want to know what the staff got up to in their own time as long as they worked hard when they were on shift.'

Sam raised an eyebrow at Josh: so Estelle's daddy was either in charge or owned the place. Strange a woman her age calling him Daddy; a psychiatrist would have a field day with that one.

'Is your father around to speak to?'

'He's on his way; he was on his way to London on business. As soon as I told him he turned around and began driving back.'

They reached a scuffed white door which Estelle pushed open. 'Annie's room is down the steps and straight along the corridor until you reach the end. The policeman is still outside her door. Do you want me to come down with you?'

Josh shook his head. 'No, it's okay. Thank you, I'll go and speak to him. If you could show my colleagues the exits and how to access them from the rear of the hotel, that would be great.'

Estelle nodded. Her expression was one of pure misery and Josh felt sorry for her. Waiting for her to turn and leave, he realised he should have got suited and booted; he didn't want to compromise any evidence the CSIs might later find. He went down the steps and shouted to Mickey, who popped his head around a corner at the far end of the gloomy corridor.

'Have you got any kit in your van?'

He shrugged. 'I think so; I don't know if there's enough though. You might have to wait for Claire to get here.' He threw the van keys in his direction. Josh deftly caught them and ran back up the stairs and out of the front of the hotel, relieved to see the tourists had all left for a couple of hours. His phone rang and he heard Paton's voice on the other end. At last.

'Sarge, he's done a runner.'

'For God's sake, how do you know that?'

'I spoke to him over two hours ago on the phone, when he agreed to come to the station. Said he was out walking and would make his way here. He didn't turn up. I'm so sorry.'

'No shit.' Josh wanted to punch something, anything. 'Circulate him as top wanted; I want his picture emailed to everyone and their dog. Have you been to his house?'

'Sat outside it now. There's no sign of him, but his car is here.'

'There's no chance he's coming back for it. Too obvious.'

A sickening thought filled Josh's mind: what if he'd gone to finish Annie off? He had nothing to lose now, not if he thought they were onto him.

'Go get a search warrant. I want the property searched from attic to cellar. Make sure it includes outbuildings, garages and sheds. Oh, and the car, I want it uplifted and sent for a full forensic examination.'

'Yes, boss. I'll get a couple of uniforms here to wait in case he turns up.'

Josh ended the call. He knew it wasn't much of a link to Chantel Price, but it was all they had and enough to go on for now. Innocent people don't run.

# CHAPTER THIRTY-FOUR

Carl had been dropped off at home a couple of hours ago. He'd gone inside, had a cold shower and been ready to go back out a short time later. He hadn't been *completely* lying; he had felt light-headed at the mortuary, but he'd faked passing out. Blood and guts didn't bother him – he'd got hardened to all sorts of horrific stuff doing his job, but he'd realised he had to get out of there. He couldn't watch any longer: he had much more pressing things on his mind. He needed to see her, couldn't stop thinking about her. His wife had never had the same effect on him that she had. Maybe in the early days, but not now. They used to sleep in separate bedrooms when he was on call, but now it was a permanent fixture. He was a man, he had needs. She couldn't really blame him for looking elsewhere, could she? He had no idea what he would do if she found out though.

He scrolled through Facebook, scrutinising her every photograph. She was so beautiful, so alive. There was something very satisfying in trying to decide if she was happy on the day it had been taken. It was kind of like a game, one he enjoyed playing. He showered and changed into something bland, clothes that would make him blend in with the crowd and not stand out. Discretion was the key thing in this situation. You didn't want to do anything to draw unnecessary attention to yourself. Not when you had so much fun to look forward to. He didn't want to spoil it by getting caught before he'd even got going. This could go on for quite some time, and he relished the thought of having a little excitement to look forward to in his otherwise dreary life.

Driving to her house, he wondered if he should park up and wait for her. Should he surprise her, or let her know he was there? It was about time he upped his stakes; he wanted more. He didn't know how she felt, but he was willing to take the risk for her. He just hoped she appreciated it.

# CHAPTER THIRTY-FIVE

Josh rustled his way into the hotel in an enormous triple-x-sized paper suit, the only one he could find in the back of Mickey's van. It drowned him, but he didn't want to wait any longer. He had to see the room for himself; he needed to see the fingernails and photograph in situ. He wouldn't be satisfied until he had. He trusted Mickey, of course; he'd been a copper almost as long as he had, and experience was everything in this job.

The reception area corridor which led to the staff quarters and kitchens had been cordoned off, and there was a PCSO standing outside. Guests could still use the main stairs, the lifts, go to the reception desk and enter the lounge and bar. He'd requested the PCSO guarding the entrance to the corridor to only let guests through who showed their key cards in and out of the hotel, to keep the foot traffic to a minimum. It wasn't ideal, but it was the best he could do in this situation. As much as he'd like to shut the hotel, it just wasn't possible without drawing too much attention. Thank God they thought the girl had been taken from the staff entrance around the back: it was fully sealed off and out of bounds to anyone except police officers and police staff.

As he walked down the stairs he heard a burst of laughter come from Mickey, who stifled it when Josh glared at him.

'Sorry, boss, but you look like the Marshmallow Man from *Ghostbusters* in that suit!'

'Very funny. It's the only size there was. I guess big Steely stocked the van up last. I don't have time to wait for another smaller set of overalls, I need to take a look inside. She might not have long left, that is if she isn't already dead.'

The smile left Mickey's face as the stark reality of the situation hit home. 'What are we going to do, Josh? How are we going to find her?'

Josh felt his mouth go dry. 'I don't know, but we can't give up. We've got to keep moving and hope for the best. It's all we can do really.'

Mickey signed him into the crime scene logbook, and Josh stepped inside the room, which smelled much better than the musty corridor. There were scented candles on almost every available surface and a plug-in air freshener which smelled of those pear drop sweets he used to love as a kid. He slowly looked around. Nothing looked out of place. The bedding was a tangled knot of duvet on top of the bed; there was a plastic bucket on the floor which Estelle had told him she'd put there in case Annie was sick. He couldn't see under the bed from this side. He walked around to the other side to find only a small gap between the floor and the bed frame. He bent down, pushed up the too-long sleeve of the suit and turned on the torch he was carrying. His breath caught at the back of his throat as it illuminated a normal-sized photograph decorated with the three chipped, pale green, blood-stained fingernails. Tilting the torch to get a better look at the image, his stomach churned at sight of Chantel Price's bone-white, lifeless face staring back at him. The photo must have been taken with a strong flash somewhere very dark. It was instantly clear that whoever had taken Annie was the same person who'd killed Chantel. And they wanted to make sure everybody knew it. Unable to look any longer, he glanced around the room, searching for an item of Annie's clothing to give to Jack and the dog to catch the scent. He picked up a discarded T-shirt from the bottom of the laundry bin.

There was a knock on the door, and he heard Mickey whisper, 'Boss, CSI are here, and Claire is apparently going to rip your bollocks off if you've been inside the scene before she's videoed and photographed it.'

He grimaced, straightened up and retraced his footsteps. As he walked out of the door he bumped straight into her, blocking his way with her arms folded across her chest. Mickey just shrugged and turned the other way.

'Why, Josh? You know the score better than anyone.'

'I didn't touch anything, and we don't have much time. I just needed to see for myself. It's all yours, and the hotel manager's already been in a couple of times.'

She shook her head, tutting at him but said no more. He knew she'd understand.

He walked back to the staircase and shuffled his way outside to the van where he stripped off the suit, boot covers and gloves, depositing them all into a brown paper sack as evidence. There was nothing else he could do here. He needed to think where to search; to work out who was keeping Annie captive, and fast. From Beth's findings with the fly pupa he was hoping they had maybe a couple of days before they ran out of time.

# CHAPTER THIRTY-SIX

Sam was waiting with Jack by his van and smiled as Josh crossed the road towards her. He passed the T-shirt to Jack, and they waited patiently as he let the dog out and held it under her nose. Their hearts lifted as the springer spaniel set off towards the hotel, straining at her long leash; but it wasn't long before Jack and the dog returned to where they were waiting.

'She picked up the scent a short distance outside of the hotel grounds, across the road at the back of the church and then it stopped; nothing else.'

'Dammit. He must have bundled her into a vehicle and drove away with her. Sam, can you ask the CCTV operators to check the cameras on the main street after she'd been escorted to bed?'

'Already on it.'

'Thank you. Any word on Thompson?'

'No. But I've been thinking: where he could possibly hide her? He lives in a second floor flat with no garden, has neighbours above and below him.'

He nodded. 'Are there any sheds, garages or lock-ups at the cemetery?'

She shrugged. 'Probably, should we go there now?'

Josh was already in the driver's seat clicking his seat belt in. He did a three-point turn to get out of the tight space and took off as fast as he could. The cemetery was only a few minutes away.

*

Driving through the main gates he headed straight towards the cemetery offices, hoping that they were still open. Abandoning the car so it blocked in a brand-new Jag, he didn't care; they would have to wait. Pushing open the old, creaky wooden door it made enough noise to wake the dead. The girl sitting behind an equally old desk jumped at the sudden noise.

Josh pulled out his warrant card and crossed towards her, thrusting it in her face. 'DS Josh Walker and this is my colleague DC Sam Thomas, we're investigating a high-risk missing person's case and need to know if there are any outbuildings here, in the grounds? Sheds, garages, that sort of thing…'

'Well, Jase and Barry have access to the entire site, they would know. I'm sorry, I haven't been here very long so I couldn't tell you. I'm sure Jase will be able to help you. I'll ring him for you.' She tucked the phone under her chin and looked at her watch. 'Mind you they might have gone home for the day. I was just about to leave. It is quite late.'

Josh looked at Sam, who shrugged: was it possible Thompson hadn't done a runner at all and had been here all day working? He hoped so. They waited for the girl to go through an address book and then dial the phone number. She seemed as if she was moving in slow motion, but eventually she replaced the receiver and looked across at him.

'Do you have a plan of the cemetery we could look at?

'I don't think we have one here. You might have to ask at the planning department, they would probably have one. Jase isn't picking up; should I try Barry?'

Sam smiled at her. 'If you wouldn't mind, but could you please hurry. This really is a matter of great urgency.'

The girl smiled back then looked down at the book and began running her finger down the page to find Barry's number, then repeated the process.

'Barry, can you come to the office now? There's two coppers here. They're in a bit of a rush.'

She put the phone down. 'He's up by the old chapel; he said can you meet him because he was about to clock off. He'll start walking down. Is there anything else I can help you with?'

Josh stepped outside and heard Sam thanking her for her help. They got back into the car and began the drive along the narrow, steep hill towards the chapel where it had all begun two days ago. Josh rubbed a hand across the stubble on his face; had it only been two days? They saw a man in a bright yellow safety vest walking down the hill towards them. Josh stopped the car and put the window down. Barry leaned into his open window. The metallic smell of freshly dug soil clung to him and filled the car.

'What's up, officers?'

Josh couldn't afford to be subtle; he decided honesty was the best way forward. They didn't have the luxury of time on their side and he hoped that it wouldn't come back to haunt him.

'What I'm about to tell you is highly sensitive and not to be spoken about to anyone. This is confidential between us, Barry.' He stared at him waiting for an acknowledgment of the seriousness of the situation.

Barry nodded, confirming he understood.

'A girl has gone missing and we think there's a strong possibility that the same person who put that girl in your grave might have taken her. We can't find Jason either and I'm more than a little bit concerned that he might have something to do with this whole mess.'

Barry stared at Josh, then began shaking his head. 'Nah, you're wrong. Jase is mouthy, full of himself and a lazy bastard. But he's not like that. He's not a weirdo.'

'How would you know that?'

'I work with him, don't I? You can tell a lot about a person when you work closely with them. He likes a laugh and a joke, and he's partial to the ladies but he wouldn't do that. Never.'

'Then why has he vanished off the face of the earth when one of my officers asked him to come into the station for a chat?'

'Scared, the stupid bugger. He watches too much TV, always banging on about some poor sod in America who got locked up for a murder he didn't commit.'

'Whoever killed the first girl now potentially has a new victim. There's a chance she may still be alive.' He glanced at the graveyard around them. 'We need to know if there are there any unused outbuildings here that he might have access to?'

'Well yeah, there's a couple. There's the equipment shed, then there's our little lock-up; but I'd know if there was a girl hidden away in there. I use them every day.'

'What about places you don't use?'

He shook his head. 'I'll take you to all the hidey-holes, so you can have a look for yourselves. You won't find anything out of the ordinary.'

He began to walk off and Sam whispered in Josh's ear, 'How's he so sure about all of this?'

Josh stared at her. They jumped out of the car and jogged to catch up with him, just in case he decided to do a runner as well.

# CHAPTER THIRTY-SEVEN

Beth had finished at a reasonable time today: she'd still make it to her usual self-defence class if she got a move on. She looked at the bottle of wine on the kitchen worktop. It was tempting, but she knew she wouldn't sleep unless she'd done something to properly tire herself out and burn off this nervous energy that was coursing through her veins.

Upstairs, she changed into a pair of loose-fitting gym pants and a baggy T-shirt – no tight Lycra for her, nothing to make her stand out and draw attention to herself, despite her having a good figure for a woman in her mid-thirties – she then dipped into the spare room to grab her trainers. She secretly loathed this room. It was a nursery when she'd first moved in, but it was now repainted and packed with boxes of odd junk, her weights and swinging punch bag in the corner. She'd never settled down long enough to consider having children before meeting Robert. After they'd been together a while the possibility had crossed her mind, but he had never really seemed like the paternal type; he was so particular about everything, couldn't stand mess, or noise, or sticky fingers all over his pristine life. After the attack she knew she wouldn't ever trust anyone enough again to ever try. At one time it had made her sad that she wasn't able to join in with her friends when they were talking about what little Skye or Jacob had been up to this week at nursery. But now she knew it was a blessing; some things were meant to be. As she laced up her trainers, she wondered why Josh and his wife had never had children. He'd make such a great dad – he was that kind of man.

The drive to the community hall didn't take very long but parking the car did. Even though it was after six, the car park a short walk away was full. Who wouldn't want to watch the sun setting over the lake with an ice cream or a bag of fish and chips on such a beautiful evening?

As she drove past the small street which led to the Windermere Lake Hotel she wondered why there were so many police vans parked outside. There was a PCSO standing guard at the entrance to the hotel. She checked her phone. There can't have been a sudden death, as she'd had no missed calls. Circling back around, she managed to pull into a space in front of Costa just as another car pulled out. Lots of people were milling around by the church and coffee shop. As she locked her car she headed towards the community hall. She'd ask Josh tomorrow if he knew what had gone on.

The class had already begun by the time she slipped inside. Phil glanced across at her, grinned and lifted his hand in greeting. She did the same back. He was cute in his own way, and very muscly. Not her type at all, but he was excellent at teaching women how to defend themselves against would-be attackers. She joined in with the rest of the class, who were warming up. Focusing on the exercises, she pushed today out of her head and before long she was punching, blocking and kicking, and Phil was throwing her around on the mats. She didn't mind, she was great at blocking punches now and enjoyed the power of the roughness and close contact between them. It was as close as she'd got to intimacy since the attack. Her mind wandered for a moment and she felt herself flying through the air, once more landing heavily on the mats.

'You're losing your touch, Beth.'

She looked up at Phil, aware that he could have thrown her a lot harder than he actually had. Grinning, she rolled over.

'Maybe I'm just luring you into a false sense of security.'

He laughed, holding out his hand for her and pulling her to her feet. Turning around, he told the class to practise what he'd just shown them and then turned back to her, asking quietly, 'Is everything okay? You've been a bit distant the last couple of sessions.'

She nodded. 'I'm good. Work is busy. It's my own fault I keep getting distracted, nothing's wrong. Thank you for asking.'

'Good, I worry about you. I think you work too hard and you need to have some fun. Why don't you come out for a drink with the rest of the class when we finish? It's Bob's birthday and we're going to The Stag for a couple.'

Beth always said no, Phil knew this, but Beth liked that he never stopped asking, never stopped trying to pull her back into the fold. It was nice. It made her feel as if she belonged to this mixed bunch of people who would probably never have the need to use what they got taught once or twice a week. At least, she hoped they wouldn't. Opening her mouth, no one was more shocked than she was to hear herself say: 'OK, just one drink.'

# CHAPTER THIRTY-EIGHT

Barry took them inside the lock-up where the tools and heavy machinery were kept. Josh and Sam checked it thoroughly, but there were no trap doors or concealed rooms, nothing but spades and lawnmowers. Next, he took them to a large empty shed and gave them a quick tour of the offices where the staff room and locker rooms were.

'What did I tell you? If there was a woman being held here against her will, I'd have known about it, and don't you think I'd have rung you lot? She's not here.'

'What about the old chapel?'

'It's fenced off and boarded up, but you can go look for yourself. Someone must have had a look around already; you lot have been hanging around by that grave opposite for long enough. Anyway, I check it's all secure at the beginning of every shift because of squatters. Nothing to report.'

Josh didn't want to admit defeat despite the sinking feeling in the pit of his stomach. 'Thanks for your time. If you notice anything amiss or strange…'

'…Then I'll ring you lot straight away.'

'Thank you.'

'You're welcome. Whatever that stupid bugger Jason has done it isn't what you're thinking. I'm never wrong about people, I've always had a gut instinct about them. You're wasting your time chasing him when you should be looking for the sick bastard who's doing this.'

Barry walked away, back towards the offices. Sam looked at Josh.

'He could be right, boss. What if we're barking up the wrong tree and wasting time?'

'We can't rule him out simply because good old Barry's "gut instinct is never wrong". But I think we need to keep our options open. Where else can we look?'

Before Sam could answer him, he answered himself. 'Let's pay the undertaker's a visit, Dean & Sons.'

Sam grimaced. 'I've seen enough dead bodies for one day.'

'Sorry, but I need you to charm your way in there. We'll need to have a look around if they'll do it without a warrant. Both of them are a bit odd from memory, rarely ever say more than hello, goodbye when I've had to call them out to a sudden death.'

'What makes you think they'll say more than that to me?'

'You have a way with words and the younger one – is it James? I think it is – he's the lonely type. I think he'll like you.'

'What are you trying to say?'

'I remember a few years ago there was a bit of a fuss when his brother was showing a customer around and walked in on James screwing a new member of staff on top of one of the trolleys where they put the coffins.'

'How the hell do you even know this stuff, Josh?'

'I know everything. It's called being a good copper.'

She rolled her eyes at him. 'No, it's called being a *gossip*.'

# CHAPTER THIRTY-NINE

The pub was literally thirty steps from the hall they had just come from, but Beth stayed close to Phil as they walked through the doors, her stomach full of butterflies. She knew she was being completely ridiculous. How on earth could she ever enjoy her life if she lived this way forever? He'd won if she did. He might not have succeeded in killing her that night, but would it have been better than this slow, torturous non-existence?

As they queued at the busy bar, Phil told her to go and sit with the others and he'd bring the drinks over. She shook her head: she was paying for this round. It was the least she could do.

'You didn't have to do that!? I can stoop to two halfs of lager, a blackcurrant and a glass of wine.'

She laughed. 'If you do that every week, is it even worth your while running the classes?'

'Yes, most definitely. I like to think of it as my chance to give something back to the community. I also hope I help people who've been through a terrible time gain the confidence to make sure it will never happen again.'

He picked up three glasses and walked towards the small table the others had squeezed themselves around. Beth had to blink several times to stop the tears from falling. He was right, and she wished she could thank him in a better way than buying a round of drinks. She squeezed in to a small gap next to Audrey and Bob, who both smiled at her.

'It's lovely to see you here, Beth,' said Audrey. 'We've often wondered what you do for a living. Bob thinks you're a copper.

I think you might be a doctor. Maybe a GP, but you're definitely not a housewife because you're always on call.'

All eyes were on her. She wanted to leave, but she couldn't. She needed to do this, to see what life was like on the other side of fear.

'You're quite close, Audrey, I'm a doctor of sorts.'

Audrey smiled sweetly at Bob. 'I knew it.'

'No one likes a smart-arse, babe. Don't gloat, it doesn't suit you.'

It was only then Beth realised that Audrey and Bob were a couple. She looked at their ring fingers to see the matching wedding rings and smiled; she was learning something new every day. How many months had she spoken to them, wrestled with them on the mats and hadn't even made the connection? Was she *that* self-absorbed these days? Trying to deflect the conversation away from herself, Beth asked, 'What about you, Audrey, do you work?'

Bob nodded. 'She works all right, drags me there with her most days.'

Audrey nudged him. 'Shh, you enjoy it. So don't pretend that you don't. How many pretty brides do you get to flirt with?'

He laughed, and Audrey turned to Beth. 'I'm a florist. I own the little shop near to the marina called Pretty Flowers.'

Beth smiled. 'I love the flowers from there, they're beautiful. If I'm passing, I always pop in for some.'

Audrey's face beamed. 'Thank you, make sure you tell the girls who work there you're my friend next time, and they'll give you a discount. Now, what kind of doctor did you say you were, pet?'

Beth inhaled: this was the moment of truth. Most people she told were horrified and would excuse themselves quickly after hearing what she did for a living.

'I'm a pathologist, specialising in forensic pathology.'

Phil began to laugh, which made her grin. Audrey was looking ever so pleased with herself.

'You mean, like Quincy?'

Beth had no idea what that meant. 'I'm sorry, I don't follow.'

'Oh, it might have been before your time. Quincy was an American pathologist on a television show I used to love. Such a good-looking man, and he always solved the murders. Then he'd go and confront the killers himself.'

Now it was Beth's turn to laugh. 'I do remember that show now. I'm afraid it's nothing like that. Sorry. I tell the police how the victim died. I give them as much evidence as I can, so they can go and find the killer. Thankfully, the chasing part has nothing to do with me. When they catch them, I go to court to give my evidence against them and hope that it's enough to secure a conviction.'

Bob reached forward and patted her hand. She did her best not to draw it away from him.

'You are a very clever young lady; thank you for all that you do. Especially for the people whose lives have been taken from them. I'm sure they appreciate it.'

For the second time in less than thirty minutes Beth felt her eyes fill with warm tears, and she wondered if the block of ice around her heart was finally beginning to thaw; if she might just be on the verge of remembering what it was like to be human.

Excusing herself to go to the toilet, she bumped into the man who'd come to fix her cameras. He was staring down at his phone and lifted his head to apologise.

'I'm so sorry.' He looked at her for a moment, and she smiled at him.

'The lady with the lovely lakefront house and the broken front door camera, how are you?'

She laughed. 'You have a great memory. I'm good thanks. Yourself?'

'I'll be wonderful when the part for your camera arrives tomorrow. I don't like keeping customers waiting too long. I know how unnerving it can be when you're used to the security.'

'It's fine, it's only been a couple of days, but thank you. And yes, I am very security conscious.'

'What brings you to The Stag? I haven't seen you in here before.'

'I came with some friends. They've been asking me for months and I finally decided to give it a try.'

He laughed. 'You don't know what you've been missing. I come here most evenings for a drink before going home to my lonely old house to warm up a microwave meal for one.'

'Oh dear, it sounds as if your life is as exciting as mine.' She hesitated, and then said, 'Listen, it was nice seeing you; hopefully I'll see you soon with the parts.'

She began to walk away, and he called after her: 'Can I buy you a drink?'

Beth froze and felt the hairs on the back of her neck rising, as a voice in her head whispered, *please act normal. Don't freak out.* Turning, she smiled at him.

'No, thank you, that's a very kind offer and I would love to say yes but I'm driving, and I have a busy day tomorrow. I only came in for a quick drink. Maybe another time.'

'No problem. That would be nice.'

He lifted his hand and waved at her as he turned to walk away, and she waved before returning to the table where Bob and Phil were having a heated discussion about something whilst Audrey was chatting on her phone. She'd had enough for one night and was pleased with her effort to do something a little different and socialise more than she had in a long time. Excusing herself, she left them to it, feeling as if she'd started a new chapter in her life, and she liked it.

# CHAPTER FORTY

The gates to Dean & Sons were closed. Josh stared at the intercom, drumming his fingers on the steering wheel. On one hand, he wanted to go in there and search the place from top to bottom. On the other, he knew that unless the owners were very understanding he wouldn't get to do that without a warrant, which could take hours, especially with so little real evidence to go on.

He turned to Sam. 'Do you think we're going to fuck it all up if we go in there now?'

'Honest opinion?'

He nodded.

'Then most probably, yes. They'll likely refuse us entry because we have no real grounds to go in there.'

'Or we can use Section 17 (1) of PACE—'

'I know, it gives us the power to enter premises without a warrant "in order to save life and limb". Look, Josh, I want to find her as much as you do. I've felt sick since we got the call about it, and I can't stop thinking about how terrified she must be, but…'

'But?'

'We don't have much to go on; the top brass are not going to fall for that. What if she's already dead? She's been gone since the early hours of the morning. If we barge in there and piss them off and she is in there, it's going to make everything ten times worse.'

'You're right, let's go back to the station and run it past the DI…'

Sam released the breath she'd been holding in.

'... after you've pressed this buzzer and asked if you could speak to them. Tell them you're trying to locate Jason Thompson. Ask them how well they know him, when they last saw him. You know the score, just keep them talking.'

'And whilst I do that, what are you going to be doing?'

'Just having a little mooch around the grounds, peering through a few windows. You know, that kind of thing.'

'What if you get caught, Josh?'

'I don't know. I'm not sure I care. If I hear the slightest whimper, then we'll go get a warrant... if I can't kick the bloody doors down to take a look myself first.'

'Jesus, all this for a free coffee. I've been ripped off. Remind me the next time you offer to buy me a drink that it's in exchange for my career.'

He started to laugh, then louder when she butted him in the ribs with her elbow.

'Get in the back and duck down. I'll speak to them, so they don't realise you're in the car. I wouldn't be surprised if they have cameras installed, which is bad news if this all goes wrong.'

'It won't, it will be okay.'

He was out of the driver's door and in the back of the car before Sam had unclipped her seat belt. Once she was in the driver's seat she rolled the window down, leant forward and pressed hard on the buzzer. After a few moments there was a burst of static and a deep voice filtered through.

'Hello, Dean & Sons, can I help you?'

'Yes, my name is Detective Constable Sam Thomas. I wonder if it's possible to come and have a chat with you about some enquiries I've been tasked with. It's nothing to worry about.'

'Of course, officer, I'll open the gates. Drive through and up to the house.'

She heard Josh whisper 'Bingo' from behind her as the two huge, black ornate cast-iron gates began to slowly open in front of them. She started the car and, as soon as the gap was wide enough to drive through, she put her foot down.

The grounds were beautiful, lush green lawns surrounded by rich evergreen plants and shrubs. The house had clearly been a private residence at some point before it had been turned into a funeral home. They drove along the gravel drive until they reached the front of the house where there were several empty parking bays. Getting out, Sam didn't lock the doors and left the keys in the ignition should Josh need to make an emergency getaway. Without looking back, she set off for the marble steps that led to the front entrance.

# CHAPTER FORTY-ONE

Once Sam had entered the building, Josh tried to open the car door, and swore: the bloody child locks were on. Great for keeping suspects inside the car, not so good when you're trying to be discreet. Climbing through into the front seat he managed to extract himself out of the passenger side door. He looked around; the place seemed deserted. Surely it wouldn't hurt for him to have a little peek. He headed towards the rear of the building where they must have a back entrance for bringing the bodies in and out. Staying close to the walls, he reached the end of the brickwork and turned the corner. *Bingo.* Parked around the back was a silver van with blacked-out windows with the words 'Private Ambulance' emblazoned across the side. This was the vehicle they used to transport bodies from the hospital or wherever they may have died. There was a double garage with a huge door attached to the house. He pressed his ear to it. Squeezing his eyes shut he concentrated as hard as he could, but he couldn't hear a thing.

He did the same at the back door, pulling his sleeve down over his hand to push gently on the handle. It didn't move. The whole place was locked up tight. He looked around. Behind the house, a good distance away, were more garages and sheds. He jogged over to find the main doors were locked, but the side door opened inwards. For a moment he wondered if he should leave it be, go back to the car and wait for Sam. But he couldn't do it; he needed to have a quick look inside.

Squeezing through the gap, he stepped inside and waited for his eyes to adjust to the dark interior. There were a variety of hearses, limousines, and the strong smell of petrol filled his nostrils. A row of different sized coffins was lined up against the back wall. He stared at them and shuddered. Christ, he thought his job was bad, but he only dealt with death occasionally. He crossed over to the coffins and noted that most of them had lids propped against them but not screwed down. One by one he checked them, his heart in his throat. They were empty.

When he heard voices in the distance, he realised he was pushing his luck staying here so long. Going back to the side door, he couldn't see anyone and slipped back outside, running quickly and quietly around to the side of the house in time to see the front door closing. Sam was sitting in the driver's seat of the car with her phone pressed to her ear. He felt his own begin to vibrate in his pocket. Lifting it to his ear he whispered: 'What?'

'Get back here now before you get caught, that's what.'

He ended the call and ran around the front of the building, before pausing to check with Sam. She nodded her head and waved him on. Running the rest of the way to the car, he threw open the passenger door and got inside as Sam drove off as fast as she dared without drawing any attention to them.

'Where the hell were you?'

'Checking out the garages; they had coffins of every shape and size back there.'

'It's a funeral home, they're supposed to. Any sign of Annie?'

'No, what did he say when you asked him about Jason Thompson?'

'Not a lot. Said he knew who he was, had spoken to him on several occasions but didn't really know him. Said he dealt with Barry more than him, thinks he seems like a nice lad.'

'What did you think about him?'

'Harry Dean seemed like a genuinely nice bloke. I can understand how families must feel reassured dealing with someone like that.'

'He didn't come across as a raving, homicidal maniac then?'

'Obviously not, boss.'

'Shame. Come on, drive me back to the station. I need to go through everything we have and see if we can get a warrant to come back and do a proper search of the main house.'

'Why?'

'I don't know, it's just a gut feeling that something isn't right. We're looking for someone who has no qualms about putting a woman in a box until the air runs out and she dies. It takes a special kind of psychopath to be able to do that, don't you think?'

'Well, yes it must. But it doesn't mean it's an undertaker, does it?'

'For Christ's sake, I'd rather look an idiot and be wrong than be too afraid to make the call and be right. At this moment in time I don't have any other viable suspects with the means and ability to deal with death and bodies so... so casually.'

They drove the rest of the way back in silence. As Sam pulled up outside the front of the station, Josh turned to look at her.

'Sorry, I didn't mean to snap. I'm tired, hungry and pissed off that we have no idea where she might be. Thank you for everything you've done today, I do appreciate your help.'

She rolled her eyes at him. 'Apology accepted. Let's go order some food, have a bit of a breather for ten mins and see what we can come up with. Hopefully the cameras on the main roads will have picked something up – like a number plate or a clear image of the bastard.'

# CHAPTER FORTY-TWO

He'd noticed the police from a distance, despite them driving an unmarked police car. The man in the crumpled suit was looking considerably more stressed than the woman with him. Did that mean he was in charge? He liked that, relished the fact that his actions were causing so many strangers to have a bad day. Picking up the bunch of wilting roses he'd plucked from the bargain bucket outside Pretty Flowers, and tucking the local daily paper under his arm, he strolled up the hill towards the chapel, although not too near it. He'd read about too many killers who'd been so wrapped up in what they'd done, they'd revisited the scene of the crime and got caught. Fools, all of them. As if the police hadn't cottoned on to his idea by now. Ever since they'd made the discovery of the girl in the grave there had been a white car parked up by the empty grave, watching and waiting to see who turned up. He chose a grave that was a bit unloved and bent to lay his flowers down. A flurry of excitement mingled with fear filled his veins as he pulled weeds away from the gravestone. He began to arrange the stems of flowers in a cracked vase; they were crooked and far too long, but it didn't matter. The two detectives were walking towards him with a man wearing a high vis jacket and a spade slung over his shoulder. He lifted a hand in polite greeting and the gravedigger nodded back. Lowering his face and pulling the peak of his baseball cap down, he quickly stared back down at the grave in front of him; he didn't want any of them to look too closely at him.

He didn't know if she was dead yet; he hoped that she was because it would make his life a lot easier. Physically killing his victims left too much trace evidence behind and forensics were a lot more advanced now than they'd been when he'd been a teenager. He'd sweated beneath paper overalls and three pairs of rubber gloves when he'd put the girl into that grave. It was risky to do it himself, but he had to admit that the excitement had outweighed the danger. Creating puzzles for the police sent a thrill through his body like no other.

Straightening up now the weeds had been cleared and the roses propped against the headstone, he could hear voices as the group approached. Slipping on to a bench near to the grave he'd been tending, he pressed his hands tightly together and shut his eyes. They might glance across at him but they wouldn't speak. You didn't intrude on a person's conversations with God, even if they were about murder. His steepled fingers pressed against his lips, covering the smile which had formed upon them.

# CHAPTER FORTY-THREE

Josh forked the last mouthful of chicken tikka in to his mouth, mopping up the rest of the sauce with his naan bread. Sam still had half a plate of food left, which he looked at hungrily.

'You're such a lightweight.'

'You're such a pig.'

He snorted, almost spraying the computer in front of him with mashed-up food.

'Right, what should we do now? Call a briefing, go back to the hotel, find Claire and see what she's come up with? Get a team together to go and arrest Florence Wright's concerned relative?'

Sam was staring out of the window by her desk. 'Probably hide.'

'Why?'

'Barker has just angry-slammed his car door and is heading this way with a face like a slapped arse.'

Josh stood up and peered over her shoulder.

'Shit, he looks furious.'

'I wonder why? It's not as if we've been sneaking around where we shouldn't, is it?'

'He won't know about that, how could he?'

She shrugged. 'Just a feeling. Are you going to wait around to find out, or should we just go and find somewhere else to figure out what to do?'

Josh grabbed his jacket, laptop and car keys and Sam shrugged her jacket on, picking up her bag from under the table.

'I vote we leave.'

There were two doors that led into the CID office, one at each end of the room. If the chief was coming in from the car park, he'd use the one nearest to Josh's desk, so he and Sam headed towards the other exit. But as they barrelled out of the door together, they walked straight into the brick wall that was Detective Inspector Eric Barker.

'Thought I might find you sneaking out, Walker.'

'What do you mean by that, boss? We have a valid enquiry that needs urgently following up on. I'll catch up with you later, yeah?'

Sam squeezed past and began hurrying towards the stairs. Josh tried to do the same, but Barker put his arm out.

'A word, if you don't mind. In my office. Now.'

# CHAPTER FORTY-FOUR

The smell of stale sweat filled the cramped office as Barker slammed the door shut behind them. It was hot, stuffy and the worst place possible to be stuck with an angry boss. Josh tried to keep his distance and not to inhale too much through his nose.

'So, I've just got off the phone with a very good friend of mine. It was quite an interesting, yet puzzling call.'

Josh nodded. The takeaway he'd enjoyed moments ago lay heavy in his stomach; he knew where this was going.

'Do you want to explain to me what you were doing sneaking around the back of Dean & Sons funeral home? Breaking and entering their outbuildings?'

'I didn't break in anywhere. The doors were open for anyone to get—'

'Anyone who had *permission* to go into them. Like, for instance, Harry and James Dean, or maybe their trusted employees, whose *job* it is to enter those buildings?'

Josh tried not to roll his eyes. Why didn't he just come out with it? He didn't have time for all this, not with a girl's life on the line. Instead, he nodded. 'I guess so.'

'Yeah, me too. So why then were you captured in full technicolour glory skulking around at the back of the premises whilst Sam was inside asking questions. I'm keen to know.'

'They had cameras then?'

'Yes, they did. Excellent cameras, better than the ones the constabulary paid a small fortune to have put up around the town.'

'How did you know it was me?' He hadn't meant to ask that, he'd promised himself not to antagonise him, but it just slipped out.

Barker thrust his phone towards his face and there he was, a crystal-clear still taken from the CCTV system. Damn, he was right, it was an excellent quality photo.

'Sam had nothing to do with it. She didn't know I was going to go looking. She left me in the car whilst she went in.'

'Why were you there in the first place?'

Josh felt the hairs on the back of his neck stand on end. Why did he *think* they were there? Was he for real?

'We have a high-risk missing person, which you know about, yes?' Barker nodded.

'We also have a body of a girl who was found underneath a coffin pulled up for an exhumation. The post-mortem provided by Doctor Adams concluded that the woman inside the coffin died of natural causes. Which leaves the question: who demanded she was exhumed in the first place? The killer of Chantel Price and Annie Potts's abductor is more than likely the same person, we believe. We recently discovered they left a calling card under the missing girl's bed: it was a photo of Chantel Price along with what we can safely assume are the three fingernails missing from one of her hands. The chance of having two different predators stalking the streets of Windemere are highly unlikely, don't you think? Sir.'

'I still don't see what the funeral home has to do with it.'

Josh sighed.

'It was a hunch. Doctor Adams's findings at the post-mortem of the mystery girl, now known to be Chantel Price, suggest the victim tried her best to claw her way out of a box, possibly a coffin or some kind of tomb. Dean & Sons had dealt with the burial of Florence Wright, who was exhumed on the say-so of some distant relative who is now nowhere to be found. I'm in the process of getting a search team together to go and locate that so-called relative. Call me whimsical, but I thought it was a good shout, that it was worth checking the undertaker's. Whoever this is had no qualms about being around death or dead bodies.'

The hostility left Barker instantly as he flopped down on the chair behind his desk. He looked at Josh. 'It would have been better if you'd come to me and asked for a search warrant. We're not going to get one now, are we? Did you find anything to make it worth the risk?'

It was Josh's turn to sit down, deflated. He shook his head. 'No, but I didn't go inside the main building. It's a huge house, as you know. There could be any number of places to conceal a missing person.'

'It's a huge house that belongs to the chief super's best friend, Harry Dean. I've had it in the neck off the boss, so now you've had it in the neck. He's warned us to keep well away from there.'

'He's warned *you* to tell me to keep well away from there, but what if you hadn't found me to tell me yet? Just because he's best mates with the chief it doesn't make him exempt from the law.'

Barker rolled his eyes at him. 'Doesn't it?'

'No, not really. Especially for someone like me who isn't, and doesn't, give a shit about who he might be upsetting.'

'That's the thing, Josh. I admire your commitment to the job, I really do, but our hands are tied.'

'Unless I can find some hard evidence to get a search warrant?'

'Yes, and you find a judge who agrees with you.' Barker shrugged. 'I thought you were bringing in the gravedigger anyway?'

'He's done a runner. Paton spoke to him earlier and asked him to come in for a chat. He decided against it and now we can't find him.'

'Guilty?'

'Guilty of something, I'm not convinced it's murder.'

'No, maybe not. But let's focus our media attention on him. Give the outraged public a name to focus on, and maybe they'll lead us to him. You and Sam concentrate on finding our missing woman.'

'You mean, hang him out to dry?'

'He did that to himself when he didn't play ball with us. If he'd come in like we'd asked, we wouldn't have to do this, would we?'

Josh nodded and took the silence that followed as a cue to leave.


Walking out of the office, he went to the car park to find Sam, who was sitting in the car scrolling through Facebook. He opened the car door. 'Busy?'

'Actually yes, I am. I was just checking out Jason Thompson's list of friends to see if any of them are linked to Dean & Sons in some way.'

He smiled at her.

'So, how bad was it? Judging by how long you were in there, it was pretty bad?'

He told her the gist of his conversation with the DI. 'So, whether Jason Thompson is guilty or not, he's going to regret his decision to run.'

'Christ, you can say that again. What happened to all the innocent until proven guilty stuff?'

'From what I can gather Jason Thompson isn't the chief's best friend.'

'Where does that leave us? Where does it leave Annie Potts?'

He shrugged. 'We need another lead. Let's go back to the hotel and speak to her friend again who rang it in. Something is missing, maybe she didn't tell us the whole truth. How did the killer know what state Annie was in; how did he know how to get access to the staff quarters?'

'Unless he was with them that night, or works with them?'

'Or was in the right place at the right time? He could have been out looking for his next victim and she fit the bill, too drunk to know what she was doing. He could have followed the girls home, watched Annie go into the staff entrance. Is anyone viewing the CCTV from the club?'

'Yes, we are. It wasn't open earlier: the staff don't come in until late afternoon. Let's go there now.'

# CHAPTER FORTY-FIVE

Josh's phone rang, and he passed it to Sam.

'Josh's phone, Sam Thomas speaking as he's currently driving.' She put it on loudspeaker.

'It's Paton. I'm outside the address on the exhumation licence for Florence Wright's relative. To be honest with you, I don't think anyone's home or has been for a while.'

Josh answered. 'Where are you?'

'Tarn Lake Caravan Park.'

'We're on our way. Do we need an entry team?'

'I don't think so, it's a caravan and it's all in darkness. No sign of life. I knocked on the doors of the caravans on either side, both of the occupants are elderly and neither of them have seen anyone for months. Apparently the bloke who owns it only stayed there for a short time.'

'Wait for us, we can go in together. Do you think it's possible the missing girl is inside?'

'Hard to say, boss, probably not if no one has been here for ages.'

The line went dead, and Josh looked across at Sam. 'How nice would it be just for once to catch a break, find the girl and be able to trace the killer?'

She smiled at him, and he knew she was humouring him because stuff like that happened in the movies, not in real life. At least not very often. Still, he said a silent prayer that on this occasion it would all work out.

The caravan park was unusually quiet, which was good. As Josh drove through the gates, he spotted Paton, who was wandering around. He waved at them. Parking the car, they got out and headed in his direction.

'Have you spoken to the staff at the site office?'

'It's closed, but there's a number on the door for out-of-hours enquiries, so I've left them a message. What do you want to do?'

Josh turned to Sam. 'You wait by the office, keep ringing the number on the door and hopefully someone will pick up.'

She nodded. 'What are you going to do?'

'Paton is going to show me the caravan. I just want to check it out.'

She shook her head at him, and he smiled.

'Hey, no funny business. You just stay here and keep trying to get us someone who can get us inside.'

Paton led him to an old caravan that was situated at the far end.

'That one in the middle, the washed-out green one.'

'What do you think? Can we get the door open?'

'I don't see why not; a few good kicks should do it.'

They walked towards it. Josh decided to try knocking on the front door to see for himself. He knocked; the second time he hammered on it. The old guy from the caravan next door stuck his head out.

'I told your mate, it's empty. Has been for ages.'

Josh smiled at him, then turned to Paton, who shrugged.

'In for a penny.' He launched his foot at the door several times, watching it bend under the pressure, but it didn't give.

Paton shook his head. 'Here, let me try.'

Josh stepped to one side.

Sam, who had decided to come and see what they were up to, rounded the corner just in time to see Paton running towards the door. He rammed it with his shoulder and the door buckled, sending him falling into the caravan.

Josh followed, shouting: 'Police.'

The stifling heat inside the caravan was unbearable. It was dark inside and stuffy. The air smelled stale. The old guy was right, no one had been here for weeks. Holding out his hand, Josh pulled Paton to his feet and they searched each room. There was nothing, no missing girl, no occupant, not even a scrap of food in any of the cupboards.

No one spoke, all of them were too overcome with disappointment.

# CHAPTER FORTY-SIX

Neither Sam nor Josh spoke on the way to the club; the weight of getting nowhere fast was pressing heavy on their shoulders. Josh pushed the door at the side of the hotel which led to the club, relieved it opened. He needed the camera footage right now, not in a week's time. This was the most vital evidence they would have, and he just hoped they caught a break and Annie's abductor showed his face on camera. He wanted to scrutinise it from the minute the club opened, to when Estelle and her friends entered, to the minutes after they left.

As he walked inside, followed by Sam, the smell of stale alcohol that lingered in the air made his stomach churn. He liked a drink but hated it the day after when the fumes and a pounding headache were all that was left of a good time. A huge guy walked towards them, his palms outstretched, signalling them to stop and turn around.

'Sorry, bud, we're not open until later. The cleaners haven't been in yet.'

Josh pulled his warrant card from his pocket. 'DS Josh Walker, this is my colleague DC Sam Thomas, can we have a word with you about an incident last night?'

'It's not my fault. I didn't keep on selling them the alcohol. It's the bar staff, they're a bit scared of Estelle, so they just kept on serving her. Besides, she wasn't that drunk. Anyway, why does it need CID? Don't you have a licensing officer who deals with this sort of stuff?'

Josh was tired. He looked at Sam, who shrugged her shoulders.

'Mate, I don't care about how much alcohol was served. Has anyone spoken to you about the missing girl?'

The bouncer's face visibly paled and he shook his head. Pulling his phone out of his pocket, he looked down at the screen then showed it to Josh. There were an alarming number of missed calls.

'Let's start again. Last night Estelle Carter and a group of friends were in here drinking champagne like it was tap water, yes?'

The bouncer nodded and held out his hand. 'I'm Pete.'

'Right, Pete. Well, one in the group of Estelle's friends was a bit worse for wear.'

'Annie, yes she was. She was leathered; she couldn't stand up and knocked the table and everything on it flying. I don't like to interfere with Estelle and her business, but I had to do something; they could have hurt someone, and Annie had drunk more than enough. I told them to get her out of here and that they couldn't have any more. Is she okay?'

Josh wondered if he was for real, then realised that it was more than likely if he'd been working until the early hours he wouldn't know what had happened. It was clear he hadn't answered any of his phone calls.

'She's missing.'

'I don't understand? Estelle and some guy carried her out of here. I assumed they took her back to her room in the basement. She couldn't stand on her own two feet, so I find it hard to believe she wandered off anywhere.'

Sam took over. 'We don't think she's missing of her own accord; we believe someone may have abducted her. Now we need to see the CCTV footage from last night. Can you show it to us?'

He nodded vigorously. 'Of course, I can download it onto a pen drive for you as well.'

Josh said a silent prayer; for once they might be about to catch a break. Pete led them through to a cramped back office where the monitors were stacked on top of each other. He sat down at the desk on a stool and began to load the recordings from the night before. He pulled over a coffee-stained notebook and opened it to the latest page of writing. He then began typing the time of the incident into the system.

Josh was impressed. 'You made a note of it?'

'We're supposed to record anything that happens in the incident book, that way the licensing officers from the police and council can see what's been going on. Just because Estelle's old man owns the place it doesn't mean she gets any special treatment down here. She's just another customer; she has nothing to do with the club. Her old man was quite insistent about that.'

Several images from around the club began playing on the different monitors. Pete pointed to one of them. 'That's their table; it's not a brilliant view but if you watch you'll see everything that happened.'

They watched in silence as the group of people who were laughing and enjoying themselves sipped at the champagne. Josh felt a chill run down his back; it was always this way, moments before watching something terrible captured on film. How he wished he could have been there and been the one to have gone to Annie's assistance.

Pete's thick index finger filled the screen as he placed it on a woman's head. 'That's Annie, she's really nice. I hope she's okay. I've never seen her get in a state like that before.'

As Annie fell and the glasses and champagne flew everywhere, Pete came into sight as he marched towards the table.

'What a state, she can't even stand up.'

Sam nudged Josh with her elbow. 'I've been drunk, but never like that. Look at that guy by the bar, he's taking a keen interest in what's going on.'

They watched as the guy, whose image wasn't very clear, finished his drink, put his glass down and strode towards where Estelle was trying to hold Annie up.

Josh jumped out of his seat and rushed out of the room into the club, to see if the dirty glasses were still on the bar, but the surfaces were clear. He felt as if someone had taken the air from his lungs; they could have had him: his DNA could have been on the glass.

Pete's voice filled the air. 'Sorry, mate, I always make sure the glasses are washed before I leave for the night. Habit.'

Josh nodded. He didn't really expect it to be that easy. But just this once... especially for Annie Potts.

# CHAPTER FORTY-SEVEN

They left Pete in the club and went back upstairs into the hotel, Josh clutching the pen drive.

'Would you do me a favour, Sam? Can you return this to the station and get it downloaded and circulated to everyone on an email? Then you can go home, it's been a long day and you must be tired.'

'What about you?'

He pointed to the PCSOs who were still guarding the entrance and exits to the hotel. 'I'll go and speak to Estelle then hitch a lift back with them.'

'Are you sure?'

He nodded; taking the keys from his pocket, he passed them to her with the pen drive.

'Call me if you need me, right? I don't mind. As long as I've sorted the kids out I can be back at work in no time.'

'I won't need you; go home and get some rest.'

She didn't need telling again. Walking off in the direction of the car, she left him to it.

Josh spoke to the PCSO. 'Ashley, whatever you do don't leave here without me. I need a lift back.'

She smiled at him and unhooked the set of car keys she had dangling from her radio antenna.

'I can get a lift back with Helen, you take the car, Josh.'

'Thank you, I owe you one.'

He went inside the hotel, which was deserted, much to his relief. Leaning against the reception desk he massaged his temples and yawned; he needed paracetamol and a large shot of something strong to knock him out tonight. A second yawn escaped his lips just as an equally tired-looking Estelle came out from the back office.

'Tough day?'

He nodded.

'Anything, any news?'

He shook his head, and Estelle crumpled, a sob escaping her lips. Running around the desk, Josh scooped her into his arms and guided her into a chair in the small back office.

Josh was annoyed that she'd failed to mention the guy from the nightclub who helped her with Annie, but he also realised that she was never going to forgive herself for this whole sorry mess. He wouldn't be too hard on her.

'We've just viewed the camera footage from the nightclub. Why did you not mention the guy who helped you take Annie down to her room?'

She glared at him. 'I didn't think I needed to.'

'But you and he were the last people to see Annie before she disappeared. He's a key witness and we need to speak to him. I can't understand why you didn't think of that.'

'There's nothing to it. He helped me take her to her room. I made sure she couldn't roll over and choke on her own sick. We left her on the bed, asleep. He followed me upstairs and out of the hotel.'

'Who was he? Do you know him? Have you ever seen him before?'

She shook her head. 'No, I'd never met him before. He was nice. Friendly and helpful.'

'Do you not think it's a bit convenient how he was there, at the bar alone. The CCTV footage shows him ordering drinks, but he doesn't drink them. He was taking a very keen interest in your group.'

He watched Estelle's face as a range of emotions began to wash over her.

'But he couldn't have done it.'

'Why?'

Her eyes filled with tears that she furiously tried to blink away, and when she spoke her voice was barely a whisper. 'Because he came back to my apartment with me… and we slept together.'

Josh sat up straight. 'Estelle, forgive me for asking, but did you use protection?'

If she said no then maybe there might still be some trace evidence.

'Of course I did. I didn't know him. I might be up for a good time, but not at the expense of my health.'

'I'm going to need a full description of him from you, and I also need you to come to the station to give a proper statement and to do an identification video. Is there anything in your apartment he touched, that you remember? Did you change your bedding or wash your underwear? Did he drink from anything?'

She shook her head. 'No, he came back with me and we screwed. Several times, actually, until finally I fell asleep. When I woke up late this morning he'd gone. I stripped the bed, washed everything. I've showered, flushed the condoms down the toilet and the glasses we drank out of went straight into the dishwasher. Do you… do you really think it was him?'

Josh couldn't lie to her. 'There's a strong possibility. How did he get into Annie's room though? Did you lock the door on the way out?'

'I don't remember. I didn't even look at it. He was the last one out, and I assumed he shut it behind him.'

The tears finally came as the full horror of what might have happened came crashing down on the young woman in front of him. He tried to comfort her, and she ended up hugging him as she cried, loud sobs filling the small office. The perfume she wore lingered in the air as she held on to him and it reminded him of Beth; she wore the same one. It was nice. Suddenly shocked at himself, he pulled himself from her grip. Shouldn't he have been thinking about his wife when he smelled the perfume?

# CHAPTER FORTY-EIGHT

Beth woke up early. She loved summer; the warmth, the cool breeze which sometimes rolled in off the lake; sitting on the patio sipping her morning tea, eating toast and contemplating life. However, she preferred autumn with chilly days and darker mornings which meant she got a touch more sleep. Having a wall of floor-to-ceiling windows looked fabulous from the outside, and gave a good view of the lake, but it didn't do much for her sleep pattern. Often, she'd resort to sleeping in the spare room, where she lay now thinking about her phone conversation with Josh late last night and wondering if he'd managed to get any sleep. He'd told her a woman had gone missing from the same hotel where she'd seen all the police activity and that it was likely linked to Chantel Price's murder. She wished she could do more to help him out and decided she would go and speak to the staff at Chantel's care home, as she'd planned yesterday. In fact, she would go to the undertaker's *and* the care home. She couldn't understand how they could so coldly not bother to report her missing because of her age.

She rolled over, stretched and thought about last night, how out of character it had been for her to go to the pub and socialise; how wonderfully normal it had felt. Seeing the security guy had thrown her a little, especially when he'd asked her if she wanted a drink. The voice in her head mocked her: *maybe, just maybe he finds you attractive.* Closing her eyes, she tried to remember how she'd felt when things had been different, when she'd had a partner she loved. A life filled with socialising, fun and friendships, the warm, open heart she'd built a brick wall around ever since the attack.

Everyone from that life, except for her dear friend Josh, had given up on her. They'd tried at first, visited, offered to take her out for lunch, maybe coffee or to try out a new wine bar. She'd loved them for trying, she really had. Leaving the house was bearable, but coming back to it alone and not knowing if there was someone inside waiting for her filled her with crippling terror. She knew it was wrong and didn't make sense, but she couldn't help feeling this way. Her mind drifted further back to that night in January, seven years ago, and for some reason she didn't fight the memory like she usually would. Maybe this was what she needed.

As she'd tied off the last few stitches in the teenage boy's leg she'd let her thoughts wander to Ellen's surprise party later that evening. She'd been excited about it for weeks. In fact, it was all she'd thought about for the last few hours of her shift that day. Ellen was one of her closest friends and Beth intended to fully let her hair down after a gruelling week at the hospital. Her only concern had been about her partner, Robert: the last couple of months he'd been more controlling than usual. He wasn't particularly good at socialising in large groups, preferring to be alone with her, but recently his mood would shift so fast she didn't know what he wanted. One minute he'd be quiet, the next he'd be snapping at her about what she was wearing or the length of her hair. Just days before, they'd had an almighty argument when she'd attempted to leave the house wearing the new red Dior lipstick she'd treated herself to. He'd called her a slut and sent her back inside to put on something more natural. She'd put it down to the long hours and the fact that sometimes because of their shifts they were like passing ships in the night. However, in the past few weeks his behaviour had been odd, disappearing for hours on end with no explanation as to where he'd been. He'd always been quiet, but this was taking it to a whole new level. If she was honest with herself, she was beginning to question their whole relationship. They needed to sit down and talk about where things were going, but not that night, she remembered. She needed to kick off her shoes, let her hair down and enjoy herself. The serious stuff could wait another twenty-four hours.

The party had been fun: she'd laughed, drunk champagne and danced the night away. Robert, contrary to her earlier misgivings, had been the perfect plus one despite him not being the most sociable of people and unable to drink that night because he was on call. After the party had wound down, the taxi had dropped them off outside the door of the Victorian semi in Kendal she owned, and she remembered being drunk and so happy. They'd gone inside and Robert had ushered her up to bed, helped her undress and put her silk nightdress on. He'd tucked her in, kissed the top of her head and told her he had to go to work; the perils of being an on-call consultant.

She remembered drifting off quickly and being woken by a loud thump downstairs. She'd opened her eyes to try and make sense of it; her neighbour was a taxi driver and often came in at the most peculiar times, so woozy and still a little drunk she'd turned on her side and gone back to sleep.

The second time she woke it was to a noise so loud it had to have come from inside the house. Robert would have locked up on his way out, she knew; he was very security conscious then – more so than she was at that time. Her mouth was dry, and her brain was thumping hard against her skull, begging for painkillers. Not bothering with her slippers or dressing gown, she'd gone to the bathroom and groaned at the reflection staring back at her in the bathroom mirror; her lips were stained Merlot red, her eyeliner smudged, an unexpected trace of glitter all over her hair and face. As she'd walked downstairs to get some water, she'd been thinking of how happy Ellen was: she had a fiancé, a new position in a fancy office in New York and pretty much everything she had ever wished for in her own life. Beth remembered hoping that one day she'd be just as happy…

*

Beth stopped herself there. That was enough for now. Fully awake, she lay in bed rubbing her finger along the faded, puckered scar on the side of her face. She kept it covered with her hair most of the time. It was one of the giveaways whenever she felt anxious; her fingers would seek it out, a reminder that she was alive, and of everything she'd been through to stay that way.

Climbing out of bed, she wondered if they'd found the missing woman from yesterday: she hoped to God they had. Josh would take it so personally, because that was the kind of person he was. Throwing open the curtains, she went downstairs to make some breakfast, her mind still ticking over the puzzling events of the last few days. Making a large mug of tea and buttering a freshly toasted bagel, she sat at the dining table with a large notebook and pen in front of her. Josh would be busy today, but she wasn't due in court until this afternoon and it was likely to be cancelled the way that case was going, so she began to list local places the missing girl may be held captive if, like with Chantel, the killer didn't take her life right away: abandoned buildings, boathouses, sheds – the list could go on indefinitely. How had the killer managed to gain access to the cemetery to get her body into the grave before the burial? It all pointed to someone having the authority to be in there, someone whose presence wouldn't stand out or be questioned. Which brought her back to the cemetery workers or the undertakers. She underlined the words on the sheet of paper in front of her then pulled her laptop over and googled undertakers in the vicinity who would have had access to the cemetery or whose 'clients', for want of a better word, would have access to the cemetery. It was very rare people who weren't local were buried in there, but it did happen. Occasionally, someone would request that they wanted to be buried in their favourite place, though cremation was far more popular than burials: it was cheaper, for one thing, with no transport or grave costs.

There was a grand total of four undertakers in the area, but only one was actually situated in Windermere, and close to the cemetery: Dean & Sons. She picked up her phone and rang Josh. When he didn't answer, she didn't leave a message knowing he'd ring her back when he saw he had a missed call.

Finishing the rest of her bagel, she decided to do the only thing she could think of: go and pay a visit to Harry and James Dean. It might help Josh, who would no doubt be stretching himself too far, taking responsibility for both cases. She needed to speak to them in any case about Florence Wright, to ask who had arranged her funeral and the mystery relative who'd made the accusations that set off the chain of events that led to her exhumation. She doubted Josh would even be thinking about Florence and her unnecessary exhumation with one dead girl and one missing girl already on his plate, but she couldn't stop thinking about her. She needed answers and was willing to step out of her comfort zone to find them. It would give her the perfect excuse to have a snoop around, see what she thought of the place and the two brothers who ran it. She'd heard rumours that James was a bit of a player, liked women and partied hard. Harry was the older of the two and, from what she could gather, was the one who called the shots and brought in the business. If she had time after that, she would head over to Dalton View Care Home to speak to the staff about Chantel.

Just as she was heading upstairs to get dressed, her phone rang. Hiding her disappointment that it was an unknown number and not Josh, she picked up.

'Ms Adams, this is Debbie from Safe & Secure. Just to let you know we have the part in for your camera. Is it possible to book an appointment for the engineer to come out to fit it?'

'Of course, yes. When do you have?'

'We could probably fit you in this afternoon around four. You'd be his last client of the day, so he might be running a little late.'

'That would be fabulous, thank you. I'll be here.'

Debbie thanked her then ended the call. Beth ran upstairs to get dressed, hoping that her court appearance was definitely going to get cancelled now. She didn't want to have to cancel the security guy; her safety was important. He was also was quite cute and friendly and had offered to take her out for a drink, something no one, except for Phil, had asked her in years.

# CHAPTER FORTY-NINE

The gates to Dean & Sons were wide open, so Beth drove straight through assuming she didn't need to announce her arrival on the intercom. It was a nice set-up, very nice. She supposed if you were going to spend your last days above earth somewhere it might as well be in a mansion with its own landscaped gardens. There was a row of gleaming black Bentley limousines parked outside the front. She pulled up in the last space opposite them; they were old cars but in pristine condition. As a classic car they were probably worth a small fortune and they looked elegant. She didn't like the modern boxy cars that seemed to be used by the majority of undertakers. Not that she was an expert in this industry; she dealt with the dead in a different way.

Getting out of the car, she noticed a man in a smart suit rubbing a soft cloth over the door handles of one of the cars. He smiled at her and she smiled back as she walked towards the front door of the house which was propped open. Stepping inside, she marvelled at the beautiful entrance. There was a huge wooden desk across one wall that was unattended. Ornate displays of fresh flowers filled the room with a heady smell; there were antiques, and beautiful paintings on the walls. It reminded her of a boutique hotel; if she hadn't seen the hearse outside and didn't know any better, she'd be quite happy to stay here for the weekend.

'Can I help you?'

She turned to see a very smartly dressed young woman in an expensive-looking black trouser suit and white shirt, her red hair pinned into the neatest French pleat Beth had ever seen. There wasn't a single wisp of hair out of place.

'Hello, yes, I hope so. My name is Doctor Beth Adams. I'm a pathologist and I've recently dealt with an exhumation of one of your former clients. I have a few questions and was hoping I'd be able to speak to either Harry or James.'

Beth handed over one of her business cards, which revealed she was, in fact, a forensic pathologist, but she was hoping the woman wouldn't take too much notice. She didn't want to arouse their suspicions about why she was really here.

'Harry is just about to leave for a funeral, but I'll see where James is. I'm sure he can help you, Doctor Adams.'

Beth smiled. 'Please, just call me Beth. That would be great. I appreciate how busy you both must be, so I won't take long.'

The girl nodded. 'Can I get you a drink whilst you're waiting? We have a pretty good coffee machine out the back. Oh, I'm Alex. Sorry, I forgot to introduce myself.'

'I'd love a cappuccino if it isn't too much trouble.'

'I'll be right back. Please take a seat. It might take me a little while to track Uncle James down: he's never around when you need him.'

Ah, so she was Harry's daughter. That would explain the expensive suit. She wondered if the girl enjoyed working here, surrounded by so much death, but then again, she'd no doubt have been brought up close to it. Beth knew better than most that you did get used to it eventually. Hardened to it, some would say.

The fact that James was never where he should be had piqued Beth's interest. Where was he then? She'd expected to speak with Harry, the face of the business, so she was quite looking forward to chatting with his brother.

Alex returned with a large cup, balanced on a saucer with one of those caramelised biscuits in a little packet next to it. Beth took it from her and wondered how many grieving relatives would think about eating at a time like this. She picked the biscuit up and put it on the coffee table, trying not to outwardly grimace. How many fingers had touched it? She didn't want to know, but she had no qualms about drinking the coffee. The cup was so white it looked brand new.

She'd just picked up a magazine called *Saga* when her phone rang. Embarrassed she'd forgotten to turn it onto silent, she heard an unfamiliar voice begin to explain to her she was no longer required at court that afternoon, and she felt a flutter of excitement at the prospect of seeing the security engineer again.

# CHAPTER FIFTY

The briefing room was full. Josh had stayed late last night after sending Sam home, watching the footage from the nightclub over and over to see if they had missed anything. Back at the station this morning, he pressed play for what felt like the thousandth time and watched the grainy image as it filled the whiteboard screen in front of the team.

'As you can see the quality is pretty bad. It's hard to make out any distinguishing features, scars or tattoos. He looks like a normal guy. I suppose you could say he was a bit of a gentleman or at least he was until he went back to Estelle's apartment with her and they spent the next couple of hours having – and these are her words not mine – "Pretty wild sex for an older guy".' A murmur went around the room. 'Our priority today is to locate this guy who helped get our misper down to her room. It meant he was shown how to access the staff quarters down in the basement, and knew which room she was in. According to Estelle Carter he was the last person out of the room, and she can't confirm if he shut the door properly behind him, said she was too drunk to even think about it. He is alone at the bar when he first comes into shot, which could indicate he was intentionally on the hunt for a victim. The bouncer said he'd never seen him before, that he's definitely not a regular. It looks to me as if he was waiting to find someone drunk enough he could abduct without too much fuss. Talk about timing, for him it was perfect. For Annie Potts it could prove fatal.'

A couple of hands went up. Josh looked across at Sykes. 'Yes.'

'Boss, what if she's already dead and been put into a grave?'

'We can only hope to God that she isn't.'

'But, there's a chance she's already dead, right?'

'There is a strong possibility she might be. If she's been put into a box or a coffin, then her air supply wouldn't have lasted more than six to seven hours max. If he's keeping her captive somewhere then we have a chance to get to her before he kills her. Doctor Adams explained at the post-mortem for Chantel Price that she had to have been dead at least twenty-four hours before she was put into the grave; this was because of the fly pupa Doctor Adams found in the body. We know that the last confirmed sighting of Chantel was three days before Florence Wright's funeral, so by my calculations – and if the killer is following the same MO as his first victim – we have approximately forty-eight hours before it's too late. We have to keep on looking.'

'Funeral homes would be a good place to start, boss.'

Josh debated about telling them what Barker had said to him yesterday. This was his team, they needed to know. 'They would, and it's a great idea. I actually went to Dean & Sons yesterday for an unofficial look around. Let's just say that unless we have enough to get a warrant, I'm not allowed back there.'

Laughter echoed around the room, and Josh checked outside the door to make sure Barker wasn't around or, even worse, the chief super.

'On a serious note, I want any evidence we can get our hands on; Paton, I'm not saying that you messed up not bringing Thompson in yesterday, but it could have gone a lot better. I want him located today. Task force are going to assist you in tracking him down. There's a couple of addresses to be checked out for ex-girlfriends and family members that were already on the system. Hopefully he's hiding locally and not gone too far away. I don't think he's our man per se, but he hasn't helped himself, has he? And the boss wants his picture released to the press today.'

'What about the guy from the nightclub? Is his picture being released? Someone might recognise him.'

'Absolutely not. He's a hotter suspect and we want to let him think we're barking up the wrong tree by going for Thompson. Let him think he's clever, let him get cocky and start making mistakes. I want all the shops, cafés, pubs and restaurants in the local area canvassed. There are PCSOs on their way up from Barrow and Ulverston to assist with those enquiries. Sykes, I want you speaking to every hotel employee, and a still of the mystery man shown to them in case he's stayed there, or they've noticed him hanging around in the bar. I want background checks on everyone who works at the hotel and all the local undertakers. Sam, could you go to the cemetery for me? I need to know about any burials that may have taken place yesterday or if there are any scheduled in the coming days. If there are then I'll organise a team to go undercover and keep a watch on them in case he turns up.'

He left before they could start asking too many questions. He needed something to go on and fast.

# CHAPTER FIFTY-ONE

'Good morning, Doctor Adams, I'm James Dean, still alive despite the rumours.'

He smiled at her, winked and then held out his hand. Taking it, she gripped it firmly. He was wearing shirt and trousers, no suit jacket, no tie. She was taken aback by just how good-looking he was, not what she'd been expecting. Just because he was a funeral director, it didn't mean he couldn't be good-looking, did it? She of all people knew how shallow it was to judge a person by their vocation.

'Our receptionist said you needed to speak about the recent exhumation. Would you like to come with me, and we can chat somewhere a bit more private? Would you like another coffee?'

'No, thank you. One was enough. And yes, that would be great; I have a few questions.' She stood up. The fact that he'd made no acknowledgment that the receptionist was his niece jarred her. Was he being professional, or was she picking up on some animosity between the pair of them? She placed the cup on the coffee table and followed him, throwing a quick glance to Alex, who smiled back.

Beth followed him into a large room with rows of filing cabinets lined up against the walls, a big desk and the most amazing view out of the huge windows onto the formal gardens with a view of Orrest Head, the very first Lakeland Fell that Wainright walked in the distance.

'I think I'd struggle to get any work done with a view like that, it's beautiful.'

He laughed. 'That's why the chair faces away from the window. It's far too easy to sit and daydream instead of working. So, how can I be of assistance, Doctor Adams?'

'As you know, the body of Florence Wright was exhumed three days ago after a relative made some allegations of possible misconduct surrounding her death.'

'Actually, all we knew was that there were some discrepancies brought to light. As you know, the procedure for exhumation is that an application to exhume usually takes around three months in order to ensure it's a necessary procedure. So whoever submitted the application must have given a valid reason for the application to be approved. This one seemed to go through very fast, so someone along the line must have had sufficient concern to give permission. We initially dealt with the body after it was released to us, like we deal with the hundreds of other bodies each year. She was brought here from the hospital mortuary after death, and nothing untoward was noted when she was embalmed and prepared for burial.'

'How do you know that; did you speak to the embalmer?'

'I *am* the embalmer. I prepare the bodies; wash, dress, hair and make-up. That's my department.'

'Oh, do you have an assistant?'

'I do, I have two. Both are very good, but I specifically remember dealing with Mrs Wright's body myself because both of them were off work. It was a weekend.'

'Don't they work weekends?'

He shook his head. 'No, we like to give our staff the weekends off to enjoy with their families or whatever it is they like to do to relax. At weekends the place is run by Harry, my brother who runs the front of house, and Harry's daughter, who you met on the reception. Alex has all calls routed to her mobile.'

'That's very noble of you, but surely you need a break as well?' Not even realising she was doing it, her fingers reached for her hair to make sure it was covering the scar on her face.

He shrugged. 'Thankfully, it's not always busy of a weekend. People have a nasty habit of dying all hours of the day and night. As you well know. Can I ask what any of this has to do with the exhumation?'

'Not a lot. I guess I'm just fascinated. I'm sorry. When I conducted the post-mortem there was nothing to suggest that Florence Wright had died of anything other than natural causes. Obviously, she'd been buried for eight weeks, so things had started to decompose. I thought it might be useful to speak to you and see if you had any concerns since you dealt with her immediately after her death.'

He shook his head. 'I'm sorry, I can't help you. I didn't notice anything, which was why I thought it was strange she was being exhumed. If I had, at the time of receiving her body, I'd have contacted the coroner's officer to raise my concerns.'

Beth smiled at him; he was good. 'I thought as much. You know I deal with the bodies just after death, but I've never really thought about what happens to them once I've finished the post-mortem. I just move onto the next case. Sometimes they stay with me and, thankfully, sometimes they don't. I guess it must be the same for you.'

'Yes, I suppose it is. The kids are the hardest. I don't like dealing with them. But I do because it's part of the job. So, is there anything else I can help you with?'

Beth pulled a copy of the photograph of Chantel Price that Josh had taken in the mortuary out of her bag, even though she knew this was unprofessional and Josh would probably kill her for it. Standing up, she handed it to James, who took it from her.

'This is a bit of a wild shot, but you don't know this girl, do you? Have you ever seen her around? I was hoping she might look familiar.'

A voice inside her head whispered, *you have just well and truly crossed the line, Beth Adams.* She ignored it and watched James to see if there was any reaction. He stared down at the picture of the girl and his head shook.

'I'm sorry, I don't recognise her. She isn't one of our clients. It's Harry who deals with the actual funerals. You could ask him, or do you want me to take a copy and show it to him when he gets back?'

'No, it's fine. I'll call back another time to ask Harry. Thank you, I really appreciate your time, Mr Dean.'

He stood up, handing the photograph back to her. 'Anything to help. Are you okay to see yourself out? I was in the middle of preparing a body.'

'Of course, thanks again.'

She turned and walked out into the corridor. He was close behind her. Shutting the office door, he walked off in the opposite direction to where the reception area was, and Beth headed towards it. Alex was typing on the computer. She looked up and smiled as Beth walked towards her.

'Thank you so much for all your help, Alex.'

'Was he okay with you, or was he his usual cocky self?'

Beth sensed there were some real issues between them. 'He was very polite, but unfortunately he couldn't help or answer my questions. I guess it was just a stab in the dark. That coffee was really very good, thanks.'

Alex laughed. 'It is, isn't it? That coffee machine is probably the best thing about this job. If you're ever passing feel free to pop in for one. It gets a bit lonely sitting here all day. I must be the only person who gets excited to see a Royal Mail van pull up outside.'

Beth chuckled. 'Thank you, I might just take you up on that offer.' She turned to walk out of the door and then hesitated, wondering if she should… She pulled the photograph out of her bag once more. 'I know this is probably pointless, and I don't think she would have had any reason to come here.' She passed the picture towards Alex, who took it from her and looked at it. 'But I wondered if you recognised this girl.'

'She's dead?'

'Yes.' Beth realised her mistake. Alex might not actually have much to do with the bodies if she was running the reception and suddenly regretted showing it to her.

Alex hesitated for a moment too long.

'I'm sorry, I don't know her.'

Something about the horrified expression on Alex's face told Beth that she might not be telling the whole truth. Beth could feel in her gut that Alex recognised her.

'I'm sorry, I shouldn't have bothered you.' She took the photograph from Alex. 'If you ever get that lonely you need a chat, I don't live that far away. I'll see if I can pop round for one of your lovely coffees.'

Alex grinned at her.

'Yes, do that. It would be great. Bye, Beth.'

'Bye, Alex.'

Beth stepped outside, not sure what she'd done. The fleet of limousines had left, leaving only her car, sitting on its own. She crossed towards it wondering if she should ring Josh and admit poking around outside of her remit. Driving away, she didn't look back.

# CHAPTER FIFTY-TWO

Josh wondered what time it was and reached into his pocket to retrieve his phone. It was then he found it wasn't there. Checking his desk, he realised he hadn't had it since he left the house. There was no way he could survive all day without it. No one would be able to get hold of him, so he had no choice but to go home and get it. He hadn't managed more than two bites of toast this morning and it still felt lodged like cardboard in the back of his throat. He hadn't even managed a mug of coffee to get his brain going because he felt as if he was wired enough and running on his nerves and wasn't sure what a shot of pure caffeine would do to him. It was far too early in the day to be making mistakes: he needed a clear head.

As he turned into his street, he noticed one of the CSI vans parked a few houses up. He wasn't aware of any jobs that had come in; normally someone would have mentioned it. There was nowhere to park, so he drove around to the next street and got out. Walking around the corner he scanned the street, wondering which house the CSIs were at. Not that it mattered, as long as it didn't come in as a job for him or the team it was fine. They had enough to do. They were no closer to finding Annie Potts than they had been as soon as the call had come in.

He pushed the handle of the front door down and swore when it didn't open. He knew Jodie was off work today, as he'd left her in bed and crept around so as not to disturb her. Pulling the key out of his pocket, he inserted it into the lock and swore again when it wouldn't go all the way in. She must have got up, locked it from the inside and gone back to bed. She never locked the bloody door, why today?

He went around to the back of the house: the chance of her locking both doors was slim to none. He let himself through the side gate and walked towards the kitchen door, passing the window. This door was open, thank God, and he let himself in. The kitchen was exactly as he'd left it; his plate of toast on the side, his still-full mug of coffee next to it. His phone wasn't on the table and he'd put it on silent, so he'd either left it on the corner of the bath or it was still tucked under his pillow from when he'd switched off his alarm.

Stepping out into the hall, he heard a moan. He stopped. A louder one followed, then the unmistakeable sound of a man's deep grunt. Josh's chest filled with dread, then hurt, then anger – all at once. *How could you? Behind my back. In my bed.* He stood at the bottom of the stairs, wondering who it could possibly be. Someone he knew? A stranger? He didn't know which was worse. He considered turning around and walking straight back out of the door, then he realised he couldn't; he needed his phone.

Taking the steps two at a time he reached the top where he could see their bedroom door was ajar. He looked at the heavy wooden candlestick on the small console table, but he didn't pick it up; violence was never the answer. Right now his priority was finding Annie. If he lost it and got arrested, he'd be no help to anyone. Taking a deep breath, he strode towards the door and pushed it wide open, immediately recognising the mop of black hair on the man on top of his wife. *That* was why the van was parked in the street.

Ignoring the voice of reason telling him not to, he lunged at Carl and grabbed a handful of his hair, dragging him backwards off the bed. Jodie let out a strangled scream and pulled the duvet around her to cover her nakedness. Drawing back his fist, he went to punch Carl as hard as he could – but hesitated seconds before unleashing. Carl was a pathetic wimp, cowering on the floor, his hands up to protect his face. Josh realised that neither he nor Jodie were worth it.

He dropped his arm and strode towards the bed where Jodie lay whimpering. She flinched as he reached forward – she should know him well enough to know he would never hit a woman – and reached under the pillow to grab his phone. Without a word, he then turned and walked back out of the room and into the spare room, where he kept most of his clothes. There, he pulled out a small case and stuffed it with the essentials: clothes, underwear, socks. Going into the bathroom, he grabbed his toiletries off the shelf and threw them in. Snatching his phone charger from the socket in the kitchen and his laptop off the sofa, he walked out of the door, slamming it shut behind him.

Dragging the case behind him down the street, he realised he felt a small sense of relief. It was over, all the misery and suffering were done with. Neither of them had been particularly happy for the last couple of years or had the balls to do anything about it. Well, it was over now. He had no idea where to go or what he was going to do but he could sleep at the station if he had to. He didn't know how he felt about Carl, what he was going to do about him. He just prayed he stayed out of his way for the time being. At least until the desire to smash his face in had subsided.

# CHAPTER FIFTY-THREE

Beth had rung Josh several times and it had gone straight to voice-mail. She was back home waiting for the security guy to come and repair the front camera, so she couldn't go anywhere. Grabbing a bottle of water from the fridge, she went out into the garden and walked down to the lakeside. She'd changed into a pair of cut-off denim shorts and a *Stranger Things* T-shirt. Sitting on the grass, she stared at the water, looking out at all boats on the lake. She'd purposely asked for the mooring to be removed when she bought the house, because she didn't want to risk anybody landing and coming onto her property. It was probably the only house that edged onto the lake without its own jetty. Would she actually have one now? She watched the boats big and small as they sailed along Lake Windermere. The large steamers were packed with tourists. This was a popular place to holiday; murders and missing girls didn't happen here very often. Her phone began to vibrate in her pocket, interrupting her thoughts.

'Hello.'

'It's me; sorry, I left my phone at home.'

Beth paused before answering: something was wrong. Josh's voice sounded strained. 'I did something that might make you mad, and I felt as if I needed to confess.'

'You wouldn't be the first person today. What's up?'

'It might be better to tell you in person. How's it going? Any sign of the missing woman?'

The sigh was so loud she pulled the phone away from her ear.

'No, we have a few leads we're following. But you know how this works; it's either a feast or a famine. To be honest with you I'm not holding out much hope for her: it's been almost forty-eight hours with no sightings. Where are you?'

'I'm at home waiting for the security guy to come and fix my broken camera. Have you eaten yet? I can make you something?' She didn't tell him she agreed with him that time was running out, he didn't need to be told twice.

'That, my friend, would be amazing. I'll be over soon.'

He ended the call, and Beth sat there for a few more minutes. In spite of the underlying sadness for Chantel Price and the missing woman she enjoyed the view, the fresh air and peace. Things were beginning to shift in her life, she could feel it. As if her soul was beginning to wake from its self-induced coma. She turned to look at her house, so different to the Victorian terrace where it had happened. Where *what* happened, Beth? She closed her eyes and was immediately back there...

\*

She'd been walking along the corridor towards her kitchen, squinting through her hangover in search of a glass of water, wondering why Robert had left the light on.

She'd opened the door and stepped into the large room and heard her feet rustle on what felt like thick plastic sheeting. She looked down, surprised to find she was right. Looking up she was shocked and confused to find that the entire room had been covered; clear plastic sheeting had been taped to the walls, floor, cupboards, even the kitchen table. She didn't understand.

The door that led out in to the garage opened, and she watched open-mouthed as a man stepped through it wearing a set of bright blue surgical scrubs, his face obscured with a mask, his hair covered, blue rubber gloves on his hands. For a moment Beth was certain she was having some kind of horrific nightmare, then she saw the glint of the butcher's knife in his hand and knew whatever was about to happen was real. She whimpered and stumbled back as he took a step forward and their eyes locked. Suddenly she knew what the plastic sheeting was for and fear flooded through her.

Her instincts kicked in at last and she knew if she didn't move quickly she was going to die. She had to get to a phone. She had to lock herself in a room until the police arrived. After several agonising seconds, her feet engaged, and she turned to run. She would have made it out of the door had she not slipped on the damn plastic underneath her and lost her footing. Scrabbling for purchase, she did the only thing she could think of and screamed as loud as she could over and over until the man's dead weight dropped down onto her back and his hand clamped over her mouth. She bit into it as hard as she could, sinking her teeth in and breaking the skin. He shouted out in pain and swung his fist, connecting with her temple. Beth had felt the explosion of black and silver stars as her vision blurred. She tried to throw him off her. He cursed and pulled his hand away in shock. The moment his hand left her mouth she began to scream again, clambering to throw him off her and make a run for it. He fell to the side and she crawled on all fours out into the hallway. Dragging herself up onto her feet, she ran towards the stairs and the safety of her bedroom, where her phone was in her handbag.

The heavy footsteps ran in the opposite direction and she pumped her legs even harder. Too scared to turn around and see what he was doing, she carried on, hoping she'd scared him off. The sound of the blood rushing through her head filled her ears with white noise as she told herself *don't pass out, keep going*. As she was about to reach the top step she felt a gloved hand clamp around her ankle.

His grip tight, he tugged so hard she lost her balance and began to fall back down the stairs. He fell with her and they landed in a tangled mess at the bottom, where her head smacked against the sideboard. She felt warmth as a gash opened across the side of her head and blood began to pour from it. Dazed, but not about to give up, she kicked out at her attacker, screaming again. This time he wrapped something around her mouth, pulling it so tight she dry-heaved. She kicked and fought until she felt herself slowly losing consciousness and could feel herself being dragged back towards the kitchen. Dazed and disorientated, she couldn't do anything to stop him as she finally blacked out.

When she opened her eyes again she was lying flat on her back on a hard surface, which she soon released could only be the kitchen table. She was tied down, her arms and legs fastened tightly to the table legs. Beside her, his back was to her and she wondered what he was doing. He turned around to reveal he'd exchanged the knife he'd had in his hand for a small, sharp scalpel. He crossed the room towards her, a surgeon about to perform an operation, and she began to throw her head from side to side. He lifted a finger to his lips to shush her and she knew then, without question, that her life was over.

It was at that exact moment that the noise of splintering wood had broken through her thoughts like sweet music. She heard shouting from somewhere near the front door and thanked God for sending help. Her attacker lunged for her, but someone launched themselves at him, knocking him to the floor. Armed officers were standing over the two men grappling on the floor. Josh; he'd got there in time. The room went black for the second time as she passed out, bloodied, bruised, but alive thanks to Josh and the rest of the team.

*

She opened her eyes, her heart racing at the memories and stared at the calming water of the lake until her breath returned to normal. Standing up, she grabbed her bottle and walked back towards the house, leaving the kitchen doors wide open; it was too nice to close them, and Josh would be here soon. She was definitely getting a little braver. She had Phil to thank for that; his kindness and weekly classes had gone a long way to building back her self-confidence. Busying herself, she began to chop mushrooms, onions and garlic to sauté in a pan. She put a pan of water on to boil; she would add some pasta to it when the sauce was ready.

The intercom buzzed and she went to answer it. She didn't recognise the car, but Josh turned up driving a different car almost every time he came. A hand came out of the window and waved wildly, so she opened the gates; no one but Josh did that geeky wave. Walking to the front door, she opened it and felt her mouth fall open at the sight of her friend as he climbed out of the car. He looked ashen, the stubble on his face was darker and thicker than she'd seen before. He smiled at her, but it didn't reach his eyes like it normally did. Something was terribly wrong.

'Something smells good,' he said as he reached her.

'Bugger, something smells *burnt*.' Beth hurried back towards the kitchen where the pasta was boiling over and the vegetables were sticking in the pan. She turned the pans down, threw the chopped-up chicken in with the veg and added a sachet of sauce. Turning to him, she shrugged.

'I've never said I was a good cook.'

He laughed. 'No, but you do try, and I love you for that.'

She felt her heart double beat, busying herself by slicing the fresh baguette she'd bought on her way back from the undertaker's. Josh sat down on one of the stools at the breakfast bar, and she knew without looking that he was staring out of the window at the lake. She glanced behind her; he looked so sad she had an overwhelming urge to wrap her arms around him and tell him everything was going to be okay. Only she didn't. She served up the food and carried the plates over to him.

'Do you want to eat outside?'

He shook his head. 'Here's fine, I can stare at the view without worrying about sharing my food with the flies.'

'To be honest, Josh, I don't think the flies will touch this. It isn't my finest creation.'

'It smells wonderful to me; I haven't eaten all day.'

They ate in silence. Beth didn't want to push him and put him off his food. She'd never seen him this down in all the years they'd been friends. When he'd finished everything on the plate and mopped up with several slices of bread, he carried his plate and hers over to the sink, rinsed them and then put them into the dishwasher. Beth sighed.

'Jodie has trained you well.'

He snorted. 'Yeah, you think so. She doesn't seem to appreciate it much.'

'Marriage is like that; you get used to each other. The passion goes, you end up being friends more than lovers.'

'You're quite an expert considering you've never been married.'

'Ouch, I was trying to help.'

'Sorry, that was uncalled for. I'm having the shittiest of days.'

'I know, if it helps you look like shit as well.'

'That good, eh?'

She nodded. 'So, who's going first; me or you?'

'You. I'm intrigued about what you think you've done to make me so mad, and after today nothing surprises me.'

She raised an eyebrow at his comment, wondering what had happened to put him in this mood. 'Right, well. Here goes. I was thinking about where the missing girl could be. What kind of place could someone keep Chantel Price and Annie? I thought Dean & Sons might be a good place to start because they dealt with the funeral of Florence Wright.'

'And?'

'I went and paid them a visit. I spoke to James Dean and his niece Alex. I get the impression that those two don't get along much.'

'I can't believe you went there too! I went there yesterday and got caught sneaking around on the CCTV. Got a bollocking from the boss. I'm not allowed back there unless I can get sufficient grounds for a search warrant.'

Beth smiled at him. 'Well at least that makes me feel a little better. I did walk in through the front door.'

'Did you find anything out?'

'Not really, I think it was a waste of time. I spoke to James, who said he didn't notice anything strange when he was preparing Florence's body. That's not the worst of it though. I took a photo of Chantel Price with me and asked him if he recognised her.'

Josh laughed. 'I've done a lot worse.'

'Good, you have? I feel really bad about it. Anyway, on the way out I figured in for a penny in for a pound and showed the picture to his niece, Alex. She took a lot longer looking at it than he did, and I can't say for sure, but I think there was a flicker of recognition in her eyes. I gave her my business card and told her to call me if she needed to chat, then I left. I'm sorry, are you mad?'

'No. I'm more impressed that you did it. That's interesting that we both came up with the same idea. Let's hope you've stirred something in her memory, and she gets in touch.'

'I've told you mine, now you tell me yours.' She reached and took hold of his hand. He squeezed her fingers gently.

'I forgot my phone, went home for it and found Jodie in bed with Carl from CSI.'

'Oh no, I'm sorry, Josh. You must be so hurt.'

He shrugged. 'Hurt yes, but a little bit relieved. Things haven't been good for a long time now.'

'What will you do? Have you got somewhere to go?'

'I'll find somewhere.'

'You have somewhere here, Josh, and it would be nice to have a bit of company. You can stay here as long as you like, there's plenty of room. You can eat your breakfast and stare at your favourite view every day. You might have to feed yourself, though, I'm not really the domestic type.'

Josh laughed. 'Thank you, Beth.' He stood up and walked around to where she was sitting. He bent down and kissed her on the cheek. 'I promise I won't get in your way.'

She felt her cheeks flush pink and her fingers reached up to touch the spot where he'd kissed her.

# CHAPTER FIFTY-FOUR

Josh carried the small suitcase in from the back of the car and Beth took him up to the spare room. He put the case in, thanked her again then told her he had to go. She gave him the code for the gates, and he knew that for her this was a huge step, though he'd never betray her trust. He was glad she was beginning to come out of her shell. He'd watched her hide away for far too long.

He left her waiting for the camera guy and went back to the station to see where everyone was up to with the enquiries he'd left for them to follow up. He was still angry about Carl, and the fact that he worked with him and had trusted him irritated him all the more. As he pulled into the station's car park the CSI van was nowhere to be seen. Good. Carl had better stay out of his way. Parking next to Sam's Clio, he got out and went inside. The smell of fish and chips lingered in the corridor. Something about the design of this building meant that no matter what someone ate for lunch, the rest of the building could smell it until the next meal time. He was full of Beth's pasta and grateful for her offer of a place to stay with no strings attached. Both of them worked hard, would likely pass like ships in the night and spend very little time together, so at least they wouldn't get on each other's nerves. Well, he hoped he wouldn't get on hers; he knew she could never get on his.

He sat down at his desk and logged onto the computer. He needed a break in the case and he needed it now, before anything else happened. The door opened and Sam walked in.

'Boss, there are three burials planned this week. Two of the graves have already been partially dug. The cemetery manager has put a stop on them until the morning of the funeral. Barry and the other bloke, I can't remember his name, are going to take it in turns to keep an eye on the three separate sites.'

'Good, thank you. I think I'll ask for volunteers to sit in a car in plain clothes and watch as well.'

'Is everything okay?'

He didn't want to get into it with Sam, with anyone. He didn't want the whole station speculating about his personal business. Paton arrived in the office, took one look at Josh and grimaced.

'Anything on Jason Thompson?' Josh asked.

'We've been given another ex-girlfriend's address by the ex-girlfriend we paid a visit to. She's out of the country working on a cruise ship, so it's a possibility he's hiding out at her place. Task force are on their way there to stake it out.'

Josh was about to speak but Paton cut him off.

'They can put the door through if they need to.'

'Good.'

Josh's phone began to ring; when he saw it was Beth he answered it.

'Hi, it's me. Remember the girl from the undertaker's I told you about earlier?'

He nodded. 'Yes.'

'Well, I've just had a very interesting conversation with her. She phoned me to tell me she'd like to speak to me in person, somewhere away from Dean & Sons. She thinks she recognises Chantel Price.'

Josh let out a whoop so loud it made both Sam and Paton jump as his fist smacked against the wooden desk. 'When?'

'I told her forty minutes in the coffee shop near the Windermere Lake Hotel you were at yesterday. Can you make it?'

'Yes, I'm on my way. Thank you, Beth.'

Grinning, he stood up. 'We might have a pretty decent lead; Paton, I still want you to go with task force and put that door through if you need to. Thompson isn't off the hook yet.'

'What about me?' said Sam.

'You can come with me, but you might have to wait in the car. I don't want to spook her if she has information and too many of us might tip the balance. Is that okay?'

'Fine by me.'

For the first time in hours he felt a spark of hope that things might fall into place. That this woman might give them a connection to Dean & Sons, so they could get a warrant and tear the place apart.

# CHAPTER FIFTY-FIVE

Beth met Josh at the hotel car park, and they walked across the narrow pedestrian street to the coffee shop together.

'I don't want to scare her, so if you sit a couple of tables away from me when she comes, I'll ask if she agrees to you being present. If she does, I'll give you the nod.'

'Thank you, Beth, you don't know how much this means.'

'It might not be anything, so don't get your hopes up, but you're welcome. I think you're becoming a bad influence on me, Josh. I've never felt the need to go and act all Kay Scarpetta on a case. I don't know what came over me.'

He laughed. 'Me neither, but I like it. What with me getting my arse kicked for sneaking around the other day and you going there out of the blue, if this all goes horribly wrong we can set up the best private detective agency in the UK.'

It was Beth's turn to laugh. 'God, I hope not. I don't think I could cope with the anxiety, although it would be a bit exciting. In fact this is the most exciting thing I've done in a long time. I've even had to cancel my security guy to come here; I'm *truly* living dangerously now.'

He stared at her a little too long, and she felt the heat begin to rise up her throat, turning her cheeks pink.

'You didn't have to do that.'

'I know, but I thought we'd better catch her whilst she wants to talk, in case she thinks about it and changes her mind. I also thought if you were stopping at mine I might feel a little bit safer and not quite as paranoid.'

He reached out and squeezed her arm. 'I hope so. You deserve to be happy, Beth. Not living under the shadow of what happened.'

The café was busy; the perils of a warm summer's day in the Lake District. Josh snagged a table outside on the patio whilst Beth went to get the drinks. When Alex arrived he'd leave her to it and go and sit on the church wall opposite. He looked around, he loved people watching and was sure that was what made him a good detective.

After a while Beth appeared with three cardboard cups and passed him one.

'I got you a latte with an extra shot. I thought you might need the caffeine.'

He smiled as he took it from her and stood up. 'There's nowhere to sit, so I'll go and hang around the church.'

'God, not you as well. Where were you last week?'

He spat the mouthful of hot coffee all over the front of his suit. 'Very funny for a doctor.' Shaking his head, he screwed the napkins up she'd passed him to blot up the coffee and left them on the table. He walked off and settled himself on a bench in the churchyard that looked onto the café.

# CHAPTER FIFTY-SIX

Beth sipped her latte, hoping Alex hadn't changed her mind and had second thoughts. The thought of Chantel Price's body being stuck in the mortuary fridge for the foreseeable future made her heart break. She could see Josh: he was sitting on a bench, his eyes closed, face lifted to catch the sun's rays. He didn't deserve what had happened to him this morning, even if his marriage was already on the rocks.

'Beth.'

She turned to see Alex, her face hidden behind a pair of large designer sunglasses.

'Alex, I bought you a latte. I hope that's OK?'

She nodded. 'If it contains caffeine, I'll drink it. Thank you.'

'I have to say, yours was much better this morning. Have you ever considered opening up a coffee shop?'

The woman laughed. 'I'd love to, anything to get out of the family business would be great. It wasn't my first choice of career.' Alex pulled out a chair and sat down opposite her.

'How did you end up working there then? Sorry if I'm being overly personal, just tell me to mind my own business.'

'No, it's fine. I told you, I don't get to have many conversations with living people. I kind of got sucked in to it. About three months after my mum passed away, my dad had a minor heart attack right when I was about to leave for university. I didn't want to leave him; James is lazy at the best of times and I knew he wasn't about to change. That business means everything to my dad; it was my grandad who started it. I didn't have the heart to leave him alone to run it when he wasn't in great shape.'

'That's very good of you. I don't know if I'd have been so keen to give up my chance to go to uni.'

'What about you, why did you want to be a pathologist?'

Beth decided to be frank with her: she wanted to gain her trust. 'I didn't, not at first. I was an A&E doctor. I loved the thrill of helping people, saving lives even if we were understaffed and under pressure.'

'How did you go from saving people to cutting up dead bodies? It's a bit of a leap.'

'I was attacked, and afterwards I went through a really bad time. After that, I didn't want to face people, well not living ones. So I retrained as a pathologist. I trust the dead more than the living, so it seemed easier and so much safer.'

'Oh, God. That must have been terrible. I'm sorry for asking.'

'No, don't be. It feels good to talk about it. I've sort of been living under a shell since it happened and hiding myself away. It was a few years ago now; he's in prison. Life is good, most of the time.'

They sipped their coffees, both of them silent. It was Beth who spoke first.

'You said you might have recognised the girl in the photo I showed you earlier. Would you mind telling me how? Before you answer, I have a favour to ask. I have a very good friend who happens to be the lead detective on the case. He's sitting over on that bench in the church.' She pointed to where Josh was sitting. 'Would you mind if he came and joined us? You don't have to say yes. If you'd rather it was just you and me I understand.'

Alex bit her lip and turned to look at Josh, who was watching them. He lifted a hand and waved. She lifted hers and gave a slight wave, then looked back at Beth.

'I suppose once I tell you it's going to go further anyway, so I might as well tell you both. The thing is, I don't want to upset my dad or give the company a bad name.'

'Thank you, we'll try and deal with anything you tell us as discreetly as possible.'

An overwhelming feeling of relief washed over Beth as she waved Josh over; at least it wasn't all down to her now.

# CHAPTER FIFTY-SEVEN

Josh pulled over a chair and introduced himself to Alex, who nervously smiled back at him.

'I recognise you. You're the guy caught sneaking around the garages yesterday. You nearly gave James a heart attack.'

He held up his right hand. 'Guilty as charged. I'm sorry for the intrusion, but why was James so upset?'

'He said it's because it's a funeral home. He thought it was disrespectful; although he was probably more worried you'd find the stash of weed he keeps hidden out in the garage, so my dad doesn't find it. It was him who made my dad ring up to get you in trouble. Did you?'

He laughed; he liked the young woman sitting opposite him. She was sharp and witty.

'I got a bit of a bollocking, yes.'

'Why didn't you come inside with your partner and ask to have a look around?'

'I didn't think you'd let me.'

'I wasn't there, but I would have. My dad got loads of grief off James, so he had to ring up.'

Beth spoke next. 'Alex, do you want to tell us why you wanted to speak to me away from the funeral home?'

She nodded. 'That photo, the girl in it, I'm sure I've seen her before. Look, I don't want to cause any trouble, though God knows it's probably too late anyway. If he finds out I've spoken to the police, he'll go mental. It's tough, but I can cope with him. He's such a moody, angry man at times.' Josh leaned in a little closer. 'I told Beth I don't want any bad press for the business if it's possible. All I care about is my dad.'

'I'll do my best, Alex, but I can't promise. It all depends on how serious what you have to tell me is.'

'I know. I don't know what she's called, but I've seen her with James a couple of times.'

Josh looked at Beth, then back at Alex.

'When was the last time you saw them together?'

'A couple of months ago now. She was a strange girl. She'd hang around, come in and ask if James was about. It used to irritate me. The last time they met I remember they had a bit of an argument. He took her out the back. I shouldn't have been listening, but I wanted to know why she was there and what she wanted from him.'

'What did she want from him?' asked Josh.

'Weed, sex and money mostly. I think she was lonely, though, she just wanted someone to be her friend. What happened was they argued, she called him a heartless bastard who didn't mind screwing her when he had no one else. Then she started crying and I heard him trying to shush her. A couple of minutes later I heard them having sex. I was horrified and ran off back to the reception. I mean, they were having sex in the embalming room where he prepares the bodies. I could hear her groaning; it was so embarrassing. I was praying my dad wouldn't turn up. It would have been enough to give him another heart attack. She was far too young for James; then again, he's always liked women younger than himself.' She stopped suddenly, the realisation that she'd said too much making her blush.

Josh wanted to punch the air; at last, a connection to Dean & Sons that gave them motive and a good enough reason for a search warrant.

'Thank you for being so honest. I'm sorry, but I'm going to have to act on the information you've told me. I must; there could be vital evidence. There's also another missing woman who I'm afraid might die if we don't act quickly.'

Alex's face had lost all its colour. She'd pushed her sunglasses on top of her head.

'What happened after they'd had sex?' Josh was aware there were families all around them and kept his voice quiet.

'He drove out of the gates with her sitting in the passenger seat of one of the fleet cars. I don't know where they went, sorry.'

'How long was he gone?'

'Thirty minutes, I'm not sure. The roads are bad around here; those roadworks to replace the water mains on the A592 have caused us no end of problems. I don't know whether he took her home; I don't know where she lived.'

Josh felt bad: the woman looked thoroughly miserable now. He began to wrack his brains how he could play this.

'I have an idea. I need to get a warrant and search for any forensic evidence at the funeral home, but I don't want to get you in trouble with your family. Could you phone Crimestoppers from a payphone? It's anonymous and you don't need to give them any contact details. Tell them you saw James Dean in a car with a woman who you believe has been found murdered. They will have to give us the authority to follow up on it. Then I'll take it from there. All you have to do is act surprised when we turn up. I'll act like I've never met you before, Alex.'

'I suppose that might work.' She stood up. 'Look, I need to get back now, or Dad will wonder where I've been. I'll stop off and make the phone call at the public phone box on Glebe Road. If it still works.'

She stood up then, drained the last of her drink and smiled at Beth. Josh stood up, too. He held out his hand and shook hers.

'Thank you, you've done the right thing. Hopefully it's nothing to do with James and we can rule him out. No more sneaking around.'

Beth waited until she left and was out of hearing.

'I didn't expect that.'

'No, neither did I. Thanks, Beth.'

She nodded. 'Glad to help.'


Josh took a large coffee over to Sam as a peace offering. She was leaning against the bonnet looking bored, but she took it from him and got back inside the car.

'So, was that worth an hour of your time?'

He nodded. 'Every minute'

'That good eh? Now what?'

'Now we have to go back to the station and get a search team together, then wait for the call to come in.'

'What call?'

'From Crimestoppers; it's going to drop James Dean knee-deep in shit. And it will give us enough to get a warrant to search the funeral home.'

She sipped her coffee. 'Whatever you say, boss. But what about the warning you had to keep away?'

'If it's come through Crimestoppers, they will have to act on it, because the information is far too good to ignore. The beauty of it is that it's nothing to do with me. Well, technically it isn't.'

He got in and drove back to Kendal station as fast as the speed limit allowed. He knew this could be the big break they were looking for. If they searched the undertaker's and found Annie Potts alive, then perhaps he could deal with the other crisis in his life.

# CHAPTER FIFTY-EIGHT

Beth started the drive home, relieved that Josh hadn't been angry with her and that Alex had come through with some useful information. But she didn't make it far before she slowed the car to a stop. Something was bothering her, and she didn't know what. Something at the back of her mind was calling her back to the cemetery for another look. Maybe a look at the gravesite would help her to focus on what was niggling at the edge of her consciousness. She couldn't stop thinking about Annie Potts and what might be making Josh so convinced that the same monster who killed Chantel Price had abducted her from the hotel. Maybe Josh would open up to her a little later when he came home from work.

As she pulled into the cemetery gates she saw a familiar face smiling back at her from a car exiting the cemetery. Phil pulled alongside and put the window down, looking unusually smart in a black suit and tie.

'Hey! Are you coming to the pub again tomorrow night, or did the happy couple put you off for life?'

She laughed. 'Who, Audrey and Bob? I think they're sweet actually and yes, I think I will. I enjoyed myself. Were you at a funeral?'

He shrugged. 'Yeah, my friend's dad sadly passed last week. I've just been to visit his grave and say goodbye, I couldn't make it to the funeral.' 'Sorry to hear that, it's tough. You don't ever want to have to say goodbye to a loved one, no matter how old they are. Look, I'm sorry but I need to get on, it's a work thing. I just needed to check something out. I'll see you tomorrow? Take care, Phil.'

He smiled at her, but it wasn't his usual cheery smile. He looked sad. As she drove away she realised she knew very little about him and hoped that he wasn't going home to an empty house.

Driving up the hill, she reached the chapel and parked next to the rusted fencing. It was so peaceful here. She spotted a marble memorial bench near to the still-open grave and walked over to take a seat and think everything through. The bench was dedicated to a woman named Gail O'Neill, which sounded familiar to Beth. Wondering where she knew it from, she realised it was the name of a local PCSO who'd died from cancer far too young last year. She had spoken to her a couple of times, and what she remembered most about her was her kindness; nothing had ever been too much trouble for her. The world needed more people like that, more happiness.

She stared at the open grave a few feet away from her. All that remained of what horrors they'd discovered here was the blue and white police tape that had been wrapped around either side of the graves, and the neat mound of soil next to it which had been sieved by the forensic anthropologist to make sure all the evidence had been collected. She wondered when Florence Wright was going to be reburied. Would Florence's family even want her to go back in there? If a body had been found underneath her own mum's coffin, she wasn't sure she'd want her to go back into the same hole. Not that it really mattered, she supposed, they were both dead.

Beth inhaled deeply then released her breath. She did this three times. Abe called it being mindful and raved about a meditation class he attended once a week. He'd even invited her along several times. Standing up, she wished she'd brought some flowers to lay by the grave for Chantel, but it hadn't entered her head. She would stop off at the florist's on the way home and buy a bunch to put on her dining table. Something bright and vibrant, something to make her smile and remember what it was like to be younger and carefree. She decided now was the time to pay a visit to Dalton View Care Home. She wanted to know more about the girl that no one seemed to care about except for her and Josh.

# CHAPTER FIFTY-NINE

Happy with his little gift, he crept back through the bushes just as a police van rounded the bend. He crouched down, heart pounding in his chest, a sheen of perspiration prickling his forehead as he pretended to search for something in the long grass around him. Stealing a glance at the coppers inside the van he almost laughed out loud when he realised they were too busy talking to each other to notice him. Standing tall, he stepped out onto the road and strolled back down to his car, the terror churning in his stomach quickly changing to a delicious tingle as the fear of getting caught added to the enjoyment of what he was doing. He knew he was taking excessive risks and he hoped she appreciated it. Everything he did was for her. Would she realise this when the time came? Would she appreciate his effort? He liked to think so.

He'd left the gift on her patio table knowing how much she liked to sit there with a large glass of wine and stare at the lake after a long shift. He would do the same if he had that kind of view. It truly was beautiful and such a shame he couldn't sit there with her. At one point in his life he'd thought that maybe they could, if she'd just give him a chance, but Beth Adams had time for no one but herself and that would be her downfall. It seemed her house was her only real luxury. She drove a nice car, but nothing too extravagant; she dressed nicely but nothing too showy or designer. She never took holidays, preferring to spend the days she had off work pottering around her garden. He'd been watching her for so long he felt as if he knew her better than she probably knew herself…

It was almost time; the watching and the waiting was finally about to pay off and he couldn't be more excited at the prospect of what lay ahead for him. And Beth.

# CHAPTER SIXTY

The convoy of police vehicles that drove up to Dean & Sons funeral home was pretty impressive; even Josh thought so and he'd been doing this job a long time. He wished someone had filmed the chief super's face when the message had come through from Crimestoppers and was delivered in person by Barker. Josh looked at the search warrant next to him on the seat, signed by the Right Honourable Judge Farley. They couldn't brush this under the carpet, not while there was a chance Annie Potts was still alive.

It was after closing time and the gates were shut and locked. Josh couldn't deny the buzz he felt in his stomach, and the butterflies; everything he had was depending upon this. He needed enough evidence to bring James Dean in. His car was first in the convoy, behind him was the huge van full of the task force officers who would also conduct the search of the premises. Behind that was the CSI van. It was no surprise to Josh that Carl had phoned in sick, the coward.

Josh pressed the intercom and wondered who was going to answer, hoping it would be Alex. Not that it mattered; he would search every corner and lift every coffin lid if he had to; he wasn't leaving here empty-handed.

'Can I help you?' The voice was male, older than he'd expected.

'Yes, it's the police. We have a search warrant to come in and search these premises for evidence which might link to the murder of Chantel Price and/or the disappearance of Annie Potts.'

'Who are they, and what have they got to do with Dean & Sons?'

Josh resisted the urge to say: 'You tell me.' Instead he smiled. 'If you open the gates and let me and my colleagues through I can explain it fully to you, in person.'

The intercom went quiet. After a minute the gates began to slowly open.

Sam looked at him. 'Nice one, Josh. Do you think he's shitting himself?'

'We're about to find out.'

He drove through, hoping to God they were going to find something worthwhile that might help break the case, because he had nothing else.

# CHAPTER SIXTY-ONE

Dalton View wasn't at all what Beth had expected. She'd envisioned a sprawling house in its own grounds, a smaller version of Dean & Sons maybe. What she hadn't expected was the terraced house along one of the busier town centre streets in Kendal. The three-storey house had a glass front door, the lower pane taped up with a piece of cardboard and yellow electricians' tape. It was open, so she pushed it and walked inside the tiny entrance where there was a two-seater sofa with two teenage girls sat on it listening to music on their phones. Both of them looked her up and down, decided she wasn't worth bothering about and continued staring down at their phones.

Behind a sliding glass window, two women were staring at her. She smiled at them and began to introduce herself. One of them leaned forward and slid open the glass the tiniest bit. Beth realised they hadn't heard a word of what she'd just said.

'Can I help you?'

'Yes, I hope so.' She fished a business card from her pocket and passed it to her. The woman read it, then passed it to her colleague. Beth cleared her throat.

'I'd like to talk to you about one of your former residents, a girl called Chantel Price.'

The smile disappeared from the woman's face as she stood up. 'You'd better come in. I'm Lyn and this is Sue.'

Beth found herself being let through a narrow door and led into the small office. The woman who'd opened the door waited for her to speak, and Beth wondered if she was out of her mind. This wasn't her job at all. She was truly pushing all boundaries now.

'I'm the pathologist who conducted Chantel's post-mortem when she was brought into the mortuary. I'd like to know a little bit about her background, we know so little about her.'

The women looked at each other.

Beth wondered how she was going to play this. 'I just wondered what Chantel was like as a person and why no one had even noticed she was missing? And, can I be honest with you both?'

They nodded.

'It's upset me on a very personal level and that doesn't happen very often.'

Lyn smiled. 'Bless you, lovely. I guess you never get used to it. The kids come here when they're sixteen, and they stay until their eighteenth birthday and it's hard to watch them leave when they choose to go off into the big wide world to fend for themselves. A lot of the time they think they can handle it, that they're old enough to look after themselves. The sad reality is that very few are really ready. It's a huge adjustment. They're vulnerable and people take advantage of them.'

'Why? Why did Chantel leave? Why was there no support for her just because she was eighteen?'

'A number of factors, really. It depends on the level of care each person needs. Chantel was, shall we say, very independent.'

Sue nodded. 'She was from the day she moved here. She didn't make friends very easy, kept to herself and was forever running away and not coming back; the police brought her back a few times.'

'That's true,' Lyn took up again. 'The moment she got a new boyfriend we didn't see her for days.'

Beth found herself feeling even sadder for the life this young girl led. 'Why didn't she have many friends?'

'She was a bit of a… what can you call it without being disrespectful to the dead?'

It was Sue who answered. 'She was a bitch. Liked the boys, hated the girls. She'd sleep with anything for a bit of weed. Argued with the girls over anything and everything.'

'What about her family, did she have any?'

'Her mum was the same: would sleep with anyone for drugs, vodka or money. Took men home all the time, all hours of the day and night. She'd leave Chantel on her own whilst she was out drinking and picking them up. Chantel got put into care when she was six, after she'd told the teacher at school she wanted to be a whore like her mum.'

Lyn nodded. 'It's sad, but true. You'd be amazed how many vulnerable kids are in dire situations—'

'And then they end up idolising the parents who neglect them,' Sue said.

'Where's her mum now?'

'She died a couple of years ago; overdosed on Tramadol and vodka.'

Beth nodded. 'How sad.'

The women shrugged. Sue said, 'It's life, just the norm. Well, at least it is for these kids.'

Lyn asked, 'When's Chantel's funeral?'

'I have no idea,' Beth said. 'At the moment we are keeping her at the mortuary until the police locate her next of kin and the investigation into her murder is complete.'

She stood up. 'Thank you for your time. I'm sorry to have bothered you.'

She walked out, glancing at the girls, who were now whispering to each other and staring at her. Beth didn't look back. She let the door slam shut behind her as she walked to her car and blinked back the tears for the girl who'd never stood a chance at life.

# CHAPTER SIXTY-TWO

At home Beth poured herself a glass of wine, though she knew she shouldn't have. It was becoming a habit, but she had little other way of relaxing and needed to take away the sadness inside her after visiting Dalton View. She stared at the cream envelope on the kitchen counter, the second one in a week in handwriting she knew so well. Her name and address were written in small, square, uniform block capitals. She sat down at the breakfast bar, drank a couple of mouthfuls of wine and waited for it to begin the familiar feeling of warming up her frozen insides. It took the edge off her permanently stressed state of being. She stared at the letter, willing it to spontaneously combust. It didn't.

How did he even have her new address? She'd ensured she wasn't on the electoral register when she bought the house, had even registered the land in her mother's name, though the deeds for the house were all hers. Slowly sipping the wine, she relished every single mouthful, swirling it around as if to numb her tongue, gums, teeth and lips. She wanted to numb every single living, breathing part of her body and hide from the pain that he'd caused her.

The worry.

The fear.

She shuddered anew at the memory of that night. The crinkle of the thick plastic laid down to protect every available surface from her blood spatter. Now, she knew better than most how much hard work, preparation and clean-up was involved in cutting someone open. It was her job to help loved ones come to terms with the sudden, somewhat inexplicable deaths of their nearest and dearest. She liked to think that because of her the unexpected grief was made slightly more bearable.

What was *his* excuse? She'd never asked, and didn't want to know. But she could never come to terms with why he did it to *her*. What had she done to make him hate her so much? The sleepless nights where she tossed and turned wondering exactly how he'd come to despise her so much to want to kill her had almost sent her over the edge. She was an educated woman, how had she not realised or seen the warning signs that there was something very wrong with Robert? It had plagued her for years until she'd finally realised that none of it had been her fault. There was no way she could have known about the sick fantasies he harboured inside of his mind. She'd been an emergency doctor, great at piecing people back together but clueless about how deviant minds worked.

She remembered his answers in the many police interviews and again in court, his voice echoing through her mind as she recalled his stark confession: 'To stake my place in society, to become a collector.'

She'd had no idea what that had even meant until the defence had brought out a dog-eared copy of a John Fowles novel called *The Collector* stating he wasn't of sound mind, that he lived in a fantasy world brought about by a story he'd become obsessed with. A book; a bland-seeming item of little significance that had lain around the house; he had multiple copies of it. She'd teased him about it once, she remembered. She'd even seen him reading it in bed. She'd rushed home that night to research *The Collector*, to discover what was so damaging about a work of fiction. Horrified, and puzzled, she learned that *The Collector* had been the inspiration for a number of high-profile serial killers. Christ. How many long, sleepless nights she'd struggled to get her head around *that* one. He'd wanted to kill her because of a story he'd read? He'd planned to kill her for the enjoyment of it. He was a psychopath, the defence had claimed, acting out some long-repressed fantasy owing to uncontrollable desires. He wanted his name to be forever linked to that book, to the collector, nothing more and nothing less.

Fingering the almost-empty bottle, she had an important decision to make: did she finish the wine and read his damn letter, or do what she always did? She crossed to where the envelope was propped on the worktop, staring at her. Snatching hold of it, she opened the drawer, threw the letter inside and slammed the drawer shut. Let it fester with the others. She wasn't giving him the satisfaction, not even the slightest hint how she felt about his letters. She didn't want to know whether or not he was sorry: *sorry*! He could tell her he was sorry every hour for the rest of his life, it wouldn't change the situation. She'd almost died because he'd wanted to kill her. Sending these stupid letters to her didn't make her feel any better; he could never give her closure, if that was what he wanted now.

Rinsing out the glass, she left it to drain on the side; she didn't need to finish the bottle. What would it look like if Josh came back and found her in a drunken stupor on the sofa because she'd received a letter in the post that she hadn't opened? It might not even be an apology; perhaps she was giving Robert too much credit. It could be a vile outpouring of his obsession. It didn't matter. Celebrities got hate mail all the time, it didn't mean they turned into a quivering wreck and never got on with their lives. Robert Hartshorn was her cross to bear; he had been her lover and her best friend until the day he'd decided to kill her, and then he'd become her problem. She placed her hands on her hips, determined now. She was going to make it her mission to put him out of her life for good.

# CHAPTER SIXTY-THREE

Harry Dean looked bewildered, there was no other way to describe it: his collar unbuttoned, tie pushed to one side and his normally well-groomed hair was sticking out where he'd run his fingers through it so many times.

'I'm sorry, officer.'

'Josh, please call me Josh.'

'I'm sorry, Josh, I don't understand how you think we had anything to do with the girl you found. God rest her soul. I've never seen her before in my life.'

Josh looked at Sam, who gave a slight shrug of her shoulders. 'We have had an anonymous tip that James was well acquainted with Chantel Price, that she'd been here on several occasions and, in fact, we believe that James was one of the last people to see her alive. The last confirmed sighting we have of her on record was that she was being driven away from here in a car with your brother.'

Josh acknowledged Alex as she came around the corner. She took one look at the expression on her dad's face and every ounce of colour drained from her cheeks. Harry turned to his daughter.

'Do you know what they're talking about? They're saying some dead girl was seen here, leaving with James. By the way, where the hell *is* James?'

Alex looked horrified, and Josh realised that they had pushed Harry to the limit.

'Harry, let's talk whilst my team does the search. Is James around? We really need to speak to him.'

A voice very similar to Harry's echoed around the reception. 'Just what the *hell* is going on here?'

Harry strode towards his brother, poking him in the chest with his index finger. 'What have you done this time?'

James shook his head. 'I don't know what you're talking about.'

Josh nodded at the two response officers who were waiting around. 'If you'd be so kind as to take Mr Dean to the station and get him booked in.'

James squared up to Josh. 'What are you arresting me for?'

'I'm not arresting you; I'm giving you the chance to come down and speak to me of your own free will, on a voluntary basis. If you don't want to do that, then I'll have no choice but to make it more formal. It's entirely up to you.'

James turned to Alex and glared at her, but she glared right back.

He shook his head but followed the two officers out to their waiting van. Josh took hold of Harry's elbow. 'Is there somewhere we can talk, or would you rather be present whilst the searches are being conducted?'

'Alex can take them where they need to go, I'd rather talk.'

Josh followed Harry down the corridor to an office, while Sam followed Alex and the search team down to the mortuary.

As Alex opened the door, she turned to face the officers behind her.

'There's a body in the middle of embalming; are you okay to work around him? My dad will go mad if you disturb it.'

Sam nodded. 'Of course, we'll be very careful.'

# CHAPTER SIXTY-FOUR

The visitor walked towards the main entrance of the prison until the huge cream gates with rust spots dotted all over them were towering above him. The whole area was bleak; the huge coils of barbed wire running along the top of the fence were both impressive and scary against the backdrop of Black Combe fell behind it. He couldn't help wonder why Robert had summoned him like this, out of the blue. Did he know what had happened? Had he read the news and realised what was going on? Was it a trap? He would find out soon enough.

After he'd been through the security he was shown to the visitor's reception centre and then led into the visit hall: a small, cramped room with a tea bar situated along the back wall. He sat at an empty table and waited for his old friend to be led in.

As a crowd of inmates rolled through the doors, he saw no sign of him. About to stand up and leave, he looked up to see a final solitary figure walk through the doors. Not recognising him, he looked the other way, and stood up.

'Sorry, had to wait for my meds and they don't always get them to you on time.'

He did a double take at the gaunt man with a scruffy beard peppered with grey and white.

'Robert, my God. I didn't recognise you. I thought this prison was supposed to be an easier ride?'

Robert laughed, the sound wavering halfway as he began to cough and splutter. Finally he regained his composure enough to speak. 'It is. It's good to see you too, my friend. The past year has been much kinder to you than me. I've been diagnosed with emphysema and lung cancer. I'm afraid I don't know how long I have left.'

'I'm sorry. Are you having treatment?'

Robert shook his head. 'No, I don't see the point to be honest. What good will it do if it's only going to prolong the misery I'm suffering in here?'

He had a point.

'Is that why you requested a visit? To tell me you're dying.'

Robert shook his head: steel grey hair now, he noticed. 'No, I didn't think you'd be too bothered about my health. I wanted to know what was going on; I read the headlines about the girl in the grave and the missing girl.' Leaning forward, Robert smiled at him. Clasping his fingers together, he cracked his knuckles and whispered, 'I know that it's you.'

He was still for a moment and then he slowly began to shake his head. 'No.'

'Are you sure about that? I remember how we'd talk for hours over a bottle or two of Rioja. Loose lips sink ships, my friend. You've got the police running around like headless chickens. I really just wanted to thank you. I never thought I'd see her again, but now I have a couple of newspaper cuttings tucked under my mattress that I can stare at.'

The visitor frowned at Robert. 'You know that you should never have chosen such a difficult subject for your first kill. You should have gone for something a little more straightforward like I did. You were far too ambitious, look where it got you. You should have waited until the room was ready, until you had a safe place to keep her like we'd discussed. But you let your arrogance get in the way of your common sense. Stupid, really, for such an intelligent man.'

Robert sat forward, his spine straight, his clasped hands now tightly clenched fists.

'I was always going to go back and finish what you started. You didn't think that I would let her go? She's mine now and there's nothing you can do about it. She's been ever so lonely since you messed up her life. I've been getting to know her quite well.'

Robert's face burned red, and before he knew it he had lunged across the table, throwing himself at him. Shouts echoed all around them, a cacophony of scraping chairs and cheers as the other prisoners all turned to watch the show. The effort of launching himself across the table was clearly far too much for Robert; he began to cough so hard he couldn't catch his breath. Three guards ran over to restrain him, and he fought hard against them despite the fact that he was almost suffocating.

The visitor stood up, brushed himself down and apologised to the stunned family nearest. Walking calmly past Robert, who was still thrashing against the guards' grip, he made his way to the exit without looking back.

# CHAPTER SIXTY-FIVE

Josh hadn't turned up last night and Beth had struggled not to text him to see if everything was okay this morning. She'd lain in bed wondering if he'd gone back home to Jodie. No, it was more than likely he'd pulled an all-nighter at the station. Maybe they'd found the missing girl. God, she hoped so. And if they hadn't called her out it would mean the girl was still alive. As she browned some bacon under the grill, her phone began to ring.

'Morning Ms Adams, it's Steve from Safe & Secure. I'm sorry I never got to yours yesterday, I have some trouble with the van. However, I can call by now and get your camera up and running if you'd like?'

She looked at her watch; she had an hour or so to spare before she needed to get to work. 'That's okay, I'd cancelled anyway, did they not let you know? Thank you, that would be great.'

She flipped the bacon, toasted a bagel and poured boiling water into the cafetière. Before she could load it onto a tray, the intercom buzzed. She answered it, surprised to hear Steve's voice already. Opening the gates, she watched as he drove through. He had a different van from the last time, so at least he wasn't bullshitting her. She hated nothing more than being lied to. She'd much rather him have say he couldn't be arsed and had sacked work off for the day than lie to her.

She opened the front door as he strode towards her, smiling.

'It's a lovely day again. This won't take long then I'll be on my way.'

She stepped to one side to let him in, closing the door behind him. Letting him get on with his work, she sat and ate her breakfast, feeling slightly guilty.

'Would you like a bacon sandwich and a coffee?'

Steve, who was up his ladder replacing the missing part from the camera, turned to look at her. 'I've already eaten, but I'd love a coffee if that's okay.'

She stood up, making him his drink in one of the huge mugs she'd bought and didn't really use. He finished screwing the camera back together and climbed back down. He walked into the open-plan kitchen; Beth pointed at the mug, which he picked up. Inhaling the aroma, he grinned.

'There's nothing like a decent cup of coffee to set you up for the day. I don't mind buying a sausage sarnie from greasy Joe's burger van, but I draw the line at his shite coffee.'

Beth laughed. 'Urgh, rather you than me. I'd be scared to eat something from a roadside van.'

'Needs must, I was too late to feed myself today. Hey, are you going to the pub again tonight? I'll be there; you said I could buy you a drink another time.'

She felt her cheeks turn pink. He was nice even if he was a little bit forward.

'It depends how busy work is.'

'Don't you go to self-defence on a Wednesday?'

She frowned, wondering how the hell he knew that.

'Sorry, God, that makes me sound like a right stalker. I'm not, I swear. I know Phil who runs the classes, and I was talking to him after you left the pub the other night. He mentioned that you were a regular, sorry. I wasn't talking about you. I should probably shut up now.'

His cheeks had turned even pinker than hers, and she couldn't help but smile at him.

'I do, I really enjoy it. Sometimes I fit in an extra class, but you're right: Wednesday's my usual night. I'll be going to class – work permitting – and as long as I don't get called out there's a good chance I'll be going to The Stag for a drink after.'

His smile was so big it actually melted her heart a little. 'Wow, that's cool. I'll probably see you there then.'

He finished his drink and Beth wondered how on earth she'd just managed to agree to go for drinks with the security guy. He walked to the sink and rinsed out the mug – which raised him slightly in her good books. Then he set about snapping shut his toolbox and carrying his ladders back out to the van. Beth walked him to the door; out in the drive he turned to wave at her. She lifted her hand and waved back, then closed the door and let out a laugh so loud it filled the hallway. She watched him leave on the camera and shut the gates behind him then set about rinsing her own breakfast dishes.

Once they were stacked in the dishwasher, she opened the sliding doors and stepped outside. The sun was warming up nicely over the lake and she watched as one of the steam boats full of tourists sailed past. It was busy despite it being early; this weather was clearly good for business.

As Beth turned to head back inside, she noticed something fluttering on the patio table. She strolled over to pick it up, wondering who could have left it there.

For a few seconds she couldn't take in what she was seeing, and then tilting her head she let out a gasp: now she understood what it was. She was looking at a bloodied acrylic fingernail. It had been placed on top of a photograph of a girl who'd been tied up. It was dark, and her expression showed she'd been startled and scared by the bright camera flash that had gone off inches from her face.

Beth bent to examine it more closely: she knew better than to pick up potential forensic evidence. The woman's wrists were tied together, her fingers all bloody and torn. For the first time in days

Beth felt a full-blown panic attack begin as her lungs constricted and she struggled to breathe. The longer she looked at the photo, the harder it was to suck in any air to feed her racing heart.

Who had put this there?

More to the point, how had they even got inside the perimeter of her property?

She ran back inside, slamming the doors shut and locking them. Her hands shaking, she dialled Josh's number and swore when it went straight to voicemail.

# CHAPTER SIXTY-SIX

Josh watched James Dean walk out of the station with his solicitor on the cameras inside the custody suite. They didn't have enough to hold him or charge him with, and he'd been released on bail pending further enquiries. James stopped before he got into the passenger side of the solicitor's car, turned and stuck two fingers up at the camera.

'Bastard,' Josh muttered. The custody sergeant just shrugged.

'You win some, you lose some.'

'He's an arse. I wish the search team had turned up something better.'

'Like what, a body?' The sergeant let out a snigger. Stan had filled him in on the embalmed body that had been smack bang in the middle of their fingertip search of the funeral home.

'There were plenty of bodies, just not the one I was looking for.'

Josh walked away before he lost it. He was tired, angry, hungry and wanting to argue with anyone looking for it. No sleep tended to have that effect on him. He'd sent Sam home late last night; she had a family and a life to take care of, while he had endless hours to spend questioning James.

It hadn't worked, though; not once had he tripped himself up. He admitted to associating with Chantel Price, said she would hang around, and yes he'd had sex with her a couple of times, but that was it. He didn't have any reason to hurt her and he definitely did not kill her. They had nothing of value forensically to link him to the crime. So where did that leave this investigation? Up shit creek, that's where.

Jason Thompson was nowhere to be found and a search of his flat and workplace had yielded absolutely nothing. Sykes had reported that when the care home staff had been questioned, they'd found that Chantel Price would sleep with anybody for a bit of money or recreational drugs. Walking into the office, he checked the whiteboards; someone had put a big tick next to James Dean's name, and the search of the funeral home had been ticked off. There was still a question mark next to Thompson.

Sitting down at his desk, he opened the drawer and took out his phone. It had died whilst he'd been in his marathon interview with James Dean. He plugged it into the charger and set about making a mug of coffee. He then logged onto the computer and began scrolling through the missing person's report for Annie Potts, needing to check which tasks had been completed. They couldn't perform cell site analysis on her mobile phone because it had been left behind in her room. If she'd had that on her when she'd been taken, they would have been able to pinpoint her location to within three kilometres. Something to go on, at least. They could have flooded the area with officers. But there was no trail for the dog to follow. The press release hadn't come up with any leads that helped; family and friends had been interviewed; Estelle had been in and done a video profile of the man she'd slept with. Everything was being done to trace him: the profile was being printed in tomorrow's local paper with the caption 'Do You Know This Man?' They'd drafted in extra staff to answer the phones in case they were flooded with calls in the morning. Somehow Josh didn't think it would be the case. If Annie's abductor was smart, he would have worn some kind of disguise.

Josh looked down at his notes. Most of the tasks had been completed: ticked off with no result, nothing to move the investigation forward. They were no closer to finding Annie Potts than they'd been on Monday, and the trail to Chantel's killer was as cold as his last cup of coffee. Under normal procedures, the next thing would be to draft in extra officers to organise a search of every derelict building in the area – but that was a big job, and he knew they could potentially waste valuable time. He considered what he knew about the killer, assuming still that the killer and the kidnapper were the same person, and worked up a list of further tasks to be ticked off.

*Likely to be local, knowledge of the cemetery, the area, camera aware.*
*All recently released violent offenders spoken to and their home addresses checked.*
*Possible local accent, witness Estelle Carter not a hundred per cent sure.*
*CCTV footage from the nightclub sent off to be enhanced.*
*Get a photofit made up.*
*Hotel to be searched from top to bottom again by task force and dog handler.*
*Chase up detailed site plan of the cemetery with council.*
*Any abandoned, disused buildings to be searched.*
*PCSOs out canvassing local businesses, speaking to members of the public, tourists.*

He couldn't think of anything else for the time being.

His phone began to vibrate with missed calls and messages. He glanced at it. A missed call from Beth. She'd left a voicemail, too.

# CHAPTER SIXTY-SEVEN

Beth ran to check the front door was locked. It was, thank goodness. Then, running into the kitchen she picked out the heavier of the two hammers she had in the tool drawer. She knew the score: self-defence with a household item would hold up much better in court than if she used a knife – not that she'd hesitate if she had to use a knife. Her legs were shaking, but not as much as her hands. She didn't understand how or why someone had left the photograph and the fingernail on her patio table, or how long they had sat there, exposed to the elements. She thought back over the last few hours; she'd come home last night but hadn't gone outside. She'd been in and out of the house all day, so it could have been left there at any point.

Tucking her phone in her pocket, she held her breath as she heard the floorboard above her creak ever so slightly, as if someone had put their weight on it and had stopped, mid-step. She thought about running to her safe room and locking herself in, but fear took over. She wanted to get out of here, as far away as possible and not give anyone the chance to get the better of her.

Beth's blood went cold; it was happening all over again, just like the last time. She gripped the hammer, picked up her car keys and began to edge towards the front door. Pulling out her phone, she dialled 999 and heard a voice tell her she was being directed to Cumbria Constabulary. The automated voice sounded too loud in the house, which was too quiet; whoever was up there would hear the voice on the end of the phone and she didn't want them to know she knew they were up there. She hung up, knowing that the police would trace the abandoned treble nine call and send officers round to investigate. But she couldn't take the chance of whoever was upstairs getting the upper hand. She needed to get out and she needed to get out right now.

Phil reminded them every week there was no shame in running in a dangerous situation, that it was much safer to try and run to safety than to stay and fight. She was almost at the front door, her heart pounding so hard she slid the bolt back with a loud thud and threw it open.

'Thank goodness you've come!' she screeched, and instinctively dived towards the person standing on her doorstep. She was surprised to see him but without wasting a moment she lifted her finger to her lips to keep him quiet.

He looked puzzled as she ran at him and whispered, 'There's someone in my house, we need to get out now.'

She fell into his open arms and he pulled her close then ran with her towards the car. Beth clambered inside, simultaneously starting the engine and frantically pressing the button on the remote to open the gates.

She turned in surprise when he jumped in beside her.

'What's going on?'

'I've phoned the police; there's an intruder in my house. We have to get away from here.'

He glared at her. 'There's no one inside your house.'

She slowly turned to look at him, dread filling the pit of her stomach. 'You don't know that.'

He smiled. 'I do, because I'm right here. Beth.'

She tried to open her door, but he lunged for her; grabbing a handful of her hair, he launched her head against the steering wheel so hard she felt an explosion of pain and darkness seep into her mind. She clawed at his hands, trying to get him to loosen his grip, but he pulled her hair even tighter and smashed her head into the driver's window so hard it cracked the glass. With his other hand he pulled a cloth out of his pocket and the strong, sweet smell of chemicals filled the car.

She tried to scream, but he rammed it into her mouth and under her nose. Already feeling faint and disorientated, her mind began to drift and everything turned black.

# CHAPTER SIXTY-EIGHT

Josh rang her back, but Beth's phone kept on ringing. Next, he dialled his voicemail and his blood froze as if he'd been dunked into an ice bath.

'Josh, I need you at mine now. Someone has been here. Th-there's a f-f-fingernail and photograph. Please ring me back as soon as you get this; please, Josh. Hurry.'

Josh's hands were shaking as he scrambled on his desk for his police radio.

'Control, this is 1195; send a patrol IR over to Water's Edge on Fell Road. This is urgent, I believe the occupant is in danger.'

'Sarge, we already have one on its way,' came the reply over the airwaves. 'There was an abandoned treble nine call. Over twenty minutes ago now.'

'I want as many patrols as possible sent immediately.'

'Roger.'

Josh took his CS gas from his top drawer, then handcuffs and his baton that he hadn't had cause to even think about using in at least eight years. Sam walked in, took one look at his face and did the same. She followed him out of the door as he raced down to the car park.

'Josh, what's wrong?'

'It's Beth Adams, I think she's being targeted by the killer.'

'Do you want me to drive?'

He shook his head, grabbing a set of van keys off the board by the rear doors, and ran out into the car park.

# CHAPTER SIXTY-NINE

As he drove out of the gates and along the road, his heart was racing. This had been so bold and so brilliant it couldn't have gone any better. It was broad daylight, so he couldn't take her to her final resting place until the sun set. He could take her home, but he'd rather not have her in his house; if things got out of hand it would make an awful mess and that might blow his cover. He didn't want to ruin it now he finally had her. He heard sirens coming along the quiet stretch of road from the distance and put his foot down. He needed to get away from here as quickly as possible without drawing attention to the fact that, as well as having an unconscious woman in the back seat, he was driving her car.

He'd made it a fair distance from the house before a police van came speeding towards him from the opposite direction. He held his breath, wondering if it was all over, but he slid past unnoticed. Taking the road into Bowness which would lead him down to the marina, he formed a plan; it wasn't perfect, but it would buy him plenty of time to spend with her before it got dark.

As he drove past the florist's he considered stopping off to buy her some flowers, then he realised it was too risky. It was a shame, though; another time, another place, he'd really like to get to know her more intimately. Woo her with flowers and fine wine, keep her locked up beside him. The two of them could have been so happy, but unfortunately for her he couldn't do that. If he'd had a place he could keep her captive for more than a few hours and not get caught he would have. It wouldn't work out, though, he knew. She'd battle her way out of it. He was just going to have to enjoy what precious time he had with her.

# CHAPTER SEVENTY

Robert Hartshorn began to cough – that familiar painful, throaty, chesty cough that was killing him. Opening his eyes, he had to take a moment to get his bearings; someone was helping him to sit up. He got a whiff of the strong smell of disinfectant that permanently lingered in the air of the hospital wing of the prison and realised exactly where he was. He looked at the unconcerned nurse holding his frail arm. She placed the plastic mask of the nebuliser over his nose and mouth, telling him to just breathe. He stuck a thumb up at her, and she backed away from him. Life was cruel. He'd never smoked in his life yet here he was dying of lung cancer.

It hadn't all been a waste, not at first when he'd been an excellent orthopaedic surgeon, cared for his patients and made a difference to their lives. He just wished he'd never met him. Before that day his own sick fantasies were nothing more than that: fantasies, not something he ever imagined he'd act out. Yes, he was a narcissist who'd enjoyed bullying his staff and making their lives a misery for his own pleasure. He'd thrived off belittling Beth, tearing shreds off her and then forcing her on rounds where he'd charm his patients until they were putty in his hands.

He'd been fascinated to discover several well-known killers had cited *The Collector* as the inspiration for their murders. Leonard Lake and Charles Ng had particularly made their mark on him. What had tied them and him together was that book. If that man hadn't overheard him asking for it and then offered him a copy, they never would have forged their deadly friendship. He'd wanted to feel what it was like to kill someone, to take control of them. To have the power of life or death, and Beth had seemed like the perfect victim; she had no close family, friends that were used to going weeks without seeing her and she already looked up to and trusted him. If he'd had a place to keep her captive, he would have.

Doubt had begun to creep in, though, before the night of the party; even though he'd planned it all down to the last, minute detail he had almost backed out. Aware of how selfish he was being by depriving the world of a talented doctor, a tiny seed of guilt had been planted. Now after all these years of not seeing her that seed had grown. Some would say it was his conscience kicking in. But he wouldn't.

As his breathing began to ease and the tightness in his chest became bearable, he knew what he had to do. The bitch had never replied to his letters; he didn't think she bothered to read them. He'd never considered speaking to the police about *him* before, but he knew that he had to before it was too late. She was his to kill and *he* had no right to take that one thing, the only thing from him.

He waved the nurse over. She looked at him and held up her hand to ask him to wait. He shook his head and beckoned her over again, this time more urgently. Sighing, she crossed the room towards him. Pulling down his mask, he croaked, 'Get me a guard, I need to speak to someone.'

'I will when Abby comes back off her break, I'm on my own.'

'Where's the guard who was watching this block?'

'With Abby.' She rolled her eyes.

'Phone someone and tell them it's a matter of life or death.'

'Whose life or death, Robert, how would you know?'

Lunging for her, he wrapped the elastic cord from the nebuliser around her neck, pulling it tight.

'Yours, you stupid bitch, I need to speak to someone. Now.'

The only other patient in the wing finally opened his eyes at the racket. Turning, he stared at the sight of Robert, wheezing whilst trying to strangle the nurse. He got out of bed and hobbled towards the emergency button on the wall by the nurses' desk. Slamming his palm on it, the alarm began to ring and the thundering sound of footsteps began to head their way.

Robert smiled to himself. He needed fast action and this was the quickest way to ensure he was listened to. He didn't want them to think it was the rambling of a morphine-infused brain.

The swarm of guards that rushed into the small wing was impressive. They took one look at the situation and began to shout at him to let her go.

Robert smiled at them and whispered in her ear.

'I'm not going to hurt you. I just need to talk to the governor, and this is the only way to get him to come and pay me a visit.'

She sobbed; obviously she didn't believe him. He didn't care. His chest was on fire, burning with the effort, but still he kept a tight grip on her.

'I need to speak to the governor now.'

'Come on, Robert, that's not going to happen, is it? Let her go and then we can arrange for you to speak to him.'

'No, I want to speak to him, and a copper called Josh Walker. Get hold of him, tell him it's life or death and I need to speak to him before someone he saved once before needs saving again.'

The burly guard who had stepped a little closer looked behind at the others. Turning back, he looked at the whimpering nurse being choked by the man who looked as if he could pass away at any given moment. He might be frail, but there was no telling what he could do because he had nothing to lose.

'Go get the boss.'

The younger guard, who was only on his second day as a newly trained prison officer, turned and ran as fast as he could towards the governor's office, hoping he was in.

# CHAPTER SEVENTY-ONE

Barry had a daily paper tucked under one arm and a spade under the other. He'd done nothing but worry about where that stupid bugger Jason had disappeared to. He didn't think for one minute he'd hidden that girl in the grave; for one thing he was far too lazy to go to the effort of putting a body in there and shovelling soil on top of it. No, as far as he was concerned, the daft sod was guilty of maybe shagging the girl or selling her a bit of weed. As he strolled up the hill to the new grave he was in the process of digging, he nodded at the huge monument as usual. He spotted a bunch of red roses in the cracked vase at the base of it. In all the years he'd worked here not once had he seen anyone at this grave. He hesitated then turned to look at it, walking closer. He stood there staring at the wilted roses. Why would someone come here and lay a bunch of red roses after all this time? A memory of seeing someone here the other day itched at the back of his mind. Bending down, he checked to see if there was a note with them, but there wasn't. Hadn't there been something familiar about him?

*Of Your Charity,*
*Pray for the Repose of the Soul*
*of Father Abraham Caffrey*

The date read 1888. Why would someone lay flowers here now, after all this time? He shook his head and continued walking towards the chapel. Taking out his phone, he dialled Jason's number again. Swearing when it went straight to voicemail. Again.

'Here, you stupid bugger. I know you had nowt to do with that dead girl, so get yourself back here and we'll sort it out. I need a hand, not that you did much but that's beside the point. If you get this message stop messing around and come back. I'll go with you to the cop shop, lad, and we'll put it right.'

Ending the call, he put the phone in his pocket and wiped his brow with his sleeve. It was a warm day and that hill never got any easier to climb no matter how many times a day he walked up it. Almost parallel with the open grave where it all began, he noticed another bunch of now-faded, dried-up red roses on a grave opposite. He walked towards it. They were similar to the ones left at the base of the monument to the priest. Someone called Vincent Naylor was interred here, the date on the grave stone 1945. He scratched at his head; something wasn't right. Who was leaving flowers around the graveyard? Sitting down on the marble bench opposite the chapel, he placed the spade next to him and shut his eyes. Was it the same guy? Why would a man visit two graves on different days and lay the same red roses for men who died years ago? Was there a bloke here the day the girl was found in the grave? The thought tugged at the edge of Barry's consciousness; there was something he'd missed. They had plenty of regulars at the cemetery, but this guy was new. The guy in the beige baseball cap. He'd seen him down by the mausoleums, he was sure of it.

Taking out his phone again, this time he dialled 101 and waited to be put through to Cumbria Constabulary. He needed to talk to that detective, Josh. He was pretty sure that the guy visiting the graves had been up to something. He wasn't sure what, but he needed checking out. It wasn't as if the coppers had anything better to do. They weren't exactly on fire, and judging by the story on the front of the local paper they were no closer to finding that missing woman.

# CHAPTER SEVENTY-TWO

The gates to Beth's house were wide open and Josh drove the van at speed straight through them. His heart was pounding in his throat as if he was about to regurgitate it. He didn't think he'd ever felt panic like it in his entire life. The night he'd answered the call when she was attacked he hadn't had time to think. Right now, he wanted more than anything to find her sitting on the patio, drinking wine and staring out at the lake. He knew that wasn't going to happen though. Never, in all the time he'd come to know Beth, had she ever left the entrance gates wide open.

Suddenly his mouth was dry, and his palms were sweaty. He was terrified of what he might find inside. Why hadn't he come back last night? Why had he pulled an all-nighter? He could have been here with her and protected her. Running from the van, he saw the front door ajar and knew then that he was too late. He stopped, tugged on a pair of bright blue rubber gloves and motioned for Sam to do the same. Stepping inside, he shouted, 'Beth, it's the police. Where are you?'

Sam pointed to the stairs, and he nodded. Running up them two at a time, he checked every room. No sign of Beth, but also no sign of a struggle; everywhere was as neat and clutter free as it always was. Apart from the guest room where his case was thrown on the middle of the bed looking distinctly out of place.

Sam's voice echoed up the stairs. 'She's not here.'

Josh rushed back downstairs to see for himself, his breathing starting to slow. He heard the sirens as the backup van arrived.

'Her car isn't here, maybe she's gone to the station.'

'No, her voice was panicked. She said she'd found a fingernail and a photograph; we need to find them.'

He looked around at the pristine white granite worktops, and the dining table and then he glanced outside. He gasped. He could see it on the table, the small photograph with a single, pink, bloodied nail sitting on top of it. Unlocking the door, he slid it open and stepped through the gap. He recognised the terrified woman – it was Annie Potts – and knew immediately that Beth wouldn't have left evidence this vital exposed to the elements no matter how scared she was. She'd have bagged it up or covered it up; a strong gust of wind and it could have blown down to the lake or got lost in the trees.

The two officers that came running in both stopped as he lifted his hand up.

'She's not here, but I'm treating this as a crime scene. Thank you, but you need to retrace your steps and go back outside. Can you request CSI and the DCI to attend.'

'Yes, Sarge.'

Both of them walked back out without touching anything.

Josh looked at Sam.

'I'm wondering if she left in a hurry or was taken as she was trying to leave.'

'Would she have left the house insecure though, Josh? I mean this is Beth we're talking about. I've never known anyone so security conscious.'

'True, but she has a bloody good reason for that, don't you think?'

'Yes, I didn't mean it that way. It's not a criticism. What I meant is she's spent the last few years of her life living in fear, so I don't think she'd run out of here and leave the door open no matter how spooked she was. If she had wouldn't she be on the phone to you or the control room right now? What about her safe room, did you check that?'

He nodded. 'It's empty. Yes, she would. She wouldn't run away and hide, it's not her style. So she got scared, ran to the front door to leave.'

'And got ambushed.'

'How did they get in the gates though? In fact, how did they even get out here? It's a fair distance from civilisation. I want an area search for an abandoned car. I also want an ANPR alert put out on Beth's car.'

He pulled his radio out and began issuing orders to the control room. His heart was still racing but he'd switched into work mode. He could do this. The trail was minutes old. Walking down towards the lake, he needed to clear his head and think; he also didn't want Sam or the two officers standing by the gates to see the tears in his eyes.

As he stared out onto the calm water, he whispered, 'Hold on, Beth, I'm coming, and I'll find you.'

# CHAPTER SEVENTY-THREE

Josh's phone began to ring. He looked down at the display, begging for it to be Beth's name flashing on it.

*Unknown number*

So it must be work. He answered it.

'Sarge, there's a phone call for you. It's from a Barry Evans. He said you were talking to him the other day about the missing girl. Should I put him through?'

'I'm a bit busy now, tell him I'll ring him back.'

'He said you would want to know he thinks he knows who it is.'

'Put him through.'

He waited for the call to be patched through wondering what information Barry could have after so many days.

'Is this Josh?'

'It is, how can I help you, Barry?'

'You know the other day when you were here looking for that girl, did you see the man standing at the old monument just off the main path?'

'No. Why?'

'Well I been thinking, in all the years I've worked here no one has ever had reason to visit that particular grave. It's a memorial to a Catholic priest from back in 1888. It's odd, I think, and then the day we found the girl's body, when we were waiting around for you coppers to come, I saw him then, too. He was standing at a grave not too far from where we were working, a bunch of red roses like the ones left at the priest's monument in his hands.'

'Whose grave was that? Did you notice? Have you looked?'

'Yes, I did, it belongs to Vincent Naylor. He died in 1945; now I can't be a hundred per cent positive but I'm pretty sure there has never been flowers laid there either.'

Josh was trying to figure out what it meant: was there some connection between the graves and the killer?

'Barry, I'm on my way. Can you try and keep an eye on both graves until I get there? I need them to be searched by CSI.'

'Well I'll try, but they're a bit of a distance away from each other and there's only one of me.'

'Go back to the monument: that was only two days ago. If you see him then walk away, don't approach him and try not to look at him. Whoever it is they're *extremely dangerous.*'

'You don't need to tell me that. Any funny business and I'll smack him across the back of the head with my spade.'

Josh smiled and ended the call feeling hopeful. There was some connection to the cemetery; perhaps everything led back to there. He wanted a full search of the area conducted and the dogs brought back. He shouted to Sam.

'I have to go to the cemetery. Can you stay here and coordinate the search, please?'

'What are you going there for?'

'Barry has come up with some vital information, and I need to go speak to him now.'

'Yes, Josh, be careful. What if it's him?'

As he climbed inside the van he wondered if Sam had a point: Barry could well be the man they were looking for. Life would be easier if it was Barry, he thought. He had access to the graves, the experience. He also had a wife and an alibi, not that they were concrete evidence. He didn't care, though, he was pretty confident he could handle Barry if he turned all psychopathic on him.

Josh knew without a shadow of a doubt he'd risk his own life to save Beth's.

# CHAPTER SEVENTY-FOUR

The sun had disappeared behind a huge, dark cloud as Josh arrived at the cemetery gates. Never had the place looked so foreboding, which kind of matched his mood. He knew something big was going to happen and he was praying that it was good and that he wasn't too late to help both Annie and Beth. He drove slowly up the hill. The cemetery was deserted but for Barry hovering around by the huge stone monument in the distance. Parking, Josh jumped out of the van and walked towards him. He studied his face: could it be him, could Barry be responsible for the devastation that had been wreaked on this normally tranquil village?

'Thank the Lord you're here, I'm not a wuss or anything but I've been scaring myself shitless waiting for you to arrive. The place is dead, there's no one around but I keep hearing noises and looking over my shoulder in case he's creeping up on me.'

Barry's face was ashen, and he was acting all jittery: not the behaviour of a cold calculated killer.

'Thank you, I've asked for patrols to come. But there's another job on at the moment the local officers are tied up with; backup is on its way from Barrow.'

Barry looked at him. 'Barrow, Jesus Christ, let's hope we don't need them in the next ten minutes then or we've had it. I've spoken to Jason, I told you it wasn't him. He ran because he was scared, but has promised he'll come to the station with me tomorrow.'

Josh nodded, then walked towards the monument and bent down to look at the flowers. They were wrapped in pale pink paper with a layer of plastic wrapping and didn't look like the kind of flowers you picked up in the supermarket. At least that narrowed it down a little: they could check the local florists, but it would all take time. If they could identify where the flowers came from then maybe they would be able to find some better CCTV evidence of the guy who had bought them.

'Have you ever noticed him hanging around other places in here? Is there anywhere else he could go, are there any old buildings that you might have forgotten about when we were looking the other day? I've finally been sent a plan of the cemetery that I requested days ago and had a brief look. What about the crypts, could he access them?'

Barry's mouth dropped open and his face turned even paler than it already was as he let out a groan.

'The crypts and mausoleums in the old part of the cemetery, well yes, but there's no way anyone could get inside them. I'm so sorry. I never go down there. It didn't enter my head.'

Josh felt a spark of hope fire inside his chest.

Barry continued. 'They've been sealed off for years, they're not safe. We don't go down there to be honest because it's so overgrown and dangerous.'

'I need you to take me there now.'

Barry nodded. He followed Josh to the van, and they got inside. He directed him along the paths which got narrower and more overgrown as they drove towards the old part that was out of bounds.

'They're just along there, but you'll have to walk from here.'

Barry led the way, but Josh paused. The grass was flattened on one side by something heavy like a car or van. 'Do you ever drive down here?'

'No, got no reason to. It's off limits until the friends of the cemetery and the council stop arguing over who can repair and maintain it.'

'Well someone has been down here and recently.' Josh could see the crumbling, leaning row of crypts a short distance in front of him and began to run towards them, shouting, 'Beth, Beth, are you there?' As he got closer the stench of decomposition filled the air, and he heard Barry gag behind him.

'What is that smell?'

'Barry, I need you to stay there. Don't come any closer.'

He let out a groan so loud it echoed around them. 'This is my fault; I didn't even think about the mausoleums. I'm so sorry.'

Josh turned to look at the man, who was visibly trembling and on the verge of tears.

'No, this isn't your fault. If it wasn't for you we wouldn't be here right now, this is the fault of whoever decided to do this.'

He knew that Barry would forever lay the blame on himself. Just as Josh would lay the blame at his own door. They had been so close; he didn't understand why he didn't know about this place. He was going to find Annie Potts, and not the way he'd wanted to. He'd hoped she'd be alive but, judging by the strong smell and the buzzing of flies, it wasn't going to be the case. His knees threatened to sag under his weight he felt so deflated; for once he'd have liked to have made the difference, to have beaten this sick bastard at his own game and saved Annie before it came to this. Unless there was someone else? It couldn't be Beth, could it? No, of course not. It had been less than an hour since he'd rushed to her house. Even if she'd been killed straight away it wouldn't smell like this. He looked at the row of oak doors, watching to see which one the bluebottles were flying in and out of. It didn't take long before a fat fly buzzed its way through the narrow slit in the door at the far end. He radioed the control room.

'How long before patrols arrive?'

A voice shouted up. 'Fifteen minutes, we're stuck in traffic. Even with the blues on there's nowhere to go. The roads are gridlocked because of the roadworks.'

Josh swore; he couldn't wait. Beth could be in there and need medical assistance, so he ran towards the door. The smell was almost overpowering; he'd smelled it many times before: the cloying smell of death which clung to every pore and shred of material you wore, catching in the back of your throat. Reaching out with a gloved hand, he pushed the door. It didn't move. It was stuck. He turned and waved Barry over.

'Can you help me shove it open?'

To give the man his dues, he ran over and placed his hands on the door next to Josh, and between the pair of them they shoved it hard and it creaked open. He didn't have a torch on him, and it took a couple of seconds for his eyes to adjust to the darkness inside the small stone crypt.

'Beth,' he called out. Turning the torch function on his phone, he shone it around. She wasn't here. He felt his heart sink. He'd really thought he was going to find her. There were five more to check, though, so it wasn't completely hopeless. Inside there was a stone tomb in the middle of the floor, and on a shelf along the back wall were the skeletal remains of who he assumed had once resided inside the tomb. They were old, there wasn't a scrap of body tissue on them. The heavy lid of the tomb didn't sit quite right; there were fresh marks in the stone where it had been moved. In the light it looked as if it was moving, but he realised it was the flies that were angrily buzzing and crawling all over it trying to find a way in.

He stepped towards the tomb, waving his arms around and clapping. The flies took off in a cloud of blackness and flew out of the door; several hangers-on stayed put, buzzing around the confined space. He put his phone down and bent to push the lid to one side. The smell was unbearable. Barry rushed over to help him and between the pair of them they managed to push it off enough for Josh to shine the light inside it. Picking up his phone, he hadn't realised just how much his hands were shaking until he shone it through the gap.

Barry let out a gasp next to him. The glassy, dead eyes staring up at them were indeed those of his missing girl. There was a length of material around Annie Potts's mouth which wouldn't have made it any easier to breathe. Josh felt a wave of sorrow wash over his entire body; he was too late. He could hear sirens in the distance. Glancing back down into the tomb, he watched as a bluebottle landed on Annie's nose and began to bury itself inside her nostril. This was too much for Barry, who began to vomit into his hands. He turned and ran outside, falling onto his knees, and spewed hot vomit into the long grass. Josh followed him, the horror almost too much to bear. He'd let her down. Screwed up and now Annie was dead.

So where was Beth?

# CHAPTER SEVENTY-FIVE

Beth could feel the gentle sway as her body moved slightly. She was on water, on a boat, it seemed. How had she got here? Then she felt the tight band of material inside her mouth cutting into the soft flesh of her cheeks. It all came flooding back to her. The physical pain of betrayal felt like her heart had torn in two. She'd trusted him more than anyone, put her faith in him. Why was he doing this to her and why did he kill the other girl? She tried to move her hands and feet: it was no good – they were tied up tight. Stifling a sob, she knew that crying wasn't going to help her. She wondered if Josh had got her message. She had no idea what time it was, as it was dark in the cramped space she'd been thrown into. There wasn't much room to move, even though her knees were slightly bent; if she turned her face to the left or right it was practically touching cold metal. The bastard had used chloroform to render her unconscious. The distinct smell was like no other. He'd known she'd fight him. She guessed that was why he'd chosen to knock her out with chemicals.

As she lay there in the dark she felt more hopeless than she had in years. When Robert had attacked her there had been no time to think about it. It had been a fight to survive, not like this. She was helpless, unable to do a single thing. Her only hope now was in Josh figuring it all out and rushing to save her like he did the last time. He'd been her knight in shining armour once upon a time. A tear rolled down her cheek but she didn't realise she was crying until it was closely followed by another.

The boat lurched as she heard heavy footsteps on the deck above her. What was he doing? Was it his boat? She tried to scream, but the muffled sounds were pathetic. No one was ever going to hear her over the noise of the engine and the sound of the boat as it sped through the water. Life was cruel, she knew that. Her job as a forensic pathologist had taught her just how cruel it could be – innocent children dying from cancer they had no right to suffer from; teenagers who decided life was too hard and killed themselves before it had even begun. What had made her become such a victim? Why was she so appealing to killers? She was a good person. Panic filled her lungs and she began to thrash around, trying to make as much noise as possible. A loud thud directly above her and then the hatch was lifted. She stopped moving as his huge outline towered over her and made her realise just how futile her attempts were. He could reach in and snap her neck before she could blink if he wanted to.

'Shut the fuck up, no one can hear you. No one is coming to rescue you, so I suggest you lie there and behave yourself.'

The hatch was slammed back down, and she welcomed the darkness. It was far better to be alone in the dark than have to face him. She tried to concentrate on her breath, to slow everything down. There was a thudding in her head far worse than any headache she'd ever suffered. Closing her eyes, she felt an overwhelming sense of tiredness take over.

Maybe she'd wake up to find this was all a bad dream. Or maybe she'd drift off into a world of darkness, where she would know nothing, there would be no pain, no worry and no fear.

Or maybe Josh would find her. And if he did, she would tell him how much she loved him. No more wasting time or precious years of her life.

# CHAPTER SEVENTY-SIX

Josh's phone rang again and again. He sat in the long grass and reached into his pocket to answer it.

It was a voice he'd never heard before.

'Is this Detective Sergeant Josh Walker?'

'Speaking.'

'My name is Andrew Salt, I'm the governor of Haverigg Prison. We have a bit of a situation going on here that you might be able to help with.'

'I'm sorry, Andrew, but I'm in the middle of a high-risk missing person's case. On top of that I've just discovered a body – not of the missing person. So, I'm a little tied up.' He wiped dirt from his palm.

'This is also life or death. Well, it is for the nurse who currently has a nebuliser tightly wrapped around her throat by one of the patients in our hospital wing.'

Josh felt bad for the nurse, for the governor's situation, but didn't have time for this. It wasn't in his remit in any case; he had no jurisdiction over what went on inside a prison.

'I don't know why you think this has something to do with me?'

'The prisoner is requesting to speak to you; he said it's a life or death situation and only you will do.'

'Who is this prisoner? Name?'

'I believe you know him. Robert Hartshorn.'

At the mention of a name from all those years ago, a name he'd buried along with the memory of finding Beth at the last minute – almost too late – Josh felt the hairs on the back of his neck stand on end.

'I can't get there, are you familiar with his background?'

'I am indeed, and he said that he needs to speak to you about someone called Beth.'

'Can I speak to him on the phone?'

'Just a minute.'

Josh could hear a muffled conversation in the background and then a raspy voice echoed in his ear.

'I haven't got much time; I can't hold her much longer. I don't want to hurt her, but I needed to speak to you.'

The voice on the other end began to cough: a deep, rattling cough that made Josh want to cough for him.

'What's going on, Robert?'

'He's going to take Beth and hurt her, if he hasn't already. I've spent the last few years deeply regretting the hurt and pain that I caused her. I've written to her every month telling her this, but she has never replied. I don't blame her, it was unforgivable.' He began to cough once more, and this time it took longer for him to gain his composure.

'His name is Phil Sullivan; he runs a self-defence class that Beth attends. She knows him and trusts him. I also believe he killed the girl you found in the cemetery; he took another one.'

'How? How do you know all this?' Josh was suspicious. Robert was a psychopath; how could he trust him where Beth was involved? He'd have read about the case in the paper and guessed Beth would have been involved with the autopsy. He was wasting his time.

'Because he's an old friend, and he told me a long time ago that he would. It's taken him a lot of years to pluck up the courage. He came to see me yesterday—'

'Yesterday,' Josh interrupted. The details had only gone into the paper today.

'And he told me he was going to hurt her. He said he was going to finish what I started. You have to find him and stop him before he does. Please tell Beth I'm sorry for everything, I'm trying to save her.'

Josh wondered if he should tell him, but he said it anyway. 'It's too late, she's gone.'

Then he hung up. He wasn't giving Robert Hartshorn any more of his precious time. At least they had a name now. If Hartshorn was to be believed. But why would he lie?

Josh passed the name over the airwaves and asked for intelligence checks, address checks and a team to go to Phil Sullivan's house and put the door through.

He looked at Barry sprawled out in the grass, spewing up his guts. But before he could leave the cemetery and join in with the manhunt, he had to know for sure that Beth wasn't inside one of the other crypts. It could be a trick. He knew Robert from the days he'd listened to his evidence in court. To his poisonous lies at the interviews, and his pathetic excuse that he'd got the idea from a book.

'Barry,' he said. He nodded at the crowbar lying in the grass by his feet.

They'd managed to open three of the doors, there were just two more to go.

# CHAPTER SEVENTY-SEVEN

He'd wanted to introduce Beth to Annie; it didn't matter that she was dead. It certainly wouldn't have mattered to her, she liked dead people, spent her entire working day cutting them up and getting paid for it. It made him wonder if she was a little bit sick inside, too. After all, what sort of person chose that as their job?

He'd found a bottle of the whisky that Bob had hidden away in one of the hatches. He didn't think they'd have realised the boat was missing yet. He knew Bob tinkered around on it most days, but there had been no sign of him when he'd gone to where they kept it moored at Audrey's elderly aunt's house. And there had been no sign of life when he'd checked out the house and grounds, which had left him ample opportunity to throw Beth over his shoulder and carry her onto the boat. Hiding her car had been the most difficult part: he'd had to drive it off the road through the hedging into a field a little further down the road. It wasn't as if she'd be needing it again, was it?

Pouring himself a generous measure of whisky, he tipped his head back and downed it in one. The warmth as it burned all the way down the back of his throat felt good. Instantly he felt all the tension begin to drain away, and he knew it was all going to be good. As he sat and stared at the lake he wondered whether he should just drown her and be done with it. No, that wasn't what he'd envisioned for the formidable Doctor Elizabeth Adams.

He flicked through the book on his lap, turning up the dog-eared page to re-read his favourite paragraph: the bit where the collector shows her the room he's prepared for her. Robert had understood how words could excite, could lead to new meanings the author never envisaged. He'd wanted to shout out in court at that lawyer who'd had made out Robert had used it as an excuse, a way to get off, like people who claim some kind of insanity to get out of prison. But he was as sane as the next man. *The Collector* was a masterclass in how to lure a victim into your web. And he'd lured Beth all right. She was stuck like a fly.

The lake seemed quiet now, but there were still people out and about on boats. He could hear the faint music drifting on the breeze from their radios. He looked to the water's edge and the houses along it, nodding to himself. It was time to take Beth home and finish what Robert had started all those years ago. The police would be out searching for her; though they might have left someone at the house, he doubted it. But he could take care of them. It was secluded and private, exactly the kind of place to end a life.

He lifted the anchor and began steering the boat in the direction of Water's Edge. He could get her inside, kill her and be off on the boat before the police knew what was happening.

He spotted the house after an hour of cruising up and down that stretch of water, though he'd had to check to make sure it was the right one. From where he was sitting on the deck it looked like it. There was no jetty, but that didn't matter. He'd wait to see if there was any police activity at the house, then drag her to the shore.

Rooting around, he found a pair of small binoculars. There was someone inside wearing one of those white paper suits they wore on the television, traipsing to and from the house to a van outside. They were on their own, which was interesting. After a while, whoever it was made their way through the house turning off the lights in each room. Then they went to the van and drove off through the gates. That was better. Outside the gates was another police car with a police woman leaning on the bonnet talking to the person in the van. The copper walked across to the gates, pressed some numbers on the keypad and they began to close. Perfect, they were going to leave her house unattended. He supposed if Beth wasn't there, and they had all the evidence they could find – which he knew was nothing because he'd never set foot inside of the place – what more was there to do? It wouldn't surprise him if they left the officer out the front though, someone to guard the crime scene. It was a fair distance from the gates to the house. If he was lucky the patio doors would still be unlocked. He'd be able to take her in that way without any trouble.

She was finally going to die. No more second chances for Beth Adams. It was over.

# CHAPTER SEVENTY-EIGHT

The boat lurched to a halt, throwing Beth to one side. She had spent the best part of the last hour trying to loosen her hands, ignoring the pain in her wrists from the rope burns. The scar on her temple throbbed, a sign she'd survived once before and could survive this, telling herself she was grateful for it because it meant she was still alive. She had woken up from her dreamless sleep to the realisation it was up to her. She was on her own. Josh wouldn't be able to save her from this. He wouldn't have a clue where she was. She knew if she wanted to survive – and she did, she truly did – then it was all down to her. A steely determination had filled her insides. What had been the point of the years of self-defence classes if she was going to roll over and play dead? If Phil had had to drug her to get her to this point then he must think she posed a threat. He'd taught her a little too well. She felt liberated knowing that she wasn't going to lie down and take whatever he threw at her without a fight. No way. She'd spent years living in darkness and solitude, scared to live her life and get close to anyone in case they hurt her again. That wasn't living. She knew that now. She was just beginning to enjoy life again, so she'd be damned if she was going to let Phil take it all away from her before she'd even got the chance to try. For the first time she was ready to fight to the death, and if he got the better of her, well at least she tried.

Why? The question filled her mind. What had she ever done to him? What had made him hate her so much that he wanted her dead? After everything she'd been through, the time he'd spent teaching her how to look after herself – the years she'd trusted him. None of it made any sense. But the pain of betrayal was crushing.

Finally, after much wriggling, there was some movement between the rope and her slender wrists. Not much, but enough that she could work it looser. She had to be smart: she couldn't slip out of the ropes completely or he'd notice straight away, and she couldn't fight in this tiny, enclosed space. She needed to be out on the deck to stand a chance. She could hear him moving around above her and knew that he was up to something; any moment now he would open the hatch, she just had to keep calm and bide her time. It had crossed her mind that in order to survive she might have to seriously hurt him, even kill him. She had made her peace with that decision and knew that given the choice between her or him she'd do it without a second thought. Why should he get to spend the rest of his days in a cushy prison cell like Robert? She thought of the unopened letters in the drawer back home. It was time to move on.

Suddenly the hatch was pulled up and she tried not to jump, wanting him to think she still wasn't fully awake and aware. She kept her eyes shut as his dark shadow reached in and she felt his arms grab under her armpits and drag her out on the deck. After the overpowering smell of diesel in the hold, the fresh smell of the lake outside was refreshing. He threw her onto the deck, and she rolled to keep his attention away from her wrists: they were smarting and bleeding, but she could feel they were close to coming free.

'I don't for one minute think you're not awake, so quit with the acting.'

She opened her eyes, glaring at him.

'That's better. I have a nice little surprise for you. I'm taking you home.'

Despite the pep talk she'd given herself, her blood turned to ice water. She turned her head slightly and saw they were anchored not too far from the shore near to her beautiful house. Her sanctuary.

There was one thing, she thought, if this all went wrong she'd much rather die at home than buried underneath someone else's coffin in the freezing, cold ground.

She jumped as he began to untie her feet.

'Did you know we have a mutual acquaintance?'

She stared at him, not wanting to engage with this sick monster, but needing to know why she was here.

'I went to visit him yesterday. He's not very well, you know, but he sends his love and he said to ask you why you never answered his letters? I'm a dangerous person, by the way. You should have kept your distance from me. You would have if you'd known what was running through my head.'

Fear filled her veins at the thought of him and Robert together, discussing her in a prison visiting room. But why? What had she ever done to either of them to deserve this? To have drawn the attention of two men who wanted her dead.

'Go fuck yourself,' she whispered.

He began to laugh. 'I like how feisty you can be, Beth, I've always admired that about you. Despite being scared of your own shadow, underneath it all there's a lioness waiting to be set free. I'll miss our little grapples on the mat. I failed that night. You were too loud and that was our downfall. Yet you came back for more. Do you have any idea how the excitement of straddling you on that mat each week made me feel? It was almost as good as the first time I straddled you. Robert was watching from the kitchen, but he panicked and tried to shut you up. He should have cut his losses and run away like I did. How many times have I told you there is no shame in running when it comes to self-preservation? More times than I care to remember, but you never listened and here we are all over again. Do you ever get the feeling of déjà vu? You said yourself at the trial you didn't recognise the man who walked into your house that night. Why would you? Before then you'd barely given me a second glance, too busy with your perfect little life to notice me. I wasn't a fancy doctor. I didn't fit in with your social circle despite Robert trying his best to integrate me. Now, don't go getting any funny ideas.'

Pain ripped through her chest as the horror and realisation that the only man she'd trusted since that night was the man who had been there all along. It was Phil who had attacked her. Not Robert. Though Robert had been there. Had planned it with him. How had she never figured this out? Or had she known deep down inside all along, buried it in her memory, unable to add a stranger into her personal nightmares? Was that where her fear of new people came from? Her whole body felt as if it was shrinking inside of itself and she didn't know how much more of this her mind could take. Unable to speak, she nodded.

Before she could react he grabbed her and threw her into the icy depths of the lake. She felt herself begin to sink as her entire body constricted with the shock as the coldness enveloped her. Then there was a loud splash as he jumped in after her. His strong hands grabbed her, dragging her head above the water. He was much taller than she was, able to stand up in the water that was up to his shoulders.

Grabbing her by the hair, she felt excruciating pain as he dragged her towards the shore. Then they were out of the water and she was lying on the pebbly shore shivering, soaked to the bone, her scalp on fire.

Still she didn't try and wriggle out of the loosened ropes on her wrists because she knew she had to wait until there was a chance she could make it.

# CHAPTER SEVENTY-NINE

Josh stared into the last crypt. It was empty. Well, apart from the official occupants sealed into two stone tombs. Barry and the two officers who had turned up from Barrow were dripping with sweat after using a crowbar to loosen the lids and push them to one side to expose the skeletal remains. They'd done that in every single crypt and found nothing else; Beth wasn't anywhere in sight.

*Where are you, Beth, where has he taken you?* He thought back to that night in 2012, when he'd saved her life from a maniac attempting to kill her. How could this possibly be happening again? And, to make matters worse, Robert *knew* the killer, was prepared to give him up to save Beth. Robert had said the killer wanted to finish what Robert started. What did he mean? Did he intend to keep her captive? Where would kill her? Josh felt as if his head was filled with a thick fog, but that the answer was hiding somewhere deep inside.

Josh remembered breaking down the door of Beth's old home, crashing through just in time to stop Robert from killing her in her own kitchen.

And there it was, clear as day.

But her house – her new lakeside house – had been searched, CSI had been in and done another sweep of it. There was even a police guard watching the gate. Had they missed something, had they overlooked it? How could someone hide Beth near her own house without getting caught? Then it struck him, and his hands were dialling Sam's number before he even had time to process his thoughts. 'Where are you?'

'At the station picking up the DCI to come and take a look at your crime scene. Well done on the find, by the way.'

'She's dead. We failed her.'

'You *found* her, Josh. As sad as it is, at least her family will be able to bury her, grieve for her and eventually get some closure.'

'I need to know who's at Beth's house right now?'

'Claire left a while ago. There was an officer outside guarding the entrance, but an IR came in for an RTC and they were the nearest patrol, so at this moment... technically no one. But the gates are locked, so no one can get in.'

'I think we missed him. I think this Phil Sullivan who has Beth is going to take her back home. He must be close by. He has to be.'

'But we searched everywhere.'

'Not everywhere. He could be out on the lake. On a boat. He'd have a good view of the house from there, watching us search the house with a huge grin on his face, thinking how clever he is, how he's outsmarted us all. I'm on my way back right now. Can you see if you can find anyone to back me up?'

'Every available South Lakes and Barrow patrol is on their way up here to you, Josh. I'm probably the closest, I'm on my way. I'll bring the two PCs from Barrow. Between the four of us we might be able to take him down.'

He ended the call. It would take Sam at least twenty minutes to get there. It would take him ten minutes. He just hoped he wasn't too late, because he'd never live with himself if anything happened to Beth. The guilt over Annie Potts would haunt him for the rest of his life, he knew that; Chantel Price had been dead weeks before he even knew about her, but it still weighed heavy on his mind.

But there would be no more bodies to add to his list. Not today. Not Beth.

# CHAPTER EIGHTY

He dragged her to her feet, pulling her along by her hair until they reached the patio doors. For a second, she hoped they were locked. When the door handle didn't turn it gave her the incentive she needed. Whilst Phil was busy trying to get it open, she slipped the sodden rope from around her wrists, keeping them behind her back so he couldn't see. There wasn't anything within reach she could use as a weapon; the only thing she had was the rope and her arms. She knew how hard it was to strangle someone as strong as Phil, but if she could render him unconscious, she might be able to make a break for it. Coiling the length of rope around both hands she decided against it: she would have more power using her arm as a weapon. So she dropped the rope to the ground. Taking a running jump, she lunged at his back, jumping up and wrapping her arms around his neck. She squeezed as hard as she could.

'You fucking—' was all he managed before she cut off his air supply. He was trying to throw her off, thrashing from side to side, but she kept tight hold just like he'd taught her to in class, pressing even harder, blocking his airway.

He fell to his knees gasping but still she didn't let go. Until he lurched forward, throwing her over the top of his head. She smacked into the glass doors with force and let out a groan. Phil's face was purple with the lack of oxygen, and the fury etched across it terrified her, propelling her to move. She just managed to push herself out of his reach by centimetres as he lunged for her. Then she ran for the log pile she kept around the opposite side of the house.

She heard him stumbling after her, laughing. Then shouted, 'Oh, you little star. I taught you well. How proud I feel right now. My pupil has outsmarted me. I can hand on my heart say that I'm impressed. Then again, I've always known how special you are. To men like me and Robert you pose the greatest of thrills.'

She pushed herself even faster, her lungs burning. Reaching the pile of wood, she picked up a heavy log, turned and swung it as hard as she could. Phil, his head bent forward as he ran at her, was blindsided as the wood made contact with his head in a sickening thud. She knew she had done some damage. For the second time he fell to his knees; this time she stepped forward and hit him again. He collapsed to the floor in a heap, blood seeping from the gash in his head.

Without looking back, she ran towards the gates, typing in the code with fingers slippery with both their blood. When the gap was wide enough she squeezed through it.

And ran straight into Josh.

'Oh, my God, Beth. You're hurt?'

He wrapped his arms around her, pulling her close, and she felt herself sink into the warmth of his body. Her teeth were chattering.

'He's in there, I've hurt him, Josh. I think I might have killed him.'

'Good.'

Sirens got louder as a police van rounded the bend towards them. Three officers jumped out. Josh directed them inside. They ran with tasers and batons drawn into Beth's garden ready to do battle, as Josh ushered her into the back of the van to get her into the warmth and keep her safe. She'd seen enough. She didn't need to witness any more.

She didn't speak, words wouldn't come but she held on tight to Josh's hand.

He took his jacket off, wrapping it around her. Another car pulled up and Josh was relieved to see Sam arriving to back him up. Josh waved her over to the van and she stepped inside to take over so he could go and detain Phil.

Beth watched as he walked through the gates and prayed that he would be okay.

But the killer was out cold on the floor and despite everything that had happened to her, she'd never felt more alive.

# CHAPTER EIGHTY-ONE

## Two Weeks Later

Beth tugged off the gloves and plastic apron she was wearing over the top of her scrubs; next she stripped off the scrubs and stepped under the lukewarm shower spray. Her head still smarted a little where the scalp had been grazed, and she had a couple of bald spots where her hair had been ripped out. But to be honest she didn't care. All of her injuries had been superficial, nothing lasting, nothing permanent. Her wrists had scabbed up and almost healed. She was here to tell the tale and she'd never felt so thankful in all of her life. She'd come back to work to focus on something, driven crazy by wandering around the house feeling lost. It was different this time though: this time she had fought back herself, and won.

Phil had suffered a fractured skull, some internal bleeding and concussion but he was still alive. More importantly he was locked up. He'd never see the light of day again, she hoped; he'd killed two women that they knew about and he'd tried to kill her. She was the lucky one: Chantel and Annie hadn't had the chance to fight back. She had and was back at work living and breathing for them both. She owed it to them to live the life she still had.

She stared at the pile of cream envelopes on her desk.

Drying herself off, she dressed in the white linen trouser suit she'd spent a small fortune on. She normally wore it to court, but this was equally as important. Using the hairdryer, she blasted her hair, running the straighteners over it to smooth it down then applying some make-up to try and cover the fading yellow bruises. She smiled at the woman staring back at her in the mirror. She liked what she saw, battle scars and all. Slipping on some shoes, she gave herself one last look in the mirror. It was time.

Outside she saw Josh's car double-parked with the engine running. She crossed the busy car park and opened the door.

He smiled at her as she climbed inside. 'Are you sure about this?'

'I've never been more sure of anything in my life. Thank you for picking me up.'

He reached over and brushed his lips across her cheek. 'I couldn't wait. I've been thinking about you all day. How was work?'

'Good, just a run-of-the-mill day. A couple of sudden deaths, no suspicious circumstances. It felt good to be back. How was yours?'

He laughed. 'It was okay, just a run-of-the-mill kind of day. But you know what, I'll take those any day from now on.'

He drove for the next forty minutes and they chatted about what to eat for dinner, the headlines in the newspapers and whose turn it was to choose which show to watch on Netflix. Beth smiled to herself;

she didn't think that she would ever tire of living a normal life. It was wonderful, especially when she was sharing it with Josh.

They arrived at the prison car park, and he stopped the car. 'I don't mind coming inside with you.'

She shook her head. 'I know you don't, but I need to do this. I need to tell him it's over: the mind games are over, and he no longer has any control over my life. I don't want him to know that you're a part of my life. I don't want him to know anything about me.'

She got out of the car, leant down and pulled the stack of envelopes from her handbag. She was returning them unopened to sender.

# LETTER FROM HELEN

Thank you for reading this book. It's always a little bit scary writing a new series, but I hope you enjoyed being a part of Beth Adams's life for a short time. If you'd like to be kept up date with news about future books you can sign up for my newsletter here:

www.bookouture.com/helen-phifer

I say every book was a tough one to write, but this book shall forever be known to me as the book that almost broke me. It just shows that no matter how many books you write it's always a learning curve.

I'm not a forensic pathologist although my ten-year-old self wanted to be one thanks to watching episodes of *Quincy* every week. If you are please forgive any inconsistencies. I've tried my best to research and make the forensic procedures as true to life as possible. But at the end of the day it is a story and there may be some instances I've used my creative licence to bend the truth for the sake of the plot.

As always a huge thank you to my amazing readers for buying this book. Your support is truly appreciated. If you did enjoy it I'd be eternally grateful if you could leave a quick review. They make such a huge difference and are a fabulous way to let other readers know about my books.

I'd also love to hear from you and you can get in touch with me through my Website, Facebook, Twitter or Instagram.

Love always
Helen xx

🖥 www.helenphifer.com

📘 Helenphifer1

🐦 @helenphifer1

📷 helenphifer

# ACKNOWLEDGEMENTS

I'd like to thank Phil Sullivan for offering to be my Mr Nasty – what a job turning you into a serial killer, Phil. You're far too nice; I'm not going to lie, it's been difficult. I'd also like to thank Diane Sullivan for being an amazing, inspirational woman. Much love to you both, my friends. Huge thanks to my editor, Jessie Botterill. I've certainly made you work with this book. It's been a tough one to write and you've had your work cut out for you. I appreciate all your fabulous input for making it what it is.

I'd also like to say a huge thank you to the fabulous Noelle Holten for all her hard work promoting it. You're amazing. Also thank you to Kim Nash for always being there when hugs are needed by everyone. You both work so hard for your authors and I'm truly privileged you have my back.

Another thank you to rest of the fabulous team at Bookouture; I'm so grateful I get to work with such amazing publishers.

Thank you to the book bloggers who read and support authors – you are truly wonderful and I can't tell you how appreciated you all are, there just aren't enough words.

I owe a huge debt of gratitude to my fabulous readers, my number one fans, my inspiration. You have no idea how blessed I feel to be able to do what I love. I write these stories and you, my dear friends, buy my books and read them. Which is all a writer could ever ask for. This writer thanks you from the bottom of her heart.

Thank you to Paul O'Neill – I can't tell you how much I appreciate your surveyor's reports when it comes to the final read-through. You're a lifesaver.

A special thank you to Jo Bartlett for her never-ending writing support. She is there for every wobble along the way and I'm truly grateful for your wonderful friendship.

Thank you to my dear friends Sam Thomas, Tina Sykes having coffee with you is the best therapy there is. Oh, and somehow you both ended up in this book, I hope you don't mind.

Another debt of thanks to John Paton, who always answers any questions I have. You too ended up as a character, I hope you don't mind either. I'd also like to thank Carl Langhorn for his advice and answering my strange questions without blinking an eye.

Lastly a big thank you to my Wednesday night meditation ladies, Helen, Jan, Val, Sam, Joanna you are the highlight of my week and my life savers. I wouldn't want to fall asleep in public anywhere else.